Frank Perrycoste

Towards Utopia being speculations in social evolution

Frank Perrycoste

Towards Utopia being speculations in social evolution

ISBN/EAN: 9783743376168

Manufactured in Europe, USA, Canada, Australia, Japa

Cover: Foto ©Andreas Hilbeck / pixelio.de

Manufactured and distributed by brebook publishing software (www.brebook.com)

Frank Perrycoste

Towards Utopia being speculations in social evolution

TOWARDS UTOPIA

BEING SPECULATIONS IN
SOCIAL EVOLUTION

Frank Hill Perry Coste

BY

A FREE LANCE

AUTHOR OF

THE CRY OF THE CHILDREN, AND ON THE ORGANISATION OF SCIENCE

NEW YORK
D. APPLETON AND COMPANY
1894

PREFACE

EVERYBODY is familiar with the conception of Utopia; and many among us believe that social evolution will presently culminate in an Utopia where all shall be good, wise, cultured, and affluent : but, whilst we have many popular imaginative descriptions of this *completed* future state, it is perhaps somewhat less usual to enquire what precisely are some of the individual *natural* processes by which that happy consummation can be brought about ; what, if anything, can be done by us of to-day to hasten the progress ; *and what price, if any, must be paid for Utopia.*

The present essay is a *sample* of the kind of answer which, as it seems to us, must be given to such questions ; and is occupied with the attempt to trace out, to a certain extent, by what known processes, and by what modifications of the present social state, such Utopia may be brought about. Thro'out we have endeavored to steer clear of chimerical and fanciful assumptions that, however legitimate in pure fairy-tales, and however necessary thereto, are quite out of place in speculations concerning an Utopia that is asserted to be the destined outcome of a *natural evolution* of Society : and we have sought in preference to shape our course by the polestar of science. Of one thing we are convinced—and to this we need fear little contradiction—that the prime factor in any revolution, or rather renovation, of society, must ever be a change in the ideas, feelings, sympathies, and aspirations, of the individuals who compose that society ; the first step towards any advance must be to thoroly change the *mental atmosphere* in which we live ; given so much, and the rest *must* follow, for the world of men is ruled by thoughts and feelings. If now this brief essay should be successful in inducing any appreciable change in the ideals and aspirations of its readers, if it should to any extent induce them to look on the world of men with somewhat different eyes and to reject any proffered social ideals that involve darkened lives to some of their fellows, then we shall deem our labor richly rewarded.

We may perhaps be permitted to observe that we have never yet read *Looking Backward*, or any other books of that class, except, some years ago, More's *Utopia* : whilst, with regard to Mr. Morris' *Lectures on Art*, as we have explained in notes in the body of this work, we had not the pleasure of reading that delightful book until six or eight months after the original draft of this essay was completed.[1] In revising it, however, and in rewriting chapters nine and ten, we have taken the opportunity to introduce specifically in several places Mr. Morris' own term, *simplicity*, which so thoroly expresses the ideas which had guided us thro'out : and we should perhaps add that the reference at the close of chapter nine to *Love in a Cot* was the outcome of a train of reflections that had been started, partly by Mr. Morris' book, and partly by studies of Greek life. It were clearly superfluous to express in detail our acknowledgments, in this work also, to Herbert Spencer, for the general conceptions of social evolution that we have derived from his *Study of Sociology*, his *Data of Ethics*, and his political and social essays.

A FREE LANCE.

London, *March 16, 1893.*

P.S.—We have taken the opportunity to insert several fresh illustrations that have come under our notice during the last twelve months.

April 4, 1894.

---

[1] The bulk of this essay was written in the spring of 1892 ; but, besides a general revision, the ninth chapter was almost entirely rewritten with very considerable additions, and nearly the whole of the tenth chapter added, early in 1893.

CONTENTS

"I will not cease from mental fight,
  Nor shall my *lance* sleep in my hand,
Till we have built Jerusalem
  In England's green and pleasant land."

———————

"I pray thee, then,
Write me as one that loves his fellow-men."

TOWARDS UTOPIA.

CHAPTER I.

INTRODUCTORY AND PESSIMISTIC.

> " What is all of it worth . . . . ?
> What is it all, if we all of us end, but in being our own corpse
>   coffins at last,
> Swallowed in vastness, lost in silence, drowned in the deeps of
>   a meaningless past ?
> What but a murmur of gnats in the gloom, or a moment's anger
>   of bees in their hive—?—"

> " We have foreknown the vanity of Hope,
>   Foreseen our Harvest, yet—procede to live ! "

" HOPE—and a renovation without end," were the
buoyant words that broke from Wordsworth's lips when
he gazed upon his child.   " Hope—and a renovation
without end " ; do they not embody the dreams of every
parent whose loving pride pictures the unclosed vista of
an yet-to-be opening away before his dear one ? And
with characteristically human blindness to staring facts,
and with that extraordinary ability (at which one can
never cease wondering) to ignore the hugest and most

aggressively plain lesson of existence, we proclaim by word and act our faith in a renovation *without end.* Sweet indeed it is to see a lovely bud unfolding daily before our eyes, and daily yielding richer promise of coming glories ; grand it is to train and guide the young mind, feeling well assured that there awaits it a glorious prime ; and inspiring and consolatory to him, whose own life has been clouded and scared, to realise prophetically the golden times that await his dear ones, and to paint in fancy *their* joys—advanced how much by himself thro toil and sorrow !   But here—in our rank idiocy—we ever stop, satisfied when from the watch-tower of our aëry castle we have descried our successor attain prime manhood, crowned with honor, riches, love, and renown ; and with obstinate pigheadedness we *won't* look any farther.   Yet in some inmost core of common sense we know perfectly well that there is an inevitable sequel to this joyous progress ; a stage when our hero, having reached with glory the summit of manhood, begins his decline into the hated shade of old age—when one by one all his talents, faculties, honors, and strength, must drop from him, and he slide into helpless paralysed dotage consummated by death.   All this we do really know—if only we would allow ourselves to tell it to ourselves ; but we won't : we prefer lies : we prefer to ignore the *whole* truth and to plan and plot for our child as tho no certain Nemesis of age and death awaited his happiness—achieved.   Are we not fools to exult for him ?   Where is the lasting good ?

Then reflect : as is an individual, so is finally the race : common to both are childhood, youth, prime manhood, and decline into death ; and equally futile is it to contrive with anxious care the fleeting happiness of either !

It follows then—alas ! how mournful a confession—that all these succeeding pages of buoyant hopes and joyous prophecies are blind folly, imaging a futile victory ; yet are such auguries, we confess, a very constant theme with us—their fulfilment as earnestly yearned for as is their foretaste sweet. *But,* being unable to ignore staring facts, we are mournfully conscious how vain and illusory are our hopes ; since, once the acme of humanity attained, there must follow (if not from internal causes, at any rate from physical environments) decline, degeneration, and death.

Humanity's perfection will prove to be only the halting halfway-house whence are beheld in retrospect primeval barbarism, and in prospect terminal barbarism. To use a favorite expression—Huxley's simile—existence is a double cone. Once earth bore only infusoria : once again she shall bear only infusoria : and then whirl thro space a dead, cold, barren, world—another moon. To the race as to the individual is assigned a certain death. So that optimist and meliorist evolutionists, who paint in such glowing colors the glories assigned to a future humanity, are every whit as absurd and wilfully short-sighted as the typical parent we have been instancing, who indulges so freely in dreams for his children and *won't* face the certainty that their bliss must be transient and yield to death.

After all then, what is all of it worth ? How much better could we all altogether cease to-day by some cosmic convulsion, and so die with " Hope and despair—

the torturers" for aye. Since however that consummation is not vouchsafed, we must toil on wearily, and
mechanically perform our parts in this existence-farce ;
and, since hope and care are among our parts, we—who
non ignore the facts, and feel the full weariness of our
play—yet continue in the dull mechanic round of indulging hopes that are vain tho fulfilled, and of labouring to build *for others* an edifice that time shall wreck.
And so, in full consciousness of our absurdity, we nurse
our speculations of human happiness irrevocably denied
to us and our generation : and these disjointed dreams
and hopes have taken somewhat this form.

CHAPTER II.

ON UTOPIAS.

"To whom this world of Life
Is as a garden ravaged ; and who e strife
Tills for the promise of a later birth
The wilderness of this Elysian earth."

"A brighter morn awaits the human day."

EVER since the days of Sir Thomas More, Utopia has been a familiar name: and "Utopian fancy" is the comment with which alike the heartless unimaginative Philistine, and the cool-headed reasoner, dismiss the eager schemes of too enthusiastic, too unpractical, well - meaning — nay, best - meaning — philanthropists. Yet tho More may have introduced this name, he did not introduce this conception of a model state administered by philosophers. Two thousand years before More, Plato had delineated his ideal Republic: and Plato's Republic and More's Utopia have their successors at the present day.

The tired heart of Humanity yearns mightily for a happy, good, and peaceful, consummation to its centuries of blood, persecution, torture, warfare, and

5

anguish; and eagerly follows after those imaginative prophets who soothe it with sweet fairy tales of perfect states located in unknown seas. Humanity listens and slumbers awhile to the harsh realities of actual life, lapped in precious dreams of renovated Earth: but too soon it reawakens and cries, "Ah yes—most sweet, most tender—but only a dream; only Utopia; only fairy tales."

But must this ever be? Is it fated that the good, descried by humanity's prophets from the Pisgah heights of their prescient intellect, is but a mirage, a phantasy, an unrealisable nonentity? A mirage it may be—but a mirage is only possible if there be a reality somewhere beyond : a mirage if you like; and, like a mirage, deceptive, in that the vision seems so very near, whilst the reality is so far beyond : but yet it *is* beyond, somewhere, however far, if only we have courage enough to perseveringly press on, strength enough to hew down the obstacles, intelligence enough to see the right path, and purity and singleheartedness enough to keep it.

That men have come to disbelieve in Utopia is not altogether strange : for after centuries have flown we find it all-unrealised. But do men sufficiently ask themselves *why* it is unrealised, or if it be really unrealisable? Do they reflect that, tho it may be difficult to correctly descry the characters of that distant Utopia, it is still *more difficult to define the paths that alone can lead us to it ;* that there are two distinct dangers to avoid? Firstly, there is the danger of thinking an impossible Utopia, of depicting an

Utopia such as never can exist, heedless of the fact that even Utopians are, and ever must be, conditioned by this life's environment, and that man can conquer Nature only by Nature : and secondly, there is the worse danger, that, having descried a vision of a real Utopia from the mountain-eyrie of our intellect, we may, descending into the plains and marching on, take plausible, but utterly wrong paths, that not only never never can lead us to Utopia, but must, on the contrary, increase our toils and wanderings; so that, after long years of stubborn persevering tracking thro the dark woods and over the craggy passes, we find that we are farther than ever, and must again ascend a mountain-outlook and map again our course de novo.

The path to Utopia can *never* be discovered until we have studied with earnest care the geography of that intervening country : Utopia's towers themselves can never be other than most vaguely viewed until we have learned the secret of constructing non-refracting telescopes, and dispelling the intervening mists : and the army of humanity can never be transported across the long interval of weary marching until we have studied the characters of leaders and soldiers alike, and *disciplined and educated our troops.*

Utopia can never be rightly seen otherwise than by the aid of science and a true philosophy that teach us to discriminate the possible and practicable from the impossible: the route can never be tracked by others than by pilots soundly trained in physical psychological and social science : and the march can never be performed by an army not disciplined and educated by the teachings of science, esthetics, and *ethics*. Too long have we already been delayed, hindered, and misled, by the blind paths pointed out by blind leaders, who knew *nothing* of the true route even if they knew anything at all of where Utopia lay: let us, in the future, take good heed that none delude us again into these false bypaths.

The one prime fallacy connected with so many schemes of Utopia is that the Utopia is unscientific and impossible; or that, if possible, the means suggested for reaching it are vicious and impossible because unscientific. And we should remember that, having once approximately satisfied ourselves as to what kind of place Utopia probably is, our grand concern should then be transferred to scrutinising the means of access thereto. The one emphatic duty of Utopian schemers now is to rigorously criticise every suggestion that is made as to the route.

Progress is—ah—how yearned for; and to remain stationary, marking time, is tedious; *but* so to remain stationary were immensely better than to progress in the wrong direction, necessitating a tedious and wearisome return.

Our only object in the following pages is to endeavour to descry some few of the landmarks that point the path to Utopia; and, once for all, let us say that our conception of Utopia is *not* as the best imaginable world, *but* the best possible. Humanity can never transcend the conditions of existence; and, while death exists, Perfect Happiness is unattainable. Our concern is therefor with the least possible Imperfect; and it necessarily follows that, to our thinking, Utopia can be reached only after a long journey thro semi-Utopia. It will be found that our chief immediate concern lies with this semi-Utopia.

CHAPTER III.

> "Yet Human Spirit, bravely hold thy course!
> Let virtue teach thee firmly to pursue
> The gradual path of an aspiring change."

> "And more, *think* well; do-well will follow thought;
> And, in the fatal sequence of this world,
> An evil thought may stain thy children's blood."

It has been pointed out by Herbert Spencer—who seems to have pointed out pretty nearly everything—that ideal men are *possible only* in an ideal state; and conversely that a perfect social state is possible *only* when *every unit* has achieved perfection. Perfect happiness and well being are wholly incompatible with the existence of *any* vice. This is one of those grand principles that we should do well to keep ever present in our minds; equipped with this *form* of thought, we may find almost daily in our walks and in our books, in our business and in our pleasure, ample *matter* for reflection; it co-ordinates and illumines observations that are afforded by every journey that we take, every article that we buy, every pleasure that we enjoy, every hardship that we compassionate, every detail of our households, no less than by every department of the social whole, by every social inequality, and by every scheme of philanthropy and education. In

10

passing therefor to instance a few such examples, it is only necessary to add that, whilst a perfect social state implies not only moral perfection, but also the command over natural forces that organised knowledge confers, so for its attainment are requisite not only the *moral perfection of individuals* but also a far more thoro acquaintance on their part with the physical, mental and social sciences and their applications. Yet if only men were unexceptionally virtuous, from what a vast incubus of misery and discomfort (especially in little things ; and happiness or unhappiness so largely depends upon the absence or presence of small worries) all of us would be saved !

For instance now, suppose, *pro argumento*, that we were all of us decently honest; and consider then how much misery would cease. And in all these illustrations we have to estimate the hedonic gain from a twofold stand-point ; first as regards the generality of mankind, and secondly as regards those units whose more or less unhappy occupations are necessitated by the crimes of others. Often, when speculating on a state in which all shall be happy, the thought must occur—" But happiness is impossible for men engaged in such and such occupations; how can we solve this perplexity?" But the solution is that such occupations will vanish when honesty is universal ; and thus we should attain this double hedonistic gain. And, if you like, there is a third hedonistic aspect, —that of those speculators who at present worry themselves into a despairful misery because they daily see so many brother-men chained down to drudgery and blank monotony.

Now let us take a few illustrations. Suppose that we are railway travellers. We arrive at the station, and, having, after loss of time and temper, obtained our ticket of the booking-clerk, we are stopped on our way to the platform by a barrier where we have to show our tickets to a ticket-collector who snips them : so too at the end of our journey we are again stopped by a ticket-collector who scrutinises our tickets to see that we have not come too far. Now here there are at least three distinct worries to be considered. First of all there are the worries of the booking-clerks and ticket-collectors, whose lives are one dreary tedious monotony,—doomed, as they are, to a hopelessly uninteresting occupation, to a lifework involving in itself (and not regarded as means to the end of living) sheer hedonistic loss. Putting aside altogether the worries of the ridiculous philanthropist who worries himself because such worries exist, we have secondly the worries of the railway-travellers themselves, who are perpetually losing trains because there is a long queue of passengers at the booking-offices or the barrier, and who are annoyed by being awakened at intervals to show their tickets. Thirdly we have this very serious *economic* worry, that many thousands are thus employed in utterly unproductive labour : from an economic standpoint their work is absolutely *wasted*, and there is no set off of any sort, since neither themselves nor anybody else gets the slightest satisfaction out of their labour. If any one consider how many hundreds and hundreds of railway stations there are in England alone, and how many ticket-clerks and collectors employed in each, he will have vividly brought home to him the fact that many thousands of men, in this one direction alone, are absorbed in absolutely unproductive labour: they are a standing army of labourers who—from an economic standpoint—do no work. Now it may sound rather startling at first to those to whom it has never occurred to reflect on these matters, but it is an indisputable fact that this great army of unproductive workers, whose work is a nuisance to themselves and to everyone else, are a necessity imposed upon us simply and solely by our own dishonesty; that is, they are necessary because the average honesty of civilised us is so low that, unless there were a complicated system of checks and counter checks, of ticket-granting and ticket-taking, no railway-company could reckon on keeping out of the Bankruptcy Court.

Now consider for a moment how different all this will be when the whole nation (for here mark that a general or universal minimum-standard of honesty must first be reached) shall have become honest. All these human ticket-appliances will be abolished along with the tickets: at every railway station there will be conspicuously posted a table of fares to every other station on that system: each passenger will see at a glance how much he is to pay for travelling a given distance in a given class; and he will put the requisite fare into a box, either at the commencement or end of his journey—or possibly in a box in the carriage. He will no more dream of taking the opportunity to defraud the company than he will feel tempted to cannibalism. See then what an immense access of comfort and convenience we shall thus achieve *when* we are honest; while the ticketmongering caste will be relieved from their miserable occupation, and set free for work, which, while equally bringing them their daily bread, will—as we may hope— be also more profitable to the community.

It must be remembered that this whole set of men, who do absolutely *nothing* useful, but are merely a private police and detective force necessitated by the general dishonesty, and are therefor in an utterly different category from the enginedrivers, shunters, porters, and others, who do actually useful and productive (indirectly productive) work—that this whole army of many thousands is simply—altho the uneconomically-cultured mass never heed it—*kept at the public cost.*[1]   The railway-companies keep them in the first place, and the cost of their keep—of their wages—necessitates a percentage increase on the price of each fare : ultimately therefor they are kept at the cost of the whole travelling public—that is to say, practically of the nation.   It just comes to this then, that because the majority of us cannot be trusted to abstain from thieving (for what else is it), therefor every one of us has a certain tax put upon his income: that is to say, practically, he has to work a percentage of our short life longer to gain—nothing !

Yes : we have seen in this one simple instance how considerable a gain in a threefold direction will be

[1] We have endeavoured to obtain some statistics as to the number of ticket-clerks and ticket-collectors—but, so far, in vain : since however the census returns (1881) the number of railway employés *other than* guards, drivers, stokers, pointsmen, and level-crossing-guardians, at 100,000, we might perhaps provisionally conclude that about 40,000 of these are ticket-clerks and ticket-collectors, leaving the remaining 60,000 as porters.

effected by a sufficient advance in the general honesty ; or rather, as one should say, when the minimum honesty shall have been sufficiently raised : for it must be remembered that in such matters our whole system must be a function of the minimum honesty : so long as *any* are dishonest enough to cheat the companies, the whole public must be, for practical purposes, put upon the same suspicion - level. What we need therefor is a marked rise of the minimum honesty ; and how great a moral advance this means it is almost needless to point out. At present the popular standard of honesty in *little* things is deplorably low ; for men and women who would be horrified at any actual misappropriation of another's goods will yet without compunction defraud a public company. Taking any church, probably nine-tenths of the " respectable worshippers," who perform their eminently "respectable" devotions there every Sunday, and thank God that they are children of grace and neither Turks, Jews, Socinians, nor Infidels, would have no scruple in cheating a railway-company on their way home : probably *very few indeed* of them, were they transplanted into the travellers'-Utopia that we have sketched above, would put the right fare into the box.[1]

We see then that, taking ourselves as one composite

---

[1] At present there is really a very strong case for those travellers—at least regular travellers—who seize every opportunity of cheating a railway-company : for all or nearly all of the companies swindle us in the most rascally fashion : and since it is hopeless for a private individual to commence litigation with a rich company to recover the expenses which their unpunctuality, *e.g.*, has caused him,—it seems clearly defensible, morally, to pay oneself by "cheating them." But this is *not* the reasoning which prompts many of the frauds to which we refer.

whole—the public—we richly deserve all the annoyance
and expense to which the ticket-system puts us; since it
is simply the just reward of our corporate knavery and
dishonesty.   Let us then hasten to become honest !

Well, let us continue somewhat farther our travelling
reflections.   In due time we arrive at our terminus, in
London, for instance, and perhaps avail ourselves of an
omnibus to reach a distant part of the city.   Here again
the least reflection will convince us that the omnibus-con-
ductor is in very nearly the same category as the ticket-
staff of the railways, and his profession is open to precisely the same objections, except that he is not so great
an annoyance to us as is the ticket-collector.   But he is
a worry to himself, since his occupation is detestable, and
a weary irksome monotony of idle hard work ; and the
existence of his calling is an economic worry, since here
again is a large staff of workers detailed for a perfectly
useless and unproductive occupation.[1]   Again, then, we
may reflect that the advent of general honesty will see
the omnibus and tram-conductors disappear—while passengers will put their rightful fares into a moneybox provided for that purpose.   It is superfluous to point out
that—like the ticket-collector—the omnibus-conductors
are kept at the public expense.   It may be observed that
the drivers are, *per contra*, an *useful* class of workers ; and
since they must continue as long as horses are used, it is
some satisfaction to the philanthropist to reflect that

[1] There does not seem any ready means of ascertaining the
number of omnibus-conductors in England ; but the London General Omnibus Co. alone employ about 1,000, whose wages vary from
4s. 6d. to 6s. per day : this represents about £80,000 per year
wasted on a private police by one company alone.

their occupation is somewhat less monotonously tedious than is that of the conductors.

The mention of omnibus-drivers suggests to one the thought of their confrères the cab-drivers; and it may be permissible to digress for a moment to consider them. We hope that it is already understood by our readers that two distinct considerations have prompted this investigation. In the first place, we have to consider what occupations are intrinsically wearisome and distasteful; and—unpleasant work being nonconsonant *with Utopia*— to enquire how far a general social advance will tend to abolish these occupations—general honesty being an essential component in any such advance; from this standpoint we consider the hedonic gain to the workers in question. But in the second place, we have to reckon with the *general hedonic* gain of the public, whether *direct*, as when we are relieved from much inconvenience by the abolition of ticket-regulations, or indirect, as when the general wealth is practically increased inasmuch as a demand is no longer made upon the public purse to support a large body of unproductive [1] workers.

Very well then, returning to our friend the cab-driver, we are willing to admit that there may be far worse occupations than his: assuming the receipt of decent pay, and the shortening of his hours of labour—assumptions

[1] We need not stop to ask whether these devote themselves to another unproductive occupation, or become direct producers of wealth. For, if the former, and supposing they become confectioners even, this implies that we spend our practically extra wealth upon extra sweetmeats; so that tho our income and outcome remain the same, our *enjoyments* are increased. And supposing that they—or an equivalent number in a higher class— become *artists*, or *scientific discoverers or teachers*? (*vide infra*).

which must be made regarding every occupation in even approximate Utopias—then there might be far worse occupations than cab-driving in fair weather. But, nevertheless, we are inclined to think that the social advance will see a great diminution in the number of cab-drivers—to the hedonic gain of the quondam drivers. For even if we put aside the weary intervals of waiting, and assume that, one day, supply and demand will be so well adjusted that every cabman will be employed thro'out the whole of his (shorter) day's work, and that, by some means, we shall contrive never to keep a cabman waiting outside houses and theatres—which are rather big assumptions—the fact still remains that, so far as we can foresee, cabs will be constantly required either very late at night or very early in the morning—which involves hedonic loss for the cabman, unless he be highly paid, and that involves hedonic loss by us. No, we prefer to show how, without assuming anything more Utopian than honesty (which we confess is a tolerable assumption), we may satisfactorily solve the problem. In the first place we will admit that cab-drivers may be always necessary in crowded cities during the daytime—precisely the conditions under which they are most likely to be constantly employed—since considerable skill is necessary to safe driving under such conditions; but for the rest—for suburbs, for night-work, and in all such cases—we might have *cabs without drivers*. The case is simply this: we hire a cab in order that we may get rapidly and without exertion from spot to spot; under the present system, however, we cannot hire a cab only; we must hire the cab-driver in addition. Now, as we have already seen,

the cab-driver will probably remain for long a necessity
in our crowded streets, since the average layman is wanting in the necessary skill or nerve ; but in suburbs, and
at night-time, the great majority of travellers could
themselves drive if they had the chance ; that is, if they
could hire the cab alone ; that is, in effect, if besides the
" cab complèt " there were for hire a number of cabs
minus drivers. The gain hedonically would be as usual
several-fold; the fare would gain by paying less: the men
who at present follow the occupation of driving cabs at
uncomfortable hours would gain by exchanging this
occupation for a more pleasant one ; and the community
in general would gain, since so much, at present unproductive, labour would be set free and might become productive. Why then can we not introduce, at least experimentally, this system ? Simply because—the usual
answer—we are not honest enough ; because, as a community, we cannot be trusted to drive off in cabs without
a guardian; because so many of us would systematically
cheat the cab owner by giving him less than his due, or
even—worst of all—by stealing his cab ! So that again
the fact that our corporate honesty is below the necessary
minimum standard debars us from spending less for given
accommodation. But in a thoroly honest community we
take it that the organisation of a driverless-cab-system
will be exceedingly simple. There will be large cab-
stands of driverless cabs, and at half-day one or two
ostlers will come up and change the horses. Any one
requiring such a cab will enter one and drive off. Arrived
at his journey's end, he will put the full fare into the box
provided, and then either the cab will be left on some

other stand, or else so intelligent an animal as a horse will at once start off home again. We must, however, remember that at no distant date horse-cabs will probably be partly or entirely superseded by electrical conveyances; which change will, in many respects, greatly simplify the system of driverless cabs. We do not, of course, for a moment profess that the above scheme is other than a very crude outline; but it is sufficient to show how greatly simplified this, among other social problems, becomes if we assume the whole public to be honest.

To continue our travels,—why did we come up to London? Well perhaps to visit a theatre, or a picture-gallery, or an exhibition, or some other place of amusement. Arrived here we find our moral at once pointed afresh; for, to whatever such place we go, we find an array of checktakers or guardians of some sort, whose occupations would at once be gone were the general public sufficiently honest to be trusted: *if* we were so honest that no one would dream of entering an exhibition without putting his fee in a moneybox, or of taking a more expensive seat than he had payed for in the theatre, where would be the necessity for such officials? Perhaps it may be replied that after all there are not many such employed: true; but the sum total is appreciable; and theirs is so much labour locked up in an employment not only unproductive of wealth but also useless, since ministering (except negatively) to no one's happiness. But we are not honest enough to dispense with them.

We spoke just now of the whole body of ticket-officials

as being simply a police upon us : and that suggests a reference to the national police. What could afford a more striking comment upon the loss, the double loss, of wealth entailed upon the community by the dishonesty of some of its members, than this fact that in England and Wales alone we require a total police-force of over 32,000 men![1] That is to say that the nation, as a whole, is heavily taxed in order to provide a check on the dishonesty, rowdyism, and violence, of a section of its members. Verily, in the long run anyhow, Honesty *is* the best Policy! The direct losses caused by actual deeds of violence and dishonesty seem almost trivial when compared with the grand annual loss necessary in order to prevent a reign of violence and fraud. We may, however, admit that the case as regards the police is not entirely on a par with that of the ticket-collectors and conductors ; inasmuch as the need for police is mainly due to the avowedly criminal classes ; whereas the potential sinners against honesty in the matter of travelling, etc., are to be reckoned in great numbers among the highly " respectable " classes.

As an intermediate instance we may however point to our legal organisation. Besides the stipendiary magistrates, who are simply an appendage to the police-force, we have to take into account the expenses of County Court Judges, Judges of the Higher Courts—whether Civil, Criminal, or Equity—with all their host of subordinate officers, and the general expenses of the courts ; and we then find that the cost of law and justice in

[1] According to the 1881 Census—besides 3,000 women.

the United Kingdom is about *six millions annually!* [1]
Now self-evidently this great annual burden is simply a
corollary to our general want of honesty. Because,
looked at as a nation, we have so scant a regard for
honor, honesty, and fairness, all this complicated
machinery of wigs, gowns and beadles is required—and
must be paid for. [2] Be it remembered too that this cal-

---

[1] This includes £1,500,000 for the Irish constabulary, and
£560,000 for the London Police. As wi'l be shown subsequently,
this Budget charge of £6,000,000 is very far from representing
the total expense to the nation.

[2] The grief of it all is that the rogues and sharpers, whose
evil-doings necessitate all this machinery, are not compelled to
pay for it : and one is sometimes inclined to despair of social
improvement when one observes the stolid pigheaded determination of our lawmakers to ignore the most crying abuses and to
leave chaos unreformed. It is no exaggeration, but a simple
literal statement of fact, to say that our laws are specially contrived to leave honest men at the mercy of rogues and swindlers.
We pass by the bankruptcy laws—which enable scoundrels to
thrive by their roguery—and likewise that iniquitous enactment
which prevents *both* civil *and* criminal action being taken
against fraudulent company - promoters et id omne genus—an
enactment that enables them to snap their fingers at the victims
they have fleeced—we pass by all such scandals as these since
our present purport is to point out the disgracefully backward
condition of our law as compared with that of—Scandinavia !
It is of no use for us Englishmen to plume ourselves upon leading
the van of civilisation when little Scandinavia can outstrip us
in commonsense laws, and in regard to justice puts us to shame.
There, as it seems, a man who has been committed for trial is
compelled, if found guilty, to pay for the expenses of his keep
while awaiting trial and for the expenses incurred in bringing
him to justice—a most admirable and salutary proceeding which
of course the "Glorious English constitution" will not hear of.
Here the system is so arranged that (1) a man who has been
swindled and robbed may have no criminal redress at all : and
(2) if he have, and from public spirit avail himself thereof, he
must forego any attempt to recover his money of which he has

culation embraces only the national law costs: add thereto the costs for solicitors and counsel incurred by every litigant, and what a total should we have !

But after all, this vast expenditure on a machinery of police, necessitated by the internal dishonesty and violence of our fellow-countrymen, which compels us to impoverish ourselves to this amount in order to safeguard person and

been robbed !—a monstrous and incredibly fatuous provision ; whilst (3) if there be criminal redress, he himself is left to work the expensive law-machinery ; that is, having surrendered his "natural right" to vindicate himself by force, and having paid heavy taxes all his life, the return made by the State is to allow him to do—himself—the State's work of public prosecution ! Is not this an admirable arrangement that makes the honest pay the costs incurred by the dishonest ? But (4) even if, as in rare cases, that national fraud the Public Prosecutor can be kicked and cuffed into doing his duty, even then the rogue whose prosecution entails all this expense pays not one farthing of the costs ! But, having thus shown itself far inferior to the code of little Scandinavia as an instrument for punishing rogues, English Law—in direct defiance of the maxim which it is ever-lastingly cackling over—endeavours to square the account by punishing the innocent. A man committed to prison to await his trial is treated almost as tho he were a condemned mis-creant : and, if found not guilty by the Jury, not one farthing of reparation do we make him for loss of time, loss of liberty, loss of money, and loss of home. In Scandinavia, however—where possibly the inhabitants do not thank Heaven quite so fervently or ostentatiously that they are virtuous and religious, and where apparently they devote some attention to *acting morally*—we may again find a pattern—and blush ; for there, if found not guilty, a prisoner is suitably compensated for the loss of time, comfort, and money, which he has suffered. In fact the difference is just this : England affords manifold facilities to rogues to escape from justice : and peremptorily refuses jus-tice to innocent and wronged men ; Scandinavian law punishes rogues and compensates innocent men. Compared then with Scandinavia, England seems to be still in a semi-barbarous condition !

property, is but small when compared with the terrible drain made on our resources by the army and navy: and what are these but a direct consequence of international dishonesty, violence, rapine, and bloodthirstiness: a consequence, and alas, too often a cause! Assuredly, if ever in the whole history of the world a glaring and overwhelming proof has been experimentally furnished demonstrative of the old adage that Honesty is the best Policy, we have it now in the present condition of Europe; every state bowed down, groaning, and strength-drained, by the terrible incubus of enormous armaments; the nations taxed and triply impoverished; first by being compelled to *keep* hundreds of thousands of idle men; secondly by losing exactly so many wealth-creators; thirdly by the expense of material armaments—guns, forts, ships, powder, etc., etc. : and all this awful waste simply because every nation believes—and rightly— pretty nearly every other nation to be—like itself—a robber and a murderer! The presence of standing armies in Europe of to-day is the maddest of all insanities; the demarcations of kingdoms have long since been mapped out; and excepting on the Eastern frontier of Germany, and along the Danubian frontier—where the danger exists of an inroad by the hordes of ravening savages who people that earthly hell ruled by devils incarnate and called Russia—there should be not a soldier in Europe. Look across the Atlantic and see America—happy country—almost without a soldier, and till lately perplexed how to dispose of her national income; then look back at Europe groaning and writhing in blood and impoverishment! The English army cost (in 1887) 17 millions, its adjuncts 9½ millions, and the navy 12½ millions, making a total of 39 millions—practically half our revenue spent on an international *Robber-police*. Putting aside all the other loss entailed, there is an *average* taxation of 6 or 7 pounds annually on every householder in the United Kingdom in order to keep up this Robber-police. Let any man of small income ask himself how much additional happiness this would mean to him every year; and yet this direct loss is the smallest part of the total impoverishment so caused. Verily, Honesty *is* the best Policy!

3

CHAPTER IV.

THE GREAT SERVANT-QUESTION.

" But the heart, and the mind,
  And the voice, of mankind,
  Shall arise in communion ;
  And who shall resist that proud union ?"

Now let us refer to a different category of occupations.
In the several preceding examples we have been anxious
to show how certain modes of labour, which are absolutely
unproductive of any pleasure to the public (being indeed
a nuisance), and are also in an economic sense absolutely
unproductive also, would at once disappear were men but
sufficiently honest. We want no Jules-Verne-inventions
to render possible that much improvement in society—
nothing but honesty ; in any honest society—let alone
Utopia—all police of every kind must disappear. But
our concern is now with certain occupations which are
not police-born at all, but which are simply the con-
comitants of our complex civilisation ; and altho most of
these be not productive in the economic sense, yet do
they minister to our comfort, meeting real or factitious
needs. The question is now—will such occupations
persist in a semi-Utopian society, or will they be
abolished ? The truth is that, while they seem

necessary to the comfort of the public—or of large classes thereof—they are undeniably unpleasant to the workers: and moreover with the growing refinement of evolving society, and the raising of the general minimum of refinement, these occupations may *primâ facie* be expected to become more and more distasteful to the workers. How then shall we reconcile the opposition, since, self-evidently, there can be no unpleasant occupations in any approximate Utopia? We do not propose here to avail ourselves of Spencer's principle of adaptation to the unavoidable, or to enquire whether, in spite of growing refinement, men might become reconciled to, and finally take great pleasure in, *e.g.* scavenging: since, before falling back on that last line of defence, it is at least permissible to enquire whether the seemingly unavoidable may not be modified or dispensed with.

It is not proposed to discuss in the present chapter a number of such unpleasant occupations with a view to determining their unavoidability or otherwise; such a discussion will be found in a subsequent chapter;[1] but for the present we shall find quite enough to occupy us for a couple of chapters or so in the great Servant-Question.

Everybody—both here and in America, and still more in Australia—seems to be agreed that one of the most pressing (minor) social problems of to-day is that of domestic service. Now, on this score a good deal might be said, and there are sundry aspects to the question. In the first place, if any one expect from us an assent

[1] See chapter xi, to which the reader may advantageously refer at this juncture.

to the universal mistress-cry that this scarcity of
domestic servants is a grave evil, let him make up
his mind to be disappointed. We can *not* and will *not*
cry *amen* to this caste-prayer of "Give us this day our
old-fashioned servants." We will admit to the full the
annoyance and inconvenience caused to *us*—the employers—by the changes wrought in the servant-class
during the last half century; and we very fully realise
the discomfort induced by repeated changes—tho here
it seems to us that the actual material discomfort and
worry caused are perhaps less serious than the *emotional*
evil—the impossibility of creating a feeling of personal
esteem and friendship between master and servant, of
making the servant one of the family as was the case
in former days, when the servant would speak of "*our*"
house, "*our*" children, and so on. We admit to feeling
very strongly on this point, and to yearning for the
affectionate life-long ties of old days, when a maid
entered the service of a young mistress just married,
and grew old along with her—the mutual esteem and
fellow-feeling deepening from year to year; or if anon
the maid married, she yet retained the kindly kinship-
feeling, and periodically visited her old mistress to talk
of the children and all household interests.

Yes! We confess to a very poignant regret for this
old affectionate intercourse, the possibility of which
seems destroyed, or at least indefinitely suspended, now;
but we can go no further with those who sigh for the
"old servants," nor can we endorse their indignant re-
proaches on the modern domestic. For, however happy
the results in individual cases under the old style, it

must be remembered that the long unchanged service, and the docility and submission, were all due to one cause—*viz.*, the inexperience, helplessness, and ignorance, of the servants, and the general overawedness and *always-carry-yourself-lowly-and-reverently-to-your-betters-ness* inculcated upon the poorer classes by their caste-born and caste-bound superiors. Now—except in the country where non-doffing to the squire and the parson is still high felony—all such insolent nonsense is disappearing. The " revolt " of the servants is only another effect and symptom of the same salutary social revolution that has given us strikes,[1] trade unions, extended franchise, and labour-conferences: all alike mean the shaking-off of thraldom, and the assertion of the independence of man. But housekeepers and mistresses are, as a rule, little given to philosophising on sociology—or on anything else ; and they deplore as unmixed evil what is, in great measure, very good. We have but scant patience or sympathy with that intolerant caste-spirit which can look on one side—its own side—only of the shield, and judge the goodness or badness of any change simply by the resultant effect on the comfort of the caste. On the contrary, we cannot but rejoice—however much inconvenience may at times be caused to ourselves personally—that the class of domestic servants is now in so far better a position that it is able to insist on higher wages, more extensive privileges, and the sus-

---

[1] Not, of course, that we can otherwise than deplore the frequency of *strikes*—the misery and loss entailed by them—tho we rejoice that the workmen can assert themselves and are no longer serfs.

pension of vexatious and impertinent restrictions. The
modern mistress laments not only the loss of long-
service-servants, but the loss of that *authority* and *power*
in which her mother and grandmother gloried : *the lust
of power* is rampant in the human breast, and few have
the virtue willingly to resign the sceptre. Nowadays—
far otherwise was it in the past generation—servants are
awake to their own value, and no longer cleave to their
one situation ; for they know that their supply is below
their employers' demands, and that a good servant need
never want a berth. Similarly they will not tolerate
those arrogant and insolent caste-regulations which
forbade them to wear colors; and we hope that in a
very short time they will throw off the "cap" also to
which they are at present deemed in order to mark their
place below the salt. Caps may be suitable to age, but
we have no sort of patience with those people who insist
upon a young girl putting on these hair-extinguishers,
instead of allowing—or teaching—her to dress her hair
in *the* one mode in which any woman should wear her
hair.[1] To one thing these mistresses had better make
up their minds at once—*viz.*, that if the servant-system
be fated to endure, it will be only in an abundantly
modified form. The general refining-process will give
us servants on a higher level of refinement ; and the
present insistence on a stern demarcation in personal
appearance between housemaid and daughter of the
house must collapse. Those who are horrified if a
servant, waiting at table, wear a watch and chain, and
who would faint instanto at seeing her minus a cap,

[1] *Viz.*, in a coil on the top of the head.

may rest assured that the future maid will not only appear thus, but also (in any family with a love for esthetic graces) with flowers in her hair : for life is so full of uglinesses that we can ill afford to squander the possibilities of beauty and grace.

Now it appears to us that one reason why the long-service-system has practically disappeared with the old cas'e-régime is this—that the employers, blinded and heart-hardened by their intolerable caste-notions, have steadfastly resisted, point by point and line by line, every advance of the servants, and, to the very best of their—happily limited—ability, have hindered the emancipation. It really seems absolutely impossible to make employers understand—far less realise—that servants are *not* a class specially brought into existence by a divine Providence to minister to *their* comfort. As long as they thus insist upon regarding every advance of the servants as a wilful rebellion, every new departure as both wicked and foolish, and—significantly—think the whole question summed up by deploring the "growing independence" of the servant-class—so long it is hopeless to expect any re-establishment of the old kindly feeling. For servants know perfectly well in what light their attempts at enfranchisement are regarded ; and the patent, tho smouldering, resentment of mistress raises inevitably an antipathetic feeling in maid. They know perfectly well that every privilege of theirs has been won in the teeth of opprobrium, opposition, and sarcasm,[1]

---

[1] It has been most truthfully said that, to really know—to realise—the inner life of any age, we must study its light literature. Anyone who should wish to study the social life of the

and that, were it possible, probably ninety-nine employers
out of every hundred would instantly combine to reduce
servants to the status of fifty years ago.

"But"—cries the injured mistress—"what has this to do

last half century would naturally turn to the pages of *Punch*,
the study of which is almost a liberal education by itself—at
least in that sense of "liberal" which excludes the most valuable
of all knowledge, anyhow. *Punch* is usually read for amusement
merely; but beneath the social satire and the humor lies a
moral which he who runs may read. Some forty-five years ago
there appeared in *Punch* a series of sketches entitled *Servantgalism ; or, what's to become of the Mistresses?* and here may be found
several apt illustrations of our contention—that the typical
mistress is hopelessly imbued with the notion that servants are
a lower caste, specially created by Providence as ministrants to
the comfort of the wealthier ; and that any assertion of independence or selfregard on their part is both wicked and absurd.
These sketches also illustrate our argument that part of the present discord between servant and mistress is traceable to the
sarcasm and ridicule which the dominant class have heaped upon
their incipiently self-asserting servants. It would be rather a
rash assumption to make that the satirised servants never saw
Punch : and, having seen themselves so satirised, they would be
something more, or something less, than human, did not their
relations with their employers become embittered and dis-
cordant ; altho it is doubtful whether the evils thus wrought
were so great as the *reflex-effect* of the sarcasms on the minds of
the employer-class, who thus became only the more confirmed in
their prejudices as to the one duty of servants, and the more
disposed to scorn all notions of servants' rights

First of all noting that the very title of *Servantgalism : or,
what's to become of the Mistresses?* is itself eloquent testimony to
the truth of our indictment, and alone speaks volumes for the
mental attitude—the hopelessly prejudiced, caste-born, attitude
—assumed by the typical employer, we pass to one or two
examples (the references to *Punch* are thro'out to the 3 volume
edition of *Leech's Cartoons* published 1886-1887 by Bradbury
Agnew & Co.).

Here is one entitled *An Impudent Minx* (1852) (I. p. 64). A

with it? You admit that servants are in a far better position than formerly; and you equally admit that they are nevertheless far more dissatisfied, and that the old affectionate relations cannot, under present conditions,

shocking old frump, with very scanty curls at the sides of her face, thus addresses a very pretty maid, who has combed some of her luxuriant tresses into long curls surrounding her cheeks: "Go and put up those curls directly if you please. How dare you imitate me in that manner? Impertinence!" And a practically identical example is one entitled *A Cause for Reproof* (1847) (I. p. 257). Now in both of these cases we will frankly admit that the point of the sarcasm is really directed at the mistresses, and that they, and not their blooming maidservants, are in reality gibbeted. In so far therefor one must exonerate Leech from a charge of intensifying caste-illwill. But we are anxious, so far as concerns these two cuts, to draw attention to their *truthfulness:* they exactly reflect the prejudiced intolerant caste-spirit; and at least ninety-nine mistresses out of every hundred who saw these sketches would consider the two pretty maids to be acting with great impertinence, and the two mistresses to be fully justified in their indignation. In fact so thoroly typical of the employer-spirit are these sketches that it is doubtful whether many mistresses would perceive the real humor at all — their attention being entirely occupied by the misdeeds of the maids and the just wrath of their mistresses; like the latter they would perhaps think that the whole absurdity lay in the maids' attempt to imitate (!) their mistresses' hair-dressing.

In other illustrations of *Servantgalism* however we find nothing but gibes, ridicule, and sarcasm, at the expense of the servants. In No. 7, for instance (1853) (I. p. 222), we find two violently caricatured servants calling at the house where "Hann Jenkins" is employed, to leave their cards, and express a hope that she got home all right after the ball. In No. 10 (1853) (I. p. 93) an aggressively snub-nosed heavy-built girl remarks, "With my beauty and figure I ain't agoing to stop in sarvice no longer." In No. 16 (1863) (III. p. 220) a smutty-faced, snub-nosed, remarkedly awkward-looking, maid-of-all-work, being reproved for wearing her crinoline in the morning, replies that the sweeps

be re-established : then this just proves the truth of our complaints—that the servant of to-day is far inferior to the servant of our grandmothers' time."

This may seem plausible, but the answer to it has already been implied. Let us take a parallel from the

were coming, and she couldn't think of opening the door to them—such a figure as she would have looked without her crinoline !   And finally in one entitled *Servantgalism in Australia—a Fact*, a servant, of about as ungainly a build as the preceding one, appears dressed in a riding habit (dreadful result !), and informs her mistress that, having an hour to spare, she is "going to try her new horse."

Now the first point, to which we wish to draw attention in these illustrations, is the intolerant and supercilious attitude taken up with regard to any attempted advance of the servants. The tacit assumption underlying all these satires—and essential to their very existence—is that dances, visiting cards, a good figure, and horse-riding, are so selfevidently, so palpably, the special endowment of the ruling class only, that any mention of them in connection with servants is essentially ludicrous : that assumption once made, it needs only to point the satire by a misplaced H, a snub-nose, or a bad figure, and the farce is complete. We are not for a moment denying the humour of Leech's satire— we think that we appreciate it to the very fullest—but we do emphatically protest against the intolerant caste-born mental standpoint,—so admirably illustrated by Leech—from which the struggles of the servant-class are regarded.   We will go even farther ; and, admitting that instances are to hand of genuine absurdities committed by servants, we will ask—Is it kind, is it chivalrous, to hold them up to scorn and contumely in a class-journal—they being the weaker party ? Satirise the strong as much as you like, vent your sarcasm on them to the top of your bent—for you do it at your own risk : but is it chivalrous, is it brave, is it other than meanspirited, to satirise a class below, who cannot retaliate, and whose absurdities and uncouthnesses are due simply to the want of that education and that happier social environment which you—thro no merit of your own—have enjoyed ?   What other result can follow but unnecessary and gratuitous embitterment of feeling, and illwill?

army. We read of certain great commanders addressing their soldiers as " My children," and we indulge in much sentiment over the affectionate relations thus existing, and deplore the fact that in our own army such relations are impossible. But it has most truly been pointed out [1] that such relations are symptomatic of an army where the men have no rights: " My children " is the phrase of a despot addressing soldiers whose lives are absolutely in his hands, and who have no redress against his decrees however arbitrary: it is the watchword of the " patriarchal" rule. But things are different in our army, where the lowest has legal rights and may obtain redress for injustice. "Respect for rights " has superseded patronage.

Now it appears to us that here is a strong analogy to the household relations which we are considering. Formerly a mistress, altho certainly not holding her servant's life in her hands, yet had her very tolerably under her thumb. The great difficulty of communication and of travelling in those days naturally induced dependence ; for a servant, having once secured a tolerable situation, would put up with a good deal of tyranny rather than risk her livelihood by leaving. How in those pre-cheap-newspaper, and pre-registry-office, days *could* a servant hear of a new situation, or how make her wants known ? Situations then were probably filled up on personal recommendations, and "characters" went for everything. In days when a cardinal article of faith was that " Rebellion is as the sin of witchcraft," and any

[1] We regret to have totally forgotten the author from whom we quote—and necessarily therefor we quote only in paraphrase.

attempt to assert independence was regarded as atheistical and republican, it may be well understood that a servant who resented caste-tyranny, caste-usurpations, and caste-restrictions, would stand but a poor chance of finding a second situation ; for probably the supply of servants—or of would-be-servants—then, was fully up to the demand. In those days too the doctrines of humility and of obedience to superiors were steadily engrained in children's minds, and contentment in *that* state of life inculcated, by caste-parsons who, themselves imbued with the quint-essential spirit of caste, had yet the effrontery to style themselves followers of Jesus of Nazareth, who—if he taught anything—most emphatically taught (rightly or wrongly) the fraternity and " equality " of man !

Very well then : is it not now very intelligible that the mistress, looking down from her lofty standpoint of superiority, could easily condescend affectionately to her servants—practically possessing no rights, and taught to reverence her *as* a mistress ; while naturally too a lifelong connection alone would in many instances superinduce feelings of affection.[1]

---

[1] But it is highly advisable to remember that, whilst our grandmothers drew for us touching pictures of the affectionate relations between well-conditioned mistresses and servants, we naturally hear nought of the sufferings of servants at the hands of ill-conditioned mistresses. We know of no more ridiculous example of the almost incredible lengths to which this precious caste-arrogance may go, than is afforded by a passage in one of De Quincey's autobiographical sketches, *The Female Infidel* —" My mother, by original choice, and by early training under a very aristocratic father, *recoiled as austerely from all direct communication with her servants,* as the Pythia at Delphi from the attendants that swept out the temple." (See also a passage in his *Introduction to the World of Strife*—" My mother, who

It may perhaps then be inferred that any possibility of resuming the old affectionate relations is now doomed, and that there will be a mutual standing-upon-one's-rights until the end of the chapter : such, however, is—we trust—not the case : and we introduced the comments on the caste-opposition to servants' emancipation in order to mark what appeared to us the poison-fount. The long-service-system, with its concomitant development of affection, is not—we hope—incompatible with servants' independence and servants' rights, but *only incompatible with the mutual distrust and resentment* born of the bitter opposition, manifested in the past and in the present, to the advance of the servants. So long as employers *will* take the caste-view, so long as they *will* insist that a servant is their god-appointed subject, so long will any re-establishment of good feeling remain impossible.

If this view be correct, employers *as a class* have mainly themselves to thank for all the present discomfort and irritation ; and a re-establishment may be effected when they meet the servants halfway—or more than halfway—and, by taking trouble for their comfort and by consulting their feelings, make them feel themselves real members of the family. In other words, affectionate relations were possible when servants had no rights ; and they will be possible when servants' rights and privileges are fully and loyally recognised : but they

never chose to have any direct communication with her servants, always had a housekeeper for the regulation of all domestic business.")

can hardly be expected in this transition-time when the rights are incomplete and are grudgingly conceded.

In the foregoing we may have seemed—almost necessarily perhaps — to attribute all the faults to the mistresses and all the virtues to the servants : but this of course were absurd. With all our strong sympathies for the weaker side, we recognise fully—if only from personally unpleasant experience, 'twere enough—the abundant faults of *many* servants, which render it almost impossible for the noblest-minded mistress to take an abiding interest in them, and almost preclude the possibility of granting special indulgences—the granting of which, so far from creating a reciprocal feeling of goodwill, would only be taken advantage of. We are also free to admit that nowadays many young servants constantly change their places from a mere sudden mania *for* change, and often (as we can assert from personal knowledge) very greatly to their own detriment ; while doubtlessly under the old system circumstances would have coerced them into remaining in one situation—to the advantage of themselves no less than of their employers : but this does not justify us in yearning for the return of a vicious system. For the rest, we must trust to time, and to the effects of a *real* education, and to the fact that the—far better-treated—servants of the future will probably be drawn from a higher social stratum than that which at present supplies us. Above all, let it be remembered that the wise training and friendly counsel given by a mistress to a maid in *her first situation*, may make *all* the difference for good or ill to the girl's after life : it is upon the early training given by mistresses that mistresses must in great measure rely for the fashioning of their servants.

Now the whole of the foregoing may seem a mere digression; but it is really a necessary preliminary if one desire to speculate on the probable position of servants in a higher-evolved social state. We do not so much propose to enquire now whether domestic servants in any form will exist in Utopia itself; for such enquiry were somewhat futile and would have but small bearing on the present: our concern in this essay, thro'out, is rather with a social state, tho considerably in advance of, yet evidently in touch with, our own; and we wish to examine how far we might at once realise it, if we—and others—chose.

Now clearly some preliminary conditions must be laid down. It appears to us that our efforts should be directed to the enquiry (1) how far servants may be dispensed with altogether, and (2) how far their work may be so modified as to comprise nothing essentially repugnant:—this latter condition with regard to every occupation being very important if we would have a happy social state. It is not clear—any exact data being non-existent—whether we should anticipate a greater dearth of servants at a later time, or not. Arguing from the present tendency, clearly we should; and in that case there were obvious reasons for enquiring how far we may do without them. But nevertheless it appears to us not improbable, and that for several reasons, that there may yet be an abundance of domestic servants. We take it for granted that their wages will continue to rise, and this alone will of course prove an attraction;

while the great amelioration of their lot which we anticipate will not only reconcile to domestic service large
numbers who at present prefer the independence of, *e.g.*,
factory-life, but will moreover bring into their ranks
many who now earn a miserable livelihood as tenth-rate
governesses, altho really wholly unfit for teaching.
Furthermore, for reasons which will be apparent later, it
seems to us that the number of servants employed in
any one household will rarely excede one or two, and
consequently, in so far, the demand (as compared with
the present) will be appreciably lessened and the supply
increased. However, since so many other and disturbing
factors enter into this problem, it is impossible to form
any conclusion at the present time.

Now anybody who will take the trouble to walk round
his house with his eyes open (instead of, as usually, *shut*)
may speedily discover various domestic duties which are,
in reality, *wholly unnecessary*, and could be dispensed with
at once if necessity arose. To begin with the beginning
of the day—what is a servant's first duty when she comes
downstairs? We understand that it is to clear up the
various fire-grates, and to generally prowl around with
ashes, cinders, and blacklead-pots-and-brushes—to the
no small detriment of her hands. Now it is absolutely
certain that this system is *doomed*—for our wasteful
English practice of heating by open hearths will be supplanted in favour either of a system of hot pipes connected
with one central huge fire, or of gas-stoves in each room :
either plan will abolish the whole dirty work of black-
leading.[1]

[1] And anyone who *does* keep his eyes open, and observes how

Again it is very usual to have white hearthstones, and also an array of white doorsteps, which a housemaid is compelled to periodically clean; and it is surely a piteous sight to see some young girl on a bitter bleak wintry morning kneeling out in the open air and *slaving* at those miserable doorsteps! What sort of hands can one expect to find her possessing after such work—what but coarse rough chapped hands? And why should fair hands be confined to a lady? No: rest assured that white hearthstones and white doorsteps are also *doomed*—as *everything entailing useless work, work producing neither pleasure nor profit, is doomed* in a better social state.

The next duty of the servants, we presume, would be to dust and sweep out the living-rooms; and here we do not see any escape: "matter in the wrong place" *must* always be removed, and, since intolerance of dirt is developed *pari passu* with civilisation, it is in no wise probable that higher-evolved man will remit the least proportion of this department of household work. One may possibly hope that advancing electrical science will solve this problem by some system of dust-collectors, depending on a polarisation of the dust particles; and it is even conceivable that the dust might be collected into a *dust-swallower* by some merely mechanical contrivance producing vortices or whirlwinds in each room: but since such hopes are somewhat chimerical—certainly so at the present time—we prefer not to rely upon them. One

things go in an ordinary English middleclass home when perhaps several visitors are present in cold weather, and fires are required in various rooms, will not depreciate the difference thus made in the servant's work.

may, however, make two observations on the subject of
dusting and sweeping : Firstly, that with the abolition of
smoke, the work in city-houses will be immensely de-
creased, in fact brought down almost to the country
minimum ; and secondly, that in this work there is
nothing actually unhealthy or *repugnant* (as in dirty
work) ; in fact, the sweeping is healthy exercise, and
many ladies allow none but their daughters to dust
drawing-room treasures. It seems to us especially fortunate that this department of household work, which
cannot as yet be superseded, is practically almost unobjectionable.

Let us procede with the servant's daily duties. What
would be her next task ? Probably to clean and black
the boots. Here again we may feel very well assured
that a change in the direction of abolition will occur anon.
It is—we presume—not known who was the miserable
idiot that first introduced the dirty and objectionable
practice of covering our boots with blacking ; but anyone
who likes to dip into the future may satisfy himself that
the boots for future wear will be either of patent leather
or brown, or at anyrate something *other than blacked ;* so
that here again the quantity of domestic work will be
lessened, and the quality much improved. Knife clean-
ing, and the washing-up of glass and crockery-ware, will
always be necessary ; but in such work there is—fortunately—nothing at all objectionable or onerous.

It were of course hardly feasible, and neither is it
necessary, to follow the servant thro every department
of the day's work ; our object is simply to show how
readily the quantity of household work, and consequently

the need for servants, may be diminished, and also how the quality of it—by the deletion of unsavoury portions—may be so improved that there may be nothing left in household service repugnant to the feelings of a refined and tolerably educated girl.[1]

Of course the *intellectual* girl will never be employed on housemaids' work ;—'twould be a wicked waste of her brain-power: but not *all* can be highly intellectual, and yet all may be educated and refined. Now when such a consummation as that here depicted shall have been attained, it is clear that the problem of how to admit servants to

---

[1] To give one more example,—which is certainly necessary tho unsavoury,—the most disgusting part of a housemaid's work could and would be at once—*now*—abolished, had the girls only the sense to " strike " against it. It is a disgrace to our civilisation that builders have not ages since been compelled to construct a simplest possible arrangement in every bedroom that would entirely obviate the necessity for this disgusting work—which we lay upon *young girls*. Now this, altho a disagreeable subject, is really one full of instruction and carries a significant moral. It typically illustrates that very peculiar product of the human spirit *caste-sympathy*. We deliberately ordain that young girls shall daily discharge an office of so repulsive a nature that even the by-no means-very-refined lower-middle-class Philistine *man* would resent it, and consider himself degraded by the performance of such work. Are we to assume that these young girls—tho lowly born—are so destitute of any feelings of refinement that they can adopt this phase of their work without repugnance? Surely no—in which case we are responsible for systematically disrefining and lowering them by habituating them to such work. This however is only one of many cases in point ; but for a further discussion of the subject we must refer the reader to chapter v.—at the same time asking him to note that, logically, the whole of that chapter is *immediately* sequent to this note, altho for his convenience the discussion was relegated to a separate chapter instead of being placed here as a lengthy footnote.

the "family," how to cultivate their friendship, will have been solved for good.

But however that may be in the far future, we have yet to do with the present and the near future; and it is advisable to enquire what amendments can be introduced in varied ways into the present arrangements or dis-arrangements—for servants' comfort—or discomfort.

In the first place—premising all the reforms, per *abolition*, or otherwise, that we have already indicated—we may take it that a very speedy reform will be made in the fittings of the servants' bedrooms. Any considera-tion at all of psychological effects, any regard at all for the esthetic tinting of our sombre soul-life, would teach us that the bedroom, whose aspect moulds our frame of mind at night as we gradually fall off to sleep, and at dawn when we wake, should be furnished and fitted with the most scrupulous regard for picturesqueness and comfort: yet the very common aspect of even "the boys'" bedrooms in a normal middle-class household is depressing and cold-blooded to a degree that really induces shuddering if one only think of it: fancy oneself then daily experiencing it! Instead of pictures, life, light, warmth, color, we find only bareness, ugliness, and desolation. If such then be the measure meted out to our own boys, what regard was likely to be paid to the servants? But we may rely upon it that the *reform must* come here also, and that servants' bedrooms[1] will

---

[1] It is often stated that in some West-end houses a servant sleeps in the kitchen under the dresser! As will be observed, we do not refer to such barbarism as this, but to the normal dis-comfort of a servant's room.

anon be furnished and fitted pleasantly, and warmed rationally.[1]

Again, under our present régime, the servants have no living-room other than the kitchen with its ever-present culinary smells : no builder ever has the common-sense or humanity to build, adjacent to the kitchen, a small room which might be used as a servants' sitting-room : and, if he did so, not one household in 100 would have the sense or humanity to let the servants use it. And yet how would any of us like to live in a kitchen ; what chance is there of real comfort or refinement under such conditions ? But no one ever troubles to apply the golden rule to his relations with servants. Yet it would be so easy to alleviate so greatly a servant's life : with a cosy bedroom, a cosy, well-lighted, decently-fitted, sitting-room, supplied with books—or at least book-shelves—and dedicated wholly to the servants' use ; with the abolition of dirty work as already indicated ; and with the abolition also of ridiculous and insolent restrictions, and with fair facilities for visiting and en-tertaining her friends ; surely then a servant's life in an ordinary English middle-class household would become one that might well be envied and coveted by many a young girl who must needs earn her own living. For even with all the drawbacks which we have so fully admitted, it must be remembered how immensely superior is the lot of a housemaid, living in a large,

---

[1] At present, people who pride themselves on their " common sense " will sit all the evening in a room at 70°, and then *undress* in a room at 35°! So long as they are content with this for themselves, there is clearly no hope for servants.

airy, healthy, house, in a good neighborhood, and having abundance of generous fare, to that of her sister living (sometimes perhaps with difficulty) on far inferior food, in a small stuffy unhealthy cottage or flat.

We spoke just now of liberty to receive friends; and that reminds us how cruel is the oftentimes-present treatment of servants. The doctrine (tacit or avowed) that they are born simply to minister to our comfort and not to their own, has sunk so deep into the employer-mind that in many households it is looked upon as a distinct piece of wickedness if a servant dare to receive the visits of friends in the kitchen.[1] Our own lives would be intolerable without the sunshine of loving

---

[1] Here again we may with advantage quote from *Punch*, and among Leech's drawings will be found two that are exceedingly pertinent to the subject. The first, "An Artful Excuse" (1847) (I. p. 94), is a double cut, representing, on the one side, an exterior, with a soldier waiting at the garden gate; and on the other an interior—a maid-servant entering the sitting-room with a request, "Oh, if you please, could I go out for half an hour to buy a piece of ribbon?" In the second, "Not Very Likely" (1850) (I. 108), a shocking old fright of a mistress, suddenly entering the kitchen, discovers there a redcoat (unmistakably from the Emerald Isle). With a countenance expressive of the utmost indignation and horror, she enquires, "Well! I'm sure! And pray who is that?" "Oh, if you please, ma'am, it is only my cousin who has called just to show me how to boil a potato." We know not how it may strike others, but there appears to us to be a significant moral here. So little is it tolerated that a *mere servant* should expect the ordinary joys of life, that to receive a visit from a sweetheart is considered appalling wickedness, and has to be schemed for and lied for by her. The tone of the mistress and the expression of her face alike emphasise her unbounded horror and astonishment that a young servant (living alone by-the-bye—weary life!) should desire any youthful joys.

He who runs may read!

faces; but, that a mere servant (enjoying none of our other sources of happiness, and perhaps living as a single servant too) should presume to require friends, is a shocking instance of *domestique* depravity! Of course we will very fully admit that, if the servants of near neighbors associate, the manufacture of scandal regarding their respective households will be something appalling (tho in five cases out of six they be no whit worse than their mistresses as regards either truth or charity); and we would very greatly prefer that our own servants' friends were not the servants of near neighbors; but, for the rest, we would insist upon the very heretical proposition that servants should, so far as possible, have— not one evening a fortnight but—nearly every evening to themselves, with full liberty to visit their friends or to receive them. We fail to perceive anything inherently absurd or depraved in this proposition; or anything that is *not* inherently absurd in the counter-proposition that servants should have no companions, and inherently selfish in the current practice.

This brief discussion is perhaps sufficient to outline the forms which domestic service may reasonably be expected to assume in the not very distant future. It will be seen that, once having put aside the actually dirty part of a housemaid's work, there is nothing that a girl of tolerable education and refinement might not undertake; and we confidently anticipate that in the coming time large numbers of girls of even "gentle" or fairly "gentle" birth, who find it necessary to earn their daily bread, may secure congenial and happy homes by undertaking domestic service. We would *most emphatically*

protest against the notion that there is anything "menial"
or "degrading" in a servant's occupation (reformed as
we have indicated), or anything that might not well be
undertaken by such girls. Most of all would we protest
against the notion that there is something particularly
humiliating in "waiting" at table: on the contrary, it is
a peculiarly gracious rôle to fill—a rôle formerly appro-
priated to the sons of noblemen and haughty knights:
and so strongly do we feel the many advantages accruing
to those who do thus "stand and wait," and so little do
we deem it an humiliating task, that, had we children,
we should delegate to them as much as possible the
duties of waiting upon our guests at dinner. Whosoever
deems it humiliating or unpleasant to serve a lady with
food and drink must have a somewhat jaundiced habit
of regarding the world: and pray how would such an
one comport himself *at a picnic?*

While thus anticipating abundant new recruits to the
domestique ranks by-and-bye, it must of course be admitted that such new recruits cannot possibly be expected *yet:* a mild revulsion of feelings and of manners
must precede their advent. Obviously there are indispensable preliminaries: reforms such as we have indicated, both as regards the work of servants, their
treatment, and their wages, must be instituted: considerably more regard must be paid to their comfort (as
already pointed out), and far more liberty and independence must be accorded to them; while lastly—or shall
we not say primarily—*public opinion* must be so far
revolutionised as to regard domestic service as honour-
able, and consistent with refinement, dignity, and inde-

pendence : in fact domestic servants must finally be elevated to the position now occupied by governesses.[1] It should however be clearly understood that to the success of this scheme it is in no wise essential that we should entirely cease to draw servants from—as at present—the illiterate and peasant classes, or supersede them wholly by drafts from classes that now, *e.g.*, yield us nursery-governesses. On the contrary : for, altho it appears to us highly probable that this will be the final condition—partly perhaps because (once the fashion is

[1] A day or two after writing the above we chanced upon a newspaper-paragraph, from which it appears that some progress is actually being made in this direction. It seems that a *Gentlewomen's-Employment-Association* was started in Manchester in 1891 (apparently),and altho "it has met with some practical difficulties, on the whole it seems to have made a good start. During the first week after opening the register there was an extraordinary rush of applicants ; but these gentlewomen betrayed lamentable ignorance of the requirements of employers. A considerable number wanted to be lady-companions, but no employer appeared to be in want of anything of this genteel kind. On the other hand the Association has numerous vacancies for ladies in other capacities, and the Committee are convinced that there is a promising field for the employment of gentlewomen who have only received a training in private households all that is needed being a reorganisation of domestic work, *so as to bring it within the scope of a different class*, and a recognition on the part of all concerned that there is as little loss of dignity involved here as in the work of governesses or hospital-nurses. The Committee complain that there is a strange notion abroad that a lady should be remunerated on a lower scale than is usual in the case of an ordinary domestic servant."

Certainly it is most satisfactory to find our speculative schemes re-echoed almost word for word by a *practical* association. We need hardly add how desirable it is—and the more so in face of this movement—to eliminate from our speech and our minds, as quickly as possible, such phrases as "menial" and "lackey."

instituted) we should prefer the new class, whilst the others would more and more continue to drift into factory-work and such-like occupations, but even still more, eventually, because the illiterate and unrefined class will have disappeared, owing to the descendants of those who now compose it having been *levelled up* to a higher standard [1]—yet we anticipate the advent of the new-era domestic servant long before then. Of course it is obvious that two servants drawn from such very different classes cannot associate in the same house: and in so saying we are not venting a caste-feeling but simply admitting a limitation, the necessity of which must be patent to everybody; for *companionship* between two persons in utterly different stages of refinement is quite impossible: but, admitting this, it by no means follows that the *two classes* of servants cannot co-exist: all that is necessary is to take care that in each household only one class is represented.

Now taking into account all these conditions we ask whether girls of the middleclass, who may be driven to earn their living, would not find their life far happier, far healthier — both physically and morally — far more gracious altogether, if they lived as domestic servants in (perhaps a country) home where their dignity and inde-

[1] It may be retorted that the higher classes would equally have progressed, and thus the relative differences remain the same. But this we think were incorrect. In estimating the possibilities of companionship we have to regard not so much the amount of higher education possessed (for most real ladies and real gentlemen of the present day are deplorably ignorant, and almost wholly uneducated in a true sense) as the attainment of a certain minimum stage of *refinement*—which however of course excludes " illiterateness ' or bucolicism.

pendence were fully recognised, and where perchance a good deal of tolerably intimate companionship with a cultured and gracious "mistress" fell to their lot, than if they slaved hard all day as clerks in some dark and dingy city-office, or employed themselves in many other of the methods by which such girls now earn a hard, a bitterly hard, livelihood—in competition perchance with men. It may retorted that the latter occupations are paid so vastly better : but it is forgotten that "servants" are paid chiefly in *kind*, and that their money wages represent only a small balance of their total wages. A servant, receiving twenty pounds a year, but boarded gratis on good food, and lodged in a large and healthy house, is incomparably better paid than her fellow, slaving in the City for a miserable £50 per year—and never sure of her situation.[1]

It is scarcely necessary to continue farther this part of the examination : taking as an example the housemaid, we have seen how desirable a work hers might be : and it were beyond our purpose to take in detail the duties of every servant, and determine what reforms are necessary, or how far the work may be already unimpeachable. It is sufficiently clear that a servant's duties are very compatible with the selfregard of gentle birth : whilst, since so many ladies now study cookery, and insist on superintending, or actually executing, the cookery of their own households,

[1] Besides which it must be remembered—(1) that we anticipate a somewhat higher rate of wages (and fewer servants in each home); and (2) that if the worst come, a "servant" of such a character, if living many years in one home, might confidently reckon on her savings being supplemented—when she should be past work —by a pension in either money or board and lodging.

it is clear that our new-advent-servants may very well undertake this rôle also.[1]

It will be convenient, before closing this chapter, to offer one or two very brief suggestions as to a development of family life, that may with some reason be expected in the future. Everybody will admit far greater happiness and jollity to exist in a large household than in a small one : and in a higher social state, when human nature is less selfish and disagreeable individuals are fewer, the happiness of large households will be considerably increased. But now, since it may be regarded as axiomatic [2] that in a comparatively rational and moral society families of more than two or three children will

---

[1] Sometimes a cook's duties may become exceedingly unpleasant, but one may anticipate reforms here : and after all, many *ladies* now walk the hospitals and attend the dissection room : what has the cook as bad as that? *Cf. infra* the discussion on Vegetarianism, pp. 207, and 225-8.

[2] As an abstract principle we are of course strong advocates of very small families—and that for many reasons too obvious to require discussion here : whilst it seems certainly axiomatic to us that whenever, in an ideal society, the population of the world shall have reached the maximum desirable, then, assuming every one to marry and no children to die young, the family will invariably consist of two children only, thus exactly preserving the balance of population. Moreover, even in this so excessively *non*-ideal state, our leanings are also strongly towards small families—*not* however as promoted by late marriages with all their moral and emotional loss, but by temperance after early marriage : but unfortunately the problem is, from the point of view of social desiderata, terribly complicated. If Malthusian precepts could be hammered into those who most need them and never act upon them, viz., the poor and the ignorant, then we might far more easily regenerate society : but unhappily, the more we preach Malthusianism, the more do we affect the conduct of the conscientious, highminded, and intelligent, members

be unknown, it is clear that large households of one
family each cannot exist. The solution to this difficulty
is that several families of intimate friends will combine
to form one large household. Each family will have its
own particular suite of bedrooms, and at least one private
sitting-room ; whilst there will be a large common
dining-room and drawing-room, etc. The advantages of
this system are so manifold that it is indeed strange to
find it almost unknown among us : since, by such a

of society—while we may make but little headway among those
who pre-eminently *ought* to adopt Malthus' canons. The result
is apt to be therefor that the prudent, intelligent, and generally
elevated, types of citizens have few children to inherit their good
qualities ; whilst the reckless, the stupid, the improvident, and
the clergy, have large families : so that at this rate the nation
would more and more tend to be swamped by lower types.
Here therefor is as terrible a social danger as that of over-popu-
lation to be guarded against : one must steer between Scylla and
Charybdis—but with a blind and mutinous crew ! Now in a
former work, the *Cry of the Children*, we were at pains to set
forth strongly the wickedness of begetting large families—for we
appealed especially to the poor, and the lower or average middle
classes, who usually cannot afford a family half as large as they
rear, and whose mental and other endowments are not usually
such as to make the preservation of a large posterity by any
means a source of gratulation to the State. But, lest this aspect
might receive undue prominence, we think it highly important
to call the attention of intellectual readers, and anti-Philistines
generally, to the *immense importance* of increasing the numbers
of our *intellectual* races by encouraging their members to marry
early, and to rear more than only two or three children. The
vital importance of thus painlessly supplanting the lower social
types by the higher is admirably set forth by Mr. Francis Galton
in his *Hereditary Genius, Natural Inheritance*, and *Enquiry into
Human Faculty*, to which books we refer our readers for the study
of this subject. Here we will merely quote from the last-named book
a calculation showing how thoroly and *painlessly*, in the natural
course of events, the weaker and lower types could be replaced

scheme, each family would secure the inestimable advantage of privacy whenever it wished it, with the concomitant advantage of ample society at meal-times and whenever otherwise social intercourse were desired. Each lady in turn, for a week or month at a time, would

by the higher, *provided* only that the latter marry early, and the former either marry later or (as we should desire) refrain from begetting children until a later age.

Age of Mother at marriage.	Approximate average fertility.
17	$9\cdot0 = 6 + 1\cdot5$
22	$7\cdot5 = 5$ —
27	$6\cdot0 = 4$ --
32	$4\cdot5 = 3$ —

After number of years as below.	Number of female descendants who themselves become mothers.	
	A.	B.
	100 Mothers whose marriages and those of their daughters all take place at age of 20 years.	100 Mothers whose marriages and those of their daughters all take place at age of 29 years.
	Ratio of increase in each generation being 1·5.	Ratio of *decrease* in each generation being 0·85.
108	175	61
216	299	38
324	535	23

At the same time we must express our strong feeling that, to suggest to such higher types families of five or six children, is to impose upon the mother, at least, the duty of making a very heavy personal sacrifice for the sake of benefitting a tolerably remote posterity.

function as absolute mistress of the house; and it is unnecessary to point out how greatly this arrangement
would economise labour and extend the leisure of all.
It is equally superfluous to point out that a house, large
and commodious enough to take say four or six small
families, would be very far from four or six times as expensive as a house suitable for one such family. In fact,
under this system every one would have the satisfaction
of living in a large mansion at less than the cost of a
small house.[1]

It is worth while also to point out that, not only will

[1] And we might suggest that when, with the advance of democratic feeling, it has become more and more distasteful to see a
large mansion monopolised by one family—as for instance all our
English castles and country-houses are—some such scheme as this
will be introduced to dispose of the trouble. We may rest fairly
assured then that, with increasing democracy and continuous
levelling of wealth, stately architecture will not disappear, nor
English country-houses with their splendid parks become things
of the past: but that instead of ministering, as now, to the selfish pleasures of one family, they will then be enjoyed by many.
We very confidently prophesy some such future for our English
historic piles.

Moreover, we may point out how admirable an opportunity
such a system would offer for paying long visits without the
trouble and expense of, on the one hand, removing one's *Lares
and Penates*, or, on the other, entrusting ·one's house to
caretakers: for what would be easier than periodically to arrange temporary exchange of house-room with others, so that a
family, while retaining all the peculiarly sacred feelings that
attach to a permanent—(not-rented)—home, might yet gain all
the advantages of constant changes of dwelling? When we reflect further that at present our large country-houses are deserted for half the year, and our London houses for another half,
and consider how much selfish waste of the means of happiness
this implies, we may then look forward to a very bright and
happy future for home-life: for town and country livers respectively will temporarily exchange with one another.

this scheme of joint-households minimise very considerably the difficulties of the *servant question*—both because the larger the household the fewer proportionally are the servants required, and because so far as the domestic work be done by the household themselves, the problem is simplified by the large number of members, while the trouble of setting aside a servant's sitting-room, tho it may be serious in a small house, becomes *nothing* in a large one,—*but* that it is attended with very great advantages as regards the children. For there is not only always plenty of society for them on the premises, but the system of *home teaching*, by a governess charged with a group of six or eight children, is greatly facilitated. Of this probable development we have spoken elsewhere,[1] and we shall therefor not linger here on the subject; but it is clear that if these household-clubs usually consisted of people of about the same ages, and having therefor very probably children of about the same ages too, these children would be far more companionable together than would those of one large family.

From our discussion of the servant-question it may have been inferred—and not unnaturally—that we advocated the system—very prevalent we believe in America, and now not unknown in England—of employing a class of domestics known as " Helps " who perform the household work, but are admitted into the family circle. But, altho the whole tendency of our suggestions was to some such consummation, yet we could not but see a grave difficulty—which seemed to render this solution, for the sake of both parties, hardly desirable: for the

[1] *Cry of the Children*, pp. 97, 98.

regular intrusion of such an outsider might become very irksome to the one ; while this very sense of " outsided- ness and intrusion " would gall any independent-spirited employé : some separation of sitting-rooms therefor would seem desirable. *But* now it is clear that all these difficulties are greatly lessened in a joint-household : for there, the society of the " Helps " would not seem an intrusion of outsiders as it would in a single small house- hold, while they would have *their* private sitting-room just as would each family.

It would seem probable that this joint-household-system will greatly inhibit the increase of residential clubs and hotels for bachelors and spinsters : since the home-life would be so far more marked, without involving on the one hand the sacrifice of society, or the danger of being thrown into the society of very disagreeable co-inmates on the other—a danger to which one is always liable in residential clubs and boarding-houses.[1]

[1] It is very greatly to be hoped that in the near future English- men will set themselves seriously to consider the social system now in vogue, and the possible reforms. The terrible isolation and solitariness of the man, who takes a house in a new district, is a grave evil ; and even when he has " made " a small circle of " friends " there he may see very little social life. A keen ap- preciation of the drawbacks of such isolation has led to a pro- posal to form local clubs, thro the medium of which everyone might come to know everyone else in the district. But the Englishman's wholesome horror of being robbed of his privacy, and his equally wholesome objection to be hail-fellow-well-met with every chance neighbour, are likely to seriously handicap any such scheme. The better remedy appears to us to be this— that little colonies should be formed of intimate friends, that a number of intimate friends and relatives should keep house together or take houses tolerably contiguous, so that they would suffer neither from isolation nor from " bad company," which is often *not* " better "—but worse—" than none."

5

POSTSCRIPT.

Reference may be made here to a short article on " A Reformation in Domestic Service" contributed by Mrs. Lewis to the *Nineteenth Century* for January, 1893. With the spirit that prompts this article, with its denunciation of vulgar display, pomp, and wastefulness, we are of course in thoro accord ; but we fear that Mrs. Lewis does not go far enough with us. However, our present concern is not to criticise the article, but to call attention to one happy suggestion made by Mrs. Lewis that had not occurred to us : she points out how beer-making, bread-making, laundry-work, and window-cleaning, all of which were formerly carried out by the permanent staff of household-servants, are now relegated to outside agencies, with great economy and greater efficiency.

Now why—says Mrs. Lewis—" why must there be forty fires kept up all day to boil forty saucepans of potatos (when one larger vessel would suffice) and forty cooks, more or less, in one small street ? Forty cooks, each with her accompanying waste, peculations, and temptations from tradesmen, and with all the expenses of kitchen and scullery ware and appliances to be kept up forty times over, while forty heads of households are racking their brains to write the indispensable orders ? . . . . As a remedy against so much wasteful expenditure, anxiety, and uncertainty, why should there not be a culinary depôt in each street from which the meals could be sent out after the fashion of every foreign town where *restaurateurs* and *trattori* abound ?" The suggestion is certainly well worthy of serious consideration ; and it is scarcely necessary for us to again point out how greatly the possibility of a Social Utopia is advanced by the suppression of all *waste* either of time or material. Mrs. Lewis' suggestion involves, of course, simply one more application of the division of labour, and we are inclined to think that it may be found very feasible as regards cookery at any rate : but when Mrs. Lewis further contemplates the advent of a "noble army of certificated day-housemaids performing the matutinal house-duties with promptitude, regularity, and thoroly trained skill," and disappearing " when their fairy wands have done their office," so that a couple or so of permanent house-servants per family would be sufficient for *waiting* purposes, etc.—then, while gladly acknowedging how great a reform on the present system Mrs. Lewis' scheme would imply, and while fully appreciating the moral advantages of "certificated day-housemaids," living in their own homes, over house-servants isolated from their own kinsfolk and friends, yet we cannot avoid an uneasy suspicion that Mrs. Lewis contemplates very considerably less *levelling* (up) than do we; that her social ideal, tho far above the present real, is yet far too much graduated into degrees of social status. (See chap. ix. ; see also an article in the same periodical for Feb., 1893, on "The Doom of the Domestic Cook.") [We believe that several of these *trattori* have already been instituted (1894).]

CHAPTER V.

" But now the past is out of date,
    The future not yet born;
And who can be *alone* elate,
    Whilst the *world* lies forlorn ? "

BEFORE carrying further our investigations into these
domestic economies, it may be permitted to us to break
off the direct argument and digress for a few minutes
into an enquiry that is pointedly suggested by sundry
reflections in the last chapter. We have had occasion to
point out how, under our present domestic system, there
is allotted to young girls of the housemaid-class a sphere
of duties involving very rough, or even thoroly repulsive,
work; and yet the ordinary householder is conscious of
no imputation upon his chivalry in that he allots such
work to girls; for the tone of his mind is dominated
by caste-sympathy. The ordinary Briton would never
dream of relieving a serving-maid who was struggling
along with a heavy scuttle of coals, altho he would
probably despise himself if he allowed his sister (or still
more a friend's sister) to carry a far lighter load for a
very short distance. So, too, without any compunction, he

condemns young girls to blacklead the grates and wash the hearthstone and doorsteps at terrible cost to their hands; but what would he say of the youngster who should lie snugly in bed while his own sister was washing a doorstep on a bitter morning? He would probably say that flogging were too gentle a treatment for such a mean-spirited cur. Yet pray is not our housemaid also somebody's sister? Again our French neighbours excel in politeness and courtesy; yet anyone who has travelled in France will have noticed that, if he arrive at or leave an inn where there happens to be no Boots present, his heavy portmanteau will be tackled and carried up (or down) stairs by a chamber-maid; a proceeding which an Englishman is apt to resent, preferring to function as luggage-porter himself rather than let a weak *woman* do the work for him —*for he is not accustomed to see women hauling portmanteaus about;* but he will find his polite and courteous French co-traveller handing over his heavy portmanteau as a matter of course to the maid,—*for he is as accustomed to see her so employed as we are to see our housemaids carrying heavy coal-scuttles;* and in neither case does the accustomed strike us as wrong—for custom has blunted the edge of our sympathies.

Again, you are out, and you pass your housemaid, your cook, or your children's nurse; do you doff your hat or salute her? "Of *course* not"—comes the indignant reply —" what an absurd question; as if one would bow to a *servant!*" Well, you meet your baker's wife, or your greengrocer's wife; she, at least, is not a servant; do you salute her? "Certainly not," is the angry retort. No, precisely; you stare straight before you, and utterly

ignore her ; or, perhaps, even into her face with a stony
nescient disregard. Well, we know what you would say
if your son passed his own sister, or mother, or friend's
sister, without saluting her ; but it would be interesting
to learn your opinion of the butcher, baker, candlestick-
maker, artisan, or farm-labourer, who should not lift his
hat when he met *his own* wife or sister.

Well, let us procede. You are in a London street, or
a country lane, and you meet a poor old woman, decrepid,
withered, tottering, soiled, staggering along thro the
mud, or against a bitter, biting, wind, or in the blazing
sunshine, with a heavy—oh for her how heavy !—sack
of hard-gleaned fire-wood, or of some frowzy refuse
painfully and wearisomely collected from a score of
refuse-heaps—the offal of a great city. See ! she is
toiling wearily along, footsore, heavy-burdened, her
grey hair dishonored and besmeared by the refuse she
has collected : what a sight ; what an occupation for
threescore-and-ten years ! Yet will you ease her? will you
carry her sack ? will you even help her to raise it ? No !
Well perhaps you are—like ourself—a moral coward, and
cannot command sufficient courage so to assist a pariah
in the sight of even a countryside—far less of a great
city !—Well, see here ; there is still an opportunity to
help her ; yonder is a strong boy idling ; for a copper
or two he will carry that old woman's sack ; have you
twopennyworth of sympathy ? No ? Well at least have
you the grace to feel dissatisfied with yourself : has
a shadow come between you and the sun as—holiday-
making—you pass along that fair countryside, and
clouded your lightheartedness for a time ; or in the city

has the encounter rather spoilt the satisfaction with which you have been reflecting on your banker's book? Do you not at least feel pained and distressed that poor old women can be found in such a strait? But stay.—We will not wait your answer—tho we see it in your unclouded face: We will first put you yet another question. We are in the open country, in France, in Italy, in Switzerland, or if you like, perhaps in Wales, or Scotland, or even in an English market-garden. There what do you see? a number of young women working hard in the fields, weeding, mowing, reaping, or what not. Approach a little nearer; take a good look at them; many are, or were, handsome; there are dark brunettes, and soft blondes with rounded faces; but the sun and the wind and exposure generally have worked havoc in their beauty; and their faces bewray less the soft womanliness than the seasoned manliness of expression: and then their hands—how rough—how coarse—how thoroly and permanently ingrained and stained! But—but you see all this as plainly as we do, yet you are not moved: there is no sadness in your face, and you seem quite satisfied.

Well, we will ask you one more question. Life has uncertainties which may wreck even the greatest prudence and forethought. You have a mother; she is not yet extremely aged, but she is in years; three score perhaps? Yes? We thought so. You are tenderly and reverently attached to her: you are right. More: you have sisters—fine, noble, tall, white-handed, gently-nurtured, English ladies: and you have a wife like unto them. Now what if some terrible calamity

reduced you all to beggary? What if your aged mother
whom you reverence so lovingly, were compelled for
very subsistence to scour the country-side for fuel or
to rake the city-offal-heaps in search of the unrefused
refuse, for which a few pence might somehow be obtained: what if you saw her staggering along under this
frowzy load, her grey hair dishonored and soiled by the
refuse—and *she* is only threescore years of age you said.
What if your sisters and wife must needs spend the
day labouring in the field, and those fair white hands,
which you are wont to gallantly kiss, were begrimed,
and soiled, and made coarse, by the heavy work, and
the soft beauty of their faces hardened and streaked by
the inclement weather? But there is no need for you
to answer: one can see your answer in your face and
in your whole frame: your face is suffused and burning,
and your eyes are quivering with tears that you *cannot*
stem back, and your lips are tightly drawn, and your
hands clenched, and every muscle and feature proclaim
that the few words, and the barely outlined verbal
picture, have stirred your heart to its lowest depths;
and all your energy of deep love and tenderness is
throbbing in a passionate revolt against this conjectured
suffering of your dear ones. Yet it is *only* conjectural—
very conjectural—and vanishingly improbable: whilst
the other pictures were true and real to the life: *there*
was no conjectured misery but sordid crying poverty;
yet you were moved not. The poor old woman of seventy
staggering under her filthy burden stirred not even
a feeling of sorrow or remorse in your heart: and the
women working in the fields were viewed with utmost

indifference. *Why is your sympathy so caste-bound : is not she too somebody's mother: are there not men who lovingly call them also wives and sisters?* Alas: so narrowed is sympathy by caste that a sight, which should suffice to poison all the pleasure of your day's holiday, fails utterly to move you.[1] Yet we are all alike flesh and blood, and the same passions, joys, and sorrows, are common to us as one mankind.

Now by a train of reflections of this character one may, we think, be enabled more truly and more sympathetically to appreciate the emotional standpoint of those who rank *above* us—and not to fall into the error of harshly judging *their* moral character, when we reflect how the poor might with equal justice rate us as feelingless and purely selfish—with equal justice, that is to say, with equally ample injustice. We mean in this way for instance. An average middle-class Englishman of this day, when he reads or hears of (especially bygone) princes, and powerful peers, and notes the haughty expression of face and manner, and the general antipathetic attitude of mind that they seem to imply, is apt (especially if a good radical) to hate and despise them cordially, and to insist that in such men and women all human feelings of love, gentleness, and sympathy, are choked and killed by the caste-

[1] A few hours after writing out the bulk of the above, we found—in re-reading Green's *Short History of the English People*—a passage that seems exactly to illustrate these remarks. "Chivalry exerted on him (Edward I.) a yet more fatal influence in its narrowing of his sympathy to the noble class, and in its exclusion of the peasant and the craftsman from all claims to pity. 'Knight without reproach' as he was, he looked calmly on at the massacre of the burghers of Berwick, and saw in William Wallace nothing but a common robber."

born spirit of haughtiness and disdain; and that *to no one* could they possibly be lovable and tender, or display a " purple-veined humanity." We are sure that any one —any *thinking* one we mean—who has had the opportunity of, to some extent, observing (from his own middle-class sphere) this class of whom we speak, whether personally, or in the pages of fiction, or in the journalism —especially the humorous journalism—of the day, but mainly in the pages of history, must have been seized by this feeling of recoiling from, and repugnance towards, a race so haughty and humanity-frozen, and must have found himself deeming it well-nigh incredible that even among themselves they could ever love with a hot passionate love, or be moved by keen human sympathy. And yet the foregoing discussion should—we think— make one very chary of adopting such a view: we think that we have learned that men and women may be keenly sympathetic, passionately emotional, tender and amiable, among those of their own caste, and yet callous (if only thro custom *and unimaginative want of thought*) to the sorrows and sufferings of a lower caste. The result of this enquiry is to tolerably satisfy us that sympathy may be keen and perfect *within the caste* and yet almost undeveloped out of it. If this reading be correct, the lesson is not without its value, both theoretically and practically; and especially at a time when the transition from the old caste-and-privilege-traditions to a wide democratism is going on so rapidly. To estimate justly and correctly the worth of all his fellows must be the desire of every philosophic student: and to abstain from unjust and uncharitable depreciation, that can only embitter and lengthen needlessly the already existing class-feuds, should be the earnest endeavor of every reformer. As to the justification for charges made *by the masses* we say no more: but surely no middle-class radical among us has a right to rail against *the* privileged classes as being destitute of sympathy and natural affections, till he have measured them by the standard that might be applied to measure his own relations to the poorest.

Let us pause yet another moment before quitting these phenomena of caste-sympathy and study them in yet another aspect. We will not delay here to point out how intimately bound up is such a restricted sympathy with the moral evolution of all the lower races—who acknowledge the obligations of right and wrong within only a narrow sphere, and confine their sympathies to their own clan or tribe or nation [1]—but we will point out the excedingly marked development of this spirit in a mighty people.

Perhaps the most striking illustration, that can be found anywhere, of what may result from the workings of a thoro and unequivocal *caste-sympathy*—how beautiful, noble, and lovable, the caste may be *when viewed from within ;* how hateful, arrogant and cruel when viewed from without—is to be found in the history of Greek life. We have most of us caught some glimpses of that so-beautiful Greece, glowing in the radiance of sunshine—both sky-shine and soul-shine—and exultant in the joyousness of life when this world was young ; and many a one must often have yearned for the power to roll back

[1] *Cf.* the author's *Cry of the Children* – opening statements.

the centuries and exchange this fevered civilization of to-
day for the beauty and freshness and glow of that young
life.　But it must never be forgotten, on the other hand,
that this joyous Greek life "rested upon the dark back-
ground of slavery"—that the noble life, which we picture
to ourselves, was possible, and *was expressly intended to be
possible, only for Greeks of the Greeks.*

　Compared with the warm and joyous humanity that
the Greek castes displayed *inter se*, and with the fervent
democratism that prevailed in, *e.g.*, Athens, nothing can
be more striking than their absolute exclusion of "barbarians"—*i.e.*, foreigners—and slaves from the pale of their
sympathies.　We have several "Utopias" bequeathed to
us by Greek literature; and the modern reader—more or
less purified from at least this excessive caste-sympathy
—experiences a rude shock of surprise and disgust at
finding that these "Utopias," when depicting an ideally
perfect social state, defined that perfection *as consisting
in the perfection of a mere handful of Greek citizens,*
whilst all the rest of Greece, and of the world, received,
perhaps, rather more cavalier treatment than would pigs
and oxen in a modern "Utopia."　To contemplate—as
we practically can—this remarkable type of mind—both
from inside, and from outside, the narrow circle—to experience alternately a yearning love for this tender
human Greek life of beauty, and a loathing from that
hateful inhumanity in its crass selfishness of caste, is a
most valuable social and moral discipline.　Such study
should preach a weighty lesson on the hatefulness of
caste—to those who even now live a caste-life; and on
the lovableness and warm sympathies of caste-members

inter se—to those who, standing without the pale, naturally deem caste and sympathy to be incompatible, and the members of a caste intrinsically hateful, inhuman, and loveless.[1]

---

[1] To illustrate and justify these remarks we subjoin two or three quotations from Mahaffy's *History of Classic Greek Literature.* " But with all this stran e modernness PLATO is an Hellene of the Hellenes. His prospect does not include any non-Hellenic races. . . . He shares with Isocrates the old, I had well-nigh said the vulgar, Greek admiration for the most retrograde and narrow of the Hellenes—the Spartans ; nay, he is *so exclusive* and aristocratic in spirit, that *he will hardly condescend to consider the lower classes;* and conceives, like every other Greek of that day, even *his ideal society to be a select body of equals amid a crowd of unprivileged inferiors and of slaves.* This it is which gives to Plato's communism a character so radically distinct from all the modern dreams known by the same name, or from the early Christian society described in the *Acts of the Apostles.* It was essentially an aristocratic communism, and *was based, not upon the equality of men, but upon their inherent and radical disparity.* It was really the Republic of the select few, exercising a strict and even intolerable despotism over the masses." (Vol. ii., part i., pp. 208-209.) So too Isocrates' panacea for the troubles of his day was " an invasion of Persia, —plundering its enormous wealth for the benefit of the Greeks. . . . He held, indeed, that Culture, more than Race, was the distinctive feature of real Greeks ; but, for all that, he would not have hesitated to place the most ignorant Spartan far above the most enlightened Macedonian or Egyptian." (*Ibid.*, part ii., p. 5.) Again, as to Aristotle's *Politics*, Mahaffy remarks : " What we rather wonder at is the *narrow Hellenedom* of Aristotle, who has learned nothing from contemporary history, nothing from his own studies in foreign politics, nothing from his varied foreign residences, nothing from the Macedonian Court. . . . With Aristotle Greeks alone are worthy to be free and dominant, and all foreigners are more or less adapted for slavery." . . . (*Ibid.*, p. 208.) " His reflections on slavery . . . [show] that there were already *Abolitionists* in the world, who declared that slavery was against Nature—a doctrine which Aristotle earnestly combats, tho making several important concessions very damag-

ing to his cause." (*Ibid.*, p. 206.) Finally, we may quote the following remark with reference to Aristotle's *Poetics*: "The whole question must be regarded in relation to Aristotle's theory of *intellectual and refined leisure as the chief end of man.*" (*Ibid.*, p. 199.) Now this grand desiderandum was a possibility to the Greeks—the select few—thanks to their institution of slavery : the problem for the modern Utopian is to secure the maximum possible of such *intellectual and refined leisure for each and all— not for a select few only.* We shall have frequent occasion to refer to this implicit criterion in subsequent pages.

CHAPTER VI.

THE SERVANT-QUESTION AND THE TRUE DEMOCRATIC SPIRIT: INCLUDING ADVICE UPON GARDENING.

" Duty—where a man *loves* what he commands himself to do."
— *Göthe.*

" To venture an opinion is like moving a piece at chess ; it may
be taken, but it forms the *beginning of a game that is won.*"—*Ibid.*

RETURNING now to the subject of domestic service, it has
of course been plain to the reader that we have all along
been dealing with the economy of an English middle-class
household possessing two or three or so servants ; and
that we have steadily ignored the problem of millionaire
households.[1]   This has been intentional : not only do
the middle-class households incomparably outnumber the
others ; not only are the problems—in many respects—
simplified by this narrowing ; *but*, as has already been
intimated, we may hope that the average middle-class-
competency is destined to one day supplant, alike, lower-
class poverty, and the waste, prodigality, and luxuriance,
of both the " upper 10,000 " and the commercial millionaire ; or that, at least, if wealthy capitalists continue to
exist (and their existence is in some respects desirable)
they will live no more extravagantly than their fellows.

[1] As for instance we have said nothing about servants' halls, etc.

71

It is clear then that, taking this view, there was small need to discuss the position of servants who are mere superfluous ornaments, or extravagant excrescences, and in no wise *useful.* One can hardly go into the question of luxuries and extravagances without trenching on a division of this subject which is reserved for subsequent discussion; but it may perhaps be admissible here to premise that the progress of social evolution will be marked by a tendency to the continual approximation of the respective wealth, wages, and comfort, of the various classes: the big fortunes will become rare, and the low wages equally disappear. It is assumed that, by no communistic plunder but, by the beneficent working of those natural processes whose laws are formulated by Political Economy, there will be a tendency to an approximately equal distribution of wealth, and that this will be heralded by the increase in price of labor and of those commodities whose price is a function mainly of labor-price. Without further anticipating here the details of this discussion it will be tolerably evident, on very slight reflection, that this increase of expenses will result in *the continuous abolition of those luxuries that are in no true sense conducive to our happiness.* Any readers who will follow out in detail the process of reasoning here indicated will probably admit our assumption that unnecessary servants will disappear: in so far as they minister merely to pomp, display, and extravagance, they are, let us hope, doomed; and anyhow it is no part of our concern to show how in semi-Utopia offices will be filled whose existence is an insult to Utopia: and similarly in so far as, altho workers and not ornaments, they yet can be employed by none but millionaires, they may fairly be considered outside the pale of our sympathies.

To make the matter quite plain we may indicate ladies'-maids, valets, butlers, housekeepers, footmen (the very *flunkies* and anathema to every liberal-minded man), game-keepers, and all such excrescences.[1] We cannot under-stand how any man, however rich, can be content to lavish his wealth on a parcel of useless bipedal—or other —luxuries, when all round him misery is rampant that he might relieve, abuses are crying out to Heaven that he might extirpate, and the beneficent schemes of broken-hearted moneyless reformers are languishing for want of his *squandered* gold. In the name of all commonsense what reasonable enjoyments could any man not get for £2-3000 per year[2]—and what infinite good might not our plutocrats do with their magnificent fortunes! Even putting such considerations on one side it is difficult to realise how any man, who has at all been touched by the breath of democratism, and who feels the brotherhood of man to be something more than an empty catchword, who has studied sociology and anticipates the distant Utopia—very distant, but yet not so unreal but that each of us might by however little help to fashion it if we would,—how any such man can tolerate the feeling

[1] In one of Leech's sketches (noted as a fact) a flunky, just engaged, says, "There's just one question I should like to ask your ladyship. Ham I engaged for work ; or ham I engaged for hornament !!"

[2] Between 2-300 years ago Cowley wrote : "When you have pared away all the vanity, what solid and natural contentment does there remain which may not be had for £500 a year." Of course £500 then represented a great deal more than now.

that some dozen or more of his fellow-men spend their whole lives simply in ministering to his—not needs but—"pleasures" or vanity. Never mind anything about their wages, however good ; here are twelve men whose service is absolutely devoted to one other man ; all are alike flesh and blood ; how can the one man endure such a reflection : 'twere almost insupportable to us ! Indeed so strongly was this feeling developed in our own case that we used to be worried by the thought that in our own household there lived two servants whose lives were devoted solely to subserving the comforts of two other human beings : and we overcame this worry—and that not completely—only by the reflection that there was a sort of equitable division of labor if two people, with the means of living, provided a home for two others, without any means, who in return discharged for their employers certain household services —which by the way the latter could not have performed for themselves. In fact we reconciled domestic service to our democratic proclivities only by regarding the servants as a constituent tho adopted and not native part of our household, of our home, where naturally by a division of labor each performed different duties.

Now, disregarding the retort that might be made by a merely verbal logic,—that what is true of our two servants is equally true of milord's twenty—it appears to us that altho this explanation will very fairly reconcile a democrat for the present to the employment of one or two servants (something, of course, depending upon the size of his family), such reconcilement becomes increasingly difficult with the addition of every fresh servant. Moreover such reconcilement may be endangered, not only by the gross total of the servants, but also by the respective avocations of any given servants. The employment of four or five servants in one large household may be possibly quite compatible, while the addition of a third servant to another may be highly incompatible, with this understanding. It all depends upon what work the servants perform—whether they minister to necessities, or merely to extravagances and luxuries : and moreover a servant who subserves a luxury daily enjoyed by a score of people may be approved of, while the same servant, subserving *one* man's individual luxury, will prove a thorn in the flesh to a consistent democrat. The criterion in fact must be applied with discrimination.

Perhaps this proposition will be made clearer by an example. We know of several households where in each case the family, consisting of two persons, not only is ministered to by two domestic servants, but furthermore employs a gardener. Now here is one man who works hard (for bad pay) purely to minister to the *luxury* of *two* people. We are not in any sense advocating communism but we do feel that there is in this picture something that would greatly worry us ; and we cannot but think that such phenomena as this will have become extinct long before Utopia is even sighted. Were the gardener employed on the grounds of a school, so that his labor gave pleasure to two or threescore boys or girls, one might feel very well satisfied—for here would be a division of labor such as we may expect will obtain —in semi-Utopia anyhow : but that the whole lifework of one man should simply subserve the luxury of two other people—this *does* stick in our throat abundantly.

"Is it contended then that as Utopia approaches gardens will cease to exist?" No; far from it: what is contended for is simply that new methods of gardening must supervene, and gardening by proxy become rare. Gardening may be a pleasure in itself, or it may be simply the means to an end—such end being the pleasure derived from looking at a fine parterre. To an immense number the garden-work is in itself a pleasure, [1]

---

[1] There are even—as we know from personal experience—some extraordinary individuals so constituted that they find pleasure in mowing a lawn! If such mental traits should persist, of course the abolition of most professional gardeners in Utopia would cause us no trouble; if not, there would seem no remedy but for Utopians to do without lawns. Perhaps, however, children might be turned to account, since they usually enjoy racing about with a mowing-machine. It may be worth while to extend this discussion somewhat beyond the remarks in the text, since it will afford a very good example of how very much pleasure may still be retained even compatibly with the sacrifice of such appliances—human or otherwise—to pleasure as reflection may assure us cannot persist into Utopia. The pleasures derived from a garden are fourfold (putting aside the pleasure of gardening—where it exists)—

(1) The kitchen-garden ministers to our material comfort.

(2) The flower-garden is a beautiful sight

(3) There is so much large open space in which to wander—free from street-sights and street-noises.

(4) There may be included a recreation-ground—as, *e.g.*, a tennis-lawn.

Now the first consideration we put aside altogether, since, on any large scale, kitchen-gardens are probably doomed—the requisite produce being raised very far more cheaply, better, and less wastefully, in large market-gardens, in accordance with the general principle of the division of labor; while, if anyone like to amuse himself by a little kitchen-gardening on a small scale, clearly that is a case for individual, or family, attention.

and to this extent therefor proxy-gardening were
evidently absurd : for the rest—the question will finally
remain whether the loss of a garden, or the loss of time,
and the trouble involved, in doing the necessary but distasteful garden-work, be the greater evil. It appears to
us however that, in and near cities, the small private
gardens will be to a very great extent superseded by a
central park and recreation ground common to all the
houses built round it. This appears to meet our requirements very fully : for such a park, when once wisely laid

The third want is sufficiently met by the scheme of central
quasi-parks alluded to in the text, where, by co-operation, each
may obtain the pleasure of a large park, whilst incurring the
cost only of a garden.

The fourth want may almost be bracketed with the last, so
that we are reduced to the second want only ; that is to say, the
Utopians have to solve the problem of how to keep a small
flower-garden (and lawn perhaps ?) without employing a gardener ;
or, in other words, is the pleasure of such a garden in excess of
the trouble required by it ? Remembering the existence of the
central park many people will vote for no private garden at all ;
but for the benefit of those who still want their own flower-garden
we may point out how very greatly the problem is now simplified
by this reduction.

To begin with, the first laying out of, planning, and planting,
a garden, cutting walks, piling rockery, and so on—in a word
the *creative* work of " landscape-gardening "—is pure pleasure, besides being remarkably healthy work. Even ourself—who never
do a stroke of gardening—can thoroly enjoy *this* department of
work ; for here there is the keen pleasure of *creating.* The real
monotony and trouble commence when the garden is made, and
requires keeping up, weeding, sweeping, raking, and the rest of
it. But even here the majority of English gardeners—thanks
simply to their own folly, pigheadedness, and want of taste—
vastly increase their labors. A rational man would begin by
filling up by far the greater portion of his garden with evergreens,
and flowering bushes and shrubs, which persist, make an admirable show, require almost no attention, and choke any

out, could be kept up at a vanishingly small expenditure of labor; while—since a very few gardeners would thus minister to the pleasure of scores of people—there would be a very fair division of labor, and their employment need not upset the feelings of the wildest democrat. It stands to reason that with the supersession of so many (in large part incompetent) gardeners, the wages of the remainder could be very much increased—apart from the influence exerted by other sociological factors: which only shows once more how all the parts of the social ma-

neighboring weeds. The border-space that remains he would then fill up with hardy perennials that look after themselves, and are dangerous rivals to the weeds; so that, having once planted his garden, his gardening labor is reduced to a very small minimum—consisting in little more than occasional sweeping, clipping, and weed-slaughtering. Above all he would avoid —as it were poison—that atrocious system of *bedding-out* and *geometrical gardening*, invented in an evil hour by some execrable fool who thus achieved a trinity of evils, in that he utterly wrecked all the grace, poetry, and natural beauty, of an old English garden, created a panorama of hideousness, and introduced the practice of annually wasting an enormous amount of human labor in order to successfully present a hideous glare of all incongruous colors and stiff forms during four months of the year.

But in such a system of gardening, as is sketched above, it will be seen that half an acre or more of ground may be kept full of blossom and perfume at the cost of almost no labor; and if a man have his own private half-acre full of almonds, lilacs, viburnums, rhododendrons, azaleas, roses, lilies, campanulas, and other border-flowers, and evergreens,—besides having the run of a large central park—what more *can* he want?

Of greenhouses we have said nothing hitherto. To a large extent greenhouses exist simply in order to winter the hideous artificialities destined for *bedding-out*—another example of the enormous expense to which men will go in order to uglify their possessions, and defraud themselves of beauty and perfume, in deference to an insane and wicked fashion. For the rest, if people

chine work together, and how any one advance implies, and is implied by, other and corelative advances. It may farthermore afford some satisfaction to some of us to note that, when garden-space is acquired mainly by a common park and but slightly by private gardens (the existence of which in a small degree however would pre-serve for us that privacy so dear—and rightly so dear— to Englishmen) there will be nothing to provoke that unpleasant consciousness of quasi-selfishness that worries a social reformer when he reflects that several acres of

can find appreciable pleasure in a greenhouse, they may very well be left to attend on it themselves in leisure moments : but private hothouses on the large scale as a mere appanage of pomp, and ministrant to plutocratic luxury, we consider of course irre-trievably *doomed.* One thing however must be carefully remem-bered by those who cannot imagine themselves happy, even in Utopia, without a garden, and yet cannot face the thought of ex-pending even this minimum of labor and time on it. They need to be reminded that—practically--life will be far longer in Utopia than here. We mean that the available leisure of each one will be far greater than now. The bread-winner will work but a very few hours daily ; so that, even after adding to this work the work which he now delegates to others, he will have a large balance to the good. It is highly important to remember this factor in any hedonistic estimate.

We have followed out into this so much detail what may ap-pear a very trivial subject, because it appears to us an exceedingly valuable *type-illustration* for Utopian speculators. The conclusions just reached only emphasise once more the truth of Spencer's doctrine that ideal arrangements and ideal men are possible only in ideal environments : and that Utopia can be reached *only* by a proportionable metamorphosis of the *whole* social system. For in our gardening-example we find, in last resort, that the plea-sure, which an Utopian regard for others' happiness indicates can only be acquired by one's own labor, is yet possible, and with a balance to our credit, *if* we have so much extra leisure as is possible for all only in Utopia. Utopia is always consistent with Utopianism.

fine garden, with masses of blossom and glorious trees, are dedicated to the exclusive use of perhaps himself and one or two children ; while scores of his surrounding neighbors are cooped up in narrow cages, pining and yearning for the country-sights-in-town that his garden would afford them : so that at present two or three people enjoy it—sometimes for only two or three hours a week ; and at *all times* this immense potential pleasure is to nineteen-twentieths of its extent unused.   And looking at it as statesmen, here is in any large town only so much ground, covered by so many thousand people : and of this ground only so many scores of acres are gardens — the   rest being pavingstones, bricks, and mortar.   But this limited extent of garden-ground, which might afford unflagging enjoyment to certainly very many hundreds, if not to several thousands, is the exclusive pleasure-monopoly of a very very few dozen—or perhaps even units.   Now whenever this reflection comes home to a large-garden-owner of genuine democratic[1] feeling—this animal being however, most unhappily, an *extraordinarily rare hybrid,* but one nevertheless likely to become comparatively common in the distant by-and-bye —-it will worry him to such an extent that the very sight of his garden will altogether upset his peace of mind for the rest of that day.   How much happier will his representative and descendant be in the future days of small-gardened-houses built round a common park !

---

[1] We use *democrat* in its best sense as implying one to whom all manhood is dear—who feels as a living reality the *brotherhood* of man : *philanthropist* would exactly meet our requirements but the word has become too specialised.

We are afraid that these remarks will seem but arrant communism to many; but we cannot help it, and must accept the risk. So far are we from any communistic intentions however, that, in thus speculating, we not only do not contemplate the "appropriation" (anglicé, *robbery*—if the communists, who do not think it robbery, will pardon us) of these large private gardens for more general use, but we do not even look to the municipal buying up of open spaces as the machinery for securing "central parks"[1]: on the contrary we look merely to the action of private unselfish impulse and private enterprise. Once succeed in infecting people with this feeling, and all will come easy: those fortunate possessors of large gardens will give their friends and neighbors the run of them: while public opinion will demand the new style of house planning which is here indicated.[2]

Well this question of the employment of gardeners has led us into a long digression, which is however very useful, as clearing up a typical case: to return—there is still remaining one class of servants somewhat difficult to deal with—the class namely of grooms and coachmen, of whom the 1881 Census records *over 73,000* in England and Wales alone: 73,000 domestic grooms and coachmen or over 1 per cent. of the *total male population* of

[1] Our central parks being—it must be observed—private, and limited to a certain group of residents.

[2] The misfortune is that, as regards houses, we are the very slaves of the builders, who build insane houses which we must occupy—for there are no better. Now nobody with eyes will question the evident truth that builders are—speaking generally—the most dolorously uninventive, unprogressive, and unmitigated, fools: the first reform therefor must be to abolish the present builders-class.

the country above 20 years of age! We have concluded that those miserable abortions footmen—mere useless lazy lumber—will inevitably disappear; and it is not difficult to foresee that coachmen, as such, coachmen pure and simple, will follow them : men will prefer to drive themselves rather than to incur the unnecessary expense of a beliveried, befurred, bebigbuttoned, live figurehead, who is required, not for use, but to meet the ridiculous demands of an extravagant fashion. But there is some difficulty in deciding whether *grooms* will disappear in semi-Utopia and Utopia—the difficulty being greatly due to the fact that their work is so distinctly unpleasant: since, however, horses in abundance will evidently be as necessary as now, we are inclined to think that, to a very great extent, private possession of horses will be superseded by the hiring of horses, when required, from a large public establishment—this being a far less extravagant procedure—and that those people who are so fond of horses as to require the constant use of one will do the grooming themselves.[1]

To hark back now to domestic servants more particularly, we have shown how, by the abolition of needless and nasty work, the servants' position may be rendered one that there should be not the least difficulty in filling. But there is yet another aspect of this great "servant-question" that it is important not to neglect : we have to face the possibility of two contingencies, either of which would compel us to ask the question—Can we

---

[1] It must again be noted that, their leisure-time being so much greater than ours, there is really no such aggression on their happiness as might be at first supposed.

entirely dispense with servants, and yet live happily?
We have shown reasons for thinking that the existence
of servants is consonant with even *semi-Utopia* anyhow;
whether or no *Utopia* demand their abolition, and
negative their continuance with however great modifications, is a question that will come up for consideration
very shortly. But, however consonant with semi-Utopia
may be domestic service, it does not *certainly* follow that
we should be able to obtain servants—for other causes
now unforeseen might militate against this by drawing
off our possible servants to still more pleasant occupations
—or that we should think the game (of having them)
worth the candle (of paying for them). The question
thus arises whether we can imagine ourselves happy
without servants, and we think it is very easy to understand that many families may find it far more pleasant
to dispense with servants altogether. It is obvious that
the very same reforms which will make it possible for—
well—young ladies to take service as cooks or housemaids, will render it equally easy for the ladies of the
house to do this work themselves; the same occupation
being far more beneficial and healthy to them, both
physically and morally, than their present frivolous
" pass-times " of reading trashy novels or of embroider-
ing impossible plants on unnecessary antimacassars:
whilst a comparatively rationalised, and less innately snobbish, public opinion will cease to think it impossible to
visit ladies who " keep no servants !" [1]

[1] "There is hardly any part of the present constitution of
society more essentially vicious, and more morally injurious to
both parties, than the relations between masters and servants.

When one considers that the social reconstitution going on must finally result in making the cost of living far more expensive than at present to the middle and upper classes—the increased wages to labor necessarily increasing the cost of building, of clothes, of food, and of ornaments ; this being, as we take it, the main process by which the apportioning of the national wealth will be brought about—and when one computes the really very considerable addition to the annual expenditure represented by the actual total wages of one servant, reckoning not only her—by assumption, very appreciable—money-wages, but also the cost of her board and the increased house-rent necessitated ;—then one may, we think, see strong reason for deeming that, in a very large number of cases, the household will prefer to dispense with a servant altogether. And here we must take cognisance of another factor, which only shows once more how indissolubly bound up and mutually dependent are all the component parts of social welfare. For, *at pre-*

To make this a really human and a moral relation is one of the principal desiderata in social improvement. The feeling of the vulgar of all classes that domestic service has anything in it peculiarly mean, is a feeling than which there is none meaner. In the feudal ages, youthful nobles of the highest rank thought themselves honoured by officiating in what is now called a menial capacity, about the persons of superiors of both sexes, for whom they felt respect. . . . . . Much of the daily physical work of a household, even in opulent families, if silly notions of degradation, common to all ranks, did not interfere, might very advantageously be performed by the family itself, at least by its younger members ; to whom it would give healthful exercise of the bodily powers, which has now to be sought in modes far less useful, and also a familiar acquaintance with the real work of the world," etc., etc. (J. S. Mill "On Comte," p. 167).

sent, to wholly dispense with servants would produce grave evils, since it would necessitate either always leaving some one of the household at home to "take care" of the house, or else leaving it empty, perhaps for hours at a time. The former alternative has the hedonistic drawback that the family is never able to go out together; while the latter has to reckon with the serious danger of thieves. But by hypothesis in our semi-Utopia there are no thieves : that is to say, only in so advanced a social state as may render it necessary to dispense with servants do we find that social environment (of honest people) that annihilates the—at present—one remaining strong reason for retaining servants. How very greatly a little (general) honesty may simplify social troubles is well instanced by the condition of Heligoland. According to a recent newspaper-account, the effect of Heligoland being a small isolated island is that burglars are un·known : doors are left unbolted, and houses empty and unguarded, simply because no thief could escape from the island with his plunder, and, since everybody knows everybody, rapid detection were certain.

This shows us clearly how very much expense, trouble, and vexation, we might avoid, were only every individual as honest as the Heligolanders—voluntarily or inevitably are.

POSTSCRIPT.

Some months after writing this essay, we made the acquaintance of William Morris' delightful book, *Hopes and Fears for Art :* and—having a great reverence for the opinions of a trained artist, or, indeed, of any trained specialist within his own sphere of work—we were not a little gratified to find Mr. Morris denouncing Geometrical Gardening and the Bedding-out system almost in our own words. For instance he remarks—" But there are some flowers (inventions of men, *i.e.*, florists) which are bad color altogether and *not to be used at all. Scarlet-geraniums,* for instance, or the yellow calceolaria, which indeed are not uncommonly grown together profusely, in order, I suppose, to show that even flowers can be *thoroly ugly*" (p. 127). On many other points we found Mr. Morris' opinions identical with those expressed in various places in this essay : so much so indeed that, had we read his work before writing, we should scarcely have dared to express many of our own opinions for fear of being accused of barefaced plagiarism. We need scarcely remark how great a gratification it is to us to find so able an ally, and to learn that, as regards the "arts" of life, even a wholly untrained and artistically-ignorant writer may find salvation—by the help of first principles, and a strong love of Beauty, only.

CHAPTER VII.

MANUAL AND MENTAL WORK; OR, THE UTOPIAN DIVISION OF LABOUR: WITH AN INQUIRY INTO GENIUS.

"That any citizen may so behave as not to deduct from the general welfare, it is needful that he shall perform such function or share of function as is of value equivalent at least to what he consumes."—*Herbert Spencer.*

BEFORE finally quitting the subject which has already occupied us for the last two or three chapters, it may, however, be worth while to briefly enquire whether after all—so far as we can see—there are likely to be any "servants" *of any kind* in *Utopia itself*; or, to put the question quite generally, whether it is probable that each man will then do for himself all such work as he would now pay—permanent or temporary—servants to do for him—or whether he will continue so to employ them? The answer to this question will be found, we think, to depend upon the assumptions that we make regarding Utopia, and the definitions by which we limit it.

In the first place, it is abundantly clear from the preceding discussions that, long before *Utopia* be reached, the amount of servant-performed-work will have been reduced to a minimum. Not only will all the excres-

cences and mere extravagances of display have disappeared, but people will have learned to wait upon
themselves in a thousand matters for which they now
lazily rely upon ladies'-maids, valets, and waiters.   But
beyond all these there lies the solid residuum of useful
and necessary, but purely mechanical and unintelligent,
work that must be done by somebody ; will each man do
his own share of it, or will it all be deputed to a class
of workers who do nothing else?   Here, after defining
Utopia, we must take for our guide the *great principle
of the division of labor.*   If the definition of Utopia
admit that, altho all are equally happy,[1] yet not all are
equally gifted, but some are born geniuses, others born
mediocre—then the problem is, we think, settled at once.
Economics teach us the great advantages resulting from
a division of labor, when each concentrates his energies
on what he can best do ; and since upon the most economical—*i.e,* most efficient and speedy—possible production of our requisites must depend the shortening of
our hours of labor, or in other words, our opportunities
for enjoyment, it seems clear that in Utopia, even as here,
will there be such a division of labor that the clever
man will do nothing (*no wage-earning*) but intellectual
labor, whilst the less gifted will do their share of the
manual work, and be well paid therefor.   In addition to
this consideration—of the time-economy of such division
of labor—it will be clear that a considerably more

---

[1] And by equality of happiness we should here understand
that each exercised every function with a maximum hedonistic
effect—and was quite satisfied with such function-possibilities
as nature had allotted to him.

direct and tangible hedonistic loss to the community must ensue if a portion of the working-time of any great artist-creator be spent in doing his share of manual work: for the world will lose so much of the beauty that he would otherwise have created. It seems to us, therefor, that, if we assume inequality of genius in Utopia, we are bound to assume that there will be such division of labor as corresponds to our present condition, where we have hand-laborers and head-laborers; and it will at once be evident that in endeavoring to clear up a very minor subject, *viz.*, that of the persistence of servants in a narrow sense, we have really found an answer to a very far broader question. We have only to reflect for one moment on the utter chaos that would ensue were we to commence disregarding the division of labor, insisting that every man should be his own bootmaker, tailor, haberdasher, haircutter, cook, builder, etc., etc., to receive a most salutary lesson on the absurdity of supposing that "Utopia" connotes the abolition of very thoro specialisation. Why, were we to attempt any so mad and preposterous a scheme as that just hinted at, so far from life being made happier and leisure increased, our lives would be exhausted after day-long drudgery before we had learned our multifarious trades. But if one thus admit that the specialised builder, baker, tailor, doctor, schoolmaster, *et id omne genus*, must always exist in Utopia, in order to ensure efficient and economic working, one must also, we think, admit that besides the specialisation involving distinctions between builder and baker on the one hand, and between medico and teacher on the other, there must also be that

7

twofold specialisation on which hangs the broad distinction between two great classes—of hand-workers and of head-workers. The only possible alternative to this were to hypothecate two trades, or rather one " craft " and one " profession," to every man. One must then assume that every baker is also, say, a music-master; every builder also a doctor ; every tailor also a sculptor ; and so on. But the difficulties, in which one thus becomes involved, are manifest. In the first place such a very daring attempt to circumvent the great principle of the division of labor would incur its meet punishment; for our unfortunate doctor-builder, *e.g.*, would find himself almost as greatly troubled by his twofold office as was Pooh-Bah, the Lord-High-Everything, of Gilbertian fame : assuredly the physician would be perpetually wanted in one place and the builder in another.

Secondly, far more manual laborers are wanted than mental laborers : how are we to divide the offices when there are perhaps three hand-workers and one brain-worker required ? If any one reply that each man should be baker or builder, etc., for 3-fourths of his working-day, and physician or music-master for the remaining 1-fourth —so that instead of having one whole physician we should have four quarter-physicians—then the result is surely so palpably absurd, so undeniably provocative of inefficiency and muddling, as to condemn itself.

Thirdly, and most important of all, we *cannot afford to waste genius:* and if a man have a genius for sculpture, music, surgery, teaching, research, or what not, then it were the grossest folly to insist that he shall exercise his special faculty for only a quarter of his working-time, while devoting the remaining 3-fourths to laying bricks or making breeches, that would be every whit as efficiently laid or made—probably far more efficiently—by a workman who has no gift at all for surgery, music, sculpture, or teaching.

Fourthly, it is important to remember that if every man had to learn two trades, there were so much the less of his life left for genuine "living." for enjoying himself—we mean—intellectually, esthetically, and physically. It must be sedulously borne in mind that in no Utopia can we escape a certain amount of *hard work :* there will be for each and all of us so many hours a day [1] of necessary *work*—all the glad remainder being devoted to music, art, poetry, study, riding, walking, boating, swimming, dancing, talking, and so on. Now the one grand thing to be aimed at in Utopia—and one grand factor in Utopia—is to diminish to the lowest possible minimum each one's daily *work*. But if every man had to learn two professions it is clear that there were so much more hard work (of learning) to do than would otherwise be the case : in effect then his life-time were shortened [2] and, besides this *direct* shortening of verit-

---

[1] On an average, that is : thus if three hours a day suffice, every one will really do—no doubt—five or six hours every working-day : but then he will have one or two days complete holiday every week : and long stretches of holiday for travelling : and, in such a state, there will be a rational division and alternation of holiday times thro'out the week and the year.

[2] This would perhaps be met if we adopted Spencer's principle that every activity may become a source of pleasure to us after sufficient *moulding*—so that the twofold apprenticeship would cause twofold pleasure. But even so (and we are so far striving to work out these problems without availing ourself of that principle) the study of bricklaying and learning of Materia Medica—

able *living*-time, there is the indirect shortening that must ensue if, by this dovetailing of professions, lesser efficiency and less expedition are caused.

These arguments (which probably by no means exhaust the armoury of that arch-beneficent science of economics) appear to us to amply demonstrate that in Utopia (and *a fortiori* in semi-Utopia, which is far less distant) there will be the same specialisation into headworkers, heartworkers, and handworkers, that we see at the present day : and for these reasons we feel bound to entirely dissent from Prince Krapotkin's picture of the future social state.   Looking at the case in this light, we cannot therefor admit that " whosoever he might be —scientist or artist, physician or surgeon, chemist or sociologist, historian or poet—he would be the gainer if he spent a part of his life in the workshop or the farm (the workshop *and* the farm) if he were in contact with humanity in its daily work, and had the satisfaction of knowing that he himself discharges his duties as an unprivileged producer of wealth. . . . . And how would gain the poet in his feeling of the beauties of Nature, how much better would he know the human heart, if he met the rising sun amidst the tillers of the soil, himself a tiller ; if he fought against the storm with the sailors on board ship ; if he knew the poetry of labor and rest, sorrow and joy, struggle and conquest." [1]

both *necessary* evils—are not *so* pleasurable as leisure-time studies and pursuits : so that the total possible pleasure is diminished. Moreover the apprenticeship to the medical profession is already a long one : if the probation be doubled by the learner's time being halved, then the suspense will become intolerably tedious. " Hope deferred " etc.   (See also note to p. 213.)

[1] *Nineteenth Century*, March, 1890.

No work is so exhausting as headwork; and it is therefor impossible (in any healthy society where the genius is not sacrificed for the good of others) to get more than a certain quantum of headwork per day from each such worker. But if, furthermore, his working day is to be half or three-fourths occupied in bricklaying or tailoring, then we shall have to wait a weary long while for the fruits of his work. In fact, any such proposition involves such an *extravagant waste of brain-power* (the most valuable motive-power of all) that we almost venture to think that it is only requisite to realise Prince Krapotkin's scheme in order to reject it as an impossible solution.[1]

We have not yet noticed one objection—which with some would appear the gravest of all—against such head-cum-hand-working; namely, that it almost necessarily involves—or at the very least it subjects us to the heaviest risk of—a governmental overlooking, a dragooning, an elaborate system of officialism, of restrictions, commands, rules, regulations, and interferences, such as are utterly incompatible with thoro spontaneity and individualism, and clash harshly with our healthy English notions of LIBERTY. We have not put this objection in the forefront, and cannot expect it to have

---

[1] In Prince Krapotkin's scheme the workers are—we believe—to divide not their *days*, between hand and head work, but their *lives*. Thus, after ten or fifteen years' sailoring, tailoring, or bricklaying, the worker would take up teaching, surgery, or what not. This scheme, whilst avoiding one minor absurdity, to which we have drawn attention, escapes none of the chief objections one whit, and encounters the graver objection that youth is the time for learning, and that after years of this manual work it is too late to learn a profession.

any weight with our communistic friends—who think nothing so delightful as to be ruled by the State for the State's good: but we hope that our other arguments are sufficiently satisfactory: and, since our object has been, not to prove that manual and mental labourers must co-exist in Utopia,[1] but simply to enquire, purely dispassionately, whether they would or not, we can very well afford to waive this last argument if the Communists think it untenable.

But, having cleared up this perplexity, we are at once met by another. Admitting that some will do only headwork, and some only handwork, will all be paid alike: in other words, will remuneration depend upon value (or rarity) of result, or upon quantity of labor bestowed—as in the celebrated Owenite labor-exchange? That it would be practicable in this present state of society to make price a function simply of quantity-of-labor-bestowed (*i.e.*, of length of laboring-hours) seems almost so transparent a fallacy that one wonders how an Owenite exchange could ever have been instituted. But we are inclined to think that in a *perfect Utopia* there will be, if not this scheme, at least a very close approximation to it. It is unnecessary to prove that Utopians would desire it and, so far as possible, bring it about; the only question is whether it would come about as a natural process—in

---

[1] If any communist accuse us of setting out to prove this conclusion, we can only reply that the accusation is false: we began to think out the subject, and our train of reasoning is set down exactly as it ran. We think that there is scarcely any such caste-prejudice apparent in this essay as would justify the false accusation: and we did not anticipate some of the conclusions to which our reasoning has led us.

which case alone it would flourish healthily ; for we have the most profound distrust of all *artificial schemes,* by which doctrinaires flatter themselves that they can circumvent the inevitable Nemeses of Nature. We think that—without going into details—since we hope at another time to enquire fully into this subject—we may see various indications pointing to such a state of things. The mere fact that intellectual acquirements become commoner will tend to depreciate their pay relatively to the pay of manual workers ; whilst a possibly relatively decreasing liking for manual work will inevitably force up the pay by diminishing the supply of labor. Moreover, as genius becomes commoner,[1] not only will the enormous sums now paid for works of art, and to musicians and surgeons, necessarily become smaller, but if the Utopians get into their heads the notion that only labor and not heaven-given brains [2] should be paid for, they will be on

[1] Commoner both because more geniuses will be born and because every genius that is born (and lives) will be made known. ' Mute inglorious Miltons" will not exist in Utopia.

[2] We trust that no reader will suspect us of anything so wildly preposterous as a desire to depreciate the unique value of genius, i.e., of heaven-given brains. We do not think that anyone can more fully recognize than ourself how absolutely indispensable is genius to progress in any direction, and how crying is our need for more genius ; and equally do we appreciate Mr. Galton's con-clusions (see *Hereditary Genius*—a golden book) that a greater supply of genius per million inhabitants is correlated with a heightening of each intellectual grade. But in the text we are concerned with not backward to-day but—advanced Utopia ; and, farther, in speaking of the disproportionate pay of head-work, we refer only to *certain* kinds of work which to-day are ridiculously over-paid *in comparison* with, not only simple labor, but, with other work of equal or greater genius. Not only do we think that the disproportion between the pay of, on

that account also averse to paying so highly as at present; in fact the mere desire to equalise the wages of labor will at *that stage* operate as a *natural* factor in the equalising tendency.   And lastly, the more that manual

the one hand, a celebrated painter or popular surgeon, and, on the other, that of a philosopher or scientific enquirer, will be relatively reduced ; but we also suspect that the great incomes of the lucky former few will be absolutely and considerably reduced.   Most of all, too, do we consider as incongruous (in Utopia) the huge payments made to a prima-donna, *e.g.*, who is paid, not for brain-power even, but for the lucky natural gift of a rare voice.   It is in such cases that the payment is so glaringly disproportionate to the labor.   At the same time we may point out that this question as to whether—in a strictly moral scheme, in an ideal state where men's actions will be presumably somewhat otherwise than as at present formulated by Political Economy— native Genius bestowed by Nature, or personal Labor bestowed by each man, should be reckoned pay-worthy, is an important one. At present, of course, literally the best policy for the community is to heavily reward genius, and by every means to encourage its exertion, since a constant supply of genius is the *sine quâ non* for progress in every sense, and to ill reward it is suicidal ; but possibly by and bye Genius—arrived at a correspondingly high moral stage—will decidedly object to being heavily paid and rewarded for its own good luck in having been born genius.   The case is very analogous to that of the love of fame and glory, concerning which we must speak in a later chapter. (See pp. 109-121).

We may incidentally remark here that such a conception of the claims of Genius must react more or less on our attitude towards Individualism (as opposed to Socialism) ; for tho we may admit to the fullest, with Spencer, the general postulates of a man's indefeasible right to benefit by his own *labor*, and furthermore the practical necessity that, during the struggle for existence, the best-endowed (luckiest) should profit by their *natural endowments*, yet the case of naturally-gifted men in a comparatively civilized society is very different.   At any rate, we should greatly like to see the point argued whether a born prima donna, or born genius of any sort, can with *perfect equity* amass a fortune by means of such lucky natural gifts.

wages go up, the more, that is, that the cost of living becomes increased, the less money will it be possible to pay for valuable headwork. It does, therefor, appear to us that in *perfect* Utopia there is a strong probability of all labor —manual or mental—being equally paid: and perhaps this conclusion will tend to reconcile to us the communists, who may resent our dissent from the propositions of Prince Krapotkin. At the same time, it is highly necessary to point out that this system of payment of labor could work *only in Utopia :* in our present semi-moral condition the effects of any such system (if it could even be introduced—which, of course, it could not) would be ruinous. If six hours bricklaying were paid as well as six hours teaching or six hours carving or six hours singing, very few would take the least trouble to acquire difficult arts or to train natural gifts at an expense of hard study: all improvement, all progress, would be abruptly checked, and the world might choose—perhaps—between stagnation and degeneration. The prospect of a big reward is to a large extent the stimulus by which action, invention, and progress, are born ; and, normally, only a very perfect man would be so naturally moral and conscientious as to exercise, to the very fullest, his talents and genius for the same reward that a bricklayer gets. Therefor, we have been careful to say that labor will probably be thus paid in a *perfect Utopia :* in the preliminary semi-Utopia no such system can prevail : tho of course we doubt not that the inequality of pay will be far less than now.

But it is time to remind the reader that for some pages we have been arguing upon the former of two assumptions as to, or rather definitions of, Utopia. We agreed to assume, first of all, that in Utopia men are not all equally gifted : if however we now make the second assumption that all are equally gifted, what result will follow ?   Clearly then several objections to the non-specialisation into manual and mental workers, will vanish : and it becomes simply **a** question whether it would be convenient to adopt the one system or the other.   Anyhow, it would seem certain that in this case all wages would be equal.

But, as a matter of fact, the supposition appears to us utterly improbable : for if all are equally gifted, no geniuses can exist, or (what comes to the same thing) all alike are geniuses.   If anyone should seek to escape this by hypothecating a certain limited number of geniuses, and perfect equality of gifts among all the rest, he can be at once shown to hypothecate a self-contra-dictory proposition.   A genius is not a solitary fact, but a correlate of very many preceding facts : a one genius must be preceded and followed (it is a necessary con-sequence of heredity) by many half and quarter geniuses : so that the dead level of "giftedness" is at once broken up, and our second assumption vanishes.

It is—to take a physical analogy—just like the case of a mountain-peak : a lofty peak always does, and always must, imply a somewhat less lofty mountain-range: and we might far more reasonably expect a single straight columnar peak to rise sheer 10,000 feet out of a prairie, than expect isolated geniuses to rise from an absolute dead level of clever men.   But if any would escape this dilemma by asserting that all alike are geniuses, or that none are, he does not so get out of the quagmire. Are we to understand that every man is a Shakespeare, a Raphael, a Newton, a Shelley? Then, involuntarily, bursts forth the reflection, "What an unmitigated nuisance we should all be to one another: the nineteenth century would be almost preferable to such an appallingly clever Utopia!" But if—putting aside this supposition for a moment—it be assumed that in that high dead-level of Utopia no such geniuses as these giants of the Past can again appear, then again the assumption lands one in a contradiction. What possible warrant can there be for assuming that the highly gifted future is unable to produce what the barbarous past has produced?

This is exactly as absurd as to consider Shelley and Milton more likely natives of Fiji or Australia than of civilised England : it is simply to assert that a lofty mountain-peak is more likely to occur in England than in the Alps : which is absurd.

We return, therefor, to the assumption that not only are all equally gifted in Utopia, but that all are geniuses at least equal to the greatest men of the past. But on closer examination this will also, we think, be found to involve a contradiction. What precisely do we understand by equal gifts—equal genius? Between two geniuses of the same *quality* we may certainly institute a quantitative comparison ; and we may decide that Shelley was greater than Wordsworth, Mozart than Haydn, Newton than Huyghens, Darwin than Lamarck, and so on without very much trouble. But how are we to quantitatively compare artistic or musical genius with scientific genius? How can we possibly ask which was the greatest—Shelley, Mozart, Darwin, or Raphael? It seems to us that here we are hopelessly stranded: we want to measure—is it exact enough to say—"brain-power"—or shall we say—"originality of thought"? Anyhow we want to measure some very complex and rare Brain-function; and the only possible scale (and that a most unsatisfactory one) by which we may measure it, is work produced.[1] But when the works are incommensurable we are left utterly helpless: how then can we decide as to the greatness of genius?

It is a commonplace with some people that genius is essentially the same, and that the particular direction taken by the genius is merely a chance of the environment; that Raphael and Newton, Mozart and Darwin, might, under opposite conditions, and in opposite ages, have taken each the other's place. But from this view we must utterly dissent, since it appears to us flatly contradicted both by psychology and biography: painting is the outcome of an intensely concrete mind, mathematics of an abstract mind, and so on. Surely it is sufficient to even glance at the biographies of early genius, of Mozart a musician at three or four years, and Shelley a poet at school, and numbers more of similar cases, to be convinced that music, poetry, or science, is no chance-*matter*, moulded by the *form* of one same genius, but that genius is born to its own peculiar object-matter. Again, a study of the

---

[1] And not merely, either, absolutely, but *relatively*: that is to say the value of the work produced—as a Brain-index—must be estimated by the difficulties to be overcome in producing it.

biography of genius will show that in many, if not in most, cases *artistic* genius is concomitant with a peculiar unhingement, or at least unstable equilibrium, of the mind : and Dryden's dictum that "Great wits are sure to madness near allied" seems literally true of artistic genius. The excess of passion, emotion, susceptibility, that is essential to poets, artists, musicians, marks a mind so strung that there needs but a shock to jar it altogether. The *irritabile genus* is especially a truthful epithet of artistic geniuses.

But the scientific, mathematical, or philosophic, genius is composed of very different mental elements : in him calmness, abstraction, and balance, replace the passion and unrest of the artist : and it is a striking testimony to this difference that the Bicêtre registers show that maniacs of the more educated classes consist almost entirely of priests, artists, painters, sculptors, poets, and musicians ; but in no cases, it is said, of naturalists, physicians, geometricians, or chemists.[1] It would be easy to pursue this subject much further and bring forward considerable evidence : but that would lead us out of our path : our object is simply to point out that genius is not one definite cast of mind, but that there are very many very different forms of genius. It is sufficient to

[1] Conolly as quoted by Abercrombie ; *cf.*, too, Galton's *Hereditary Genius.* According to Lombroso, however, the man of genius is nearly always more or less closely allied to insanity. *En passant* we may suggest the great service to this branch of psychology that would be done by a detailed critique of Lombroso's work by, *e.g.*, Mr. Francis Galton, who holds such very different views.

indicate the evidence that may be found, in biography and psychology, to prove this point.

But if genius be thus so very different *qualitatively*, it will be found to follow necessarily that there are profound *quantitative* differences making up this *qualitative* difference. The mind is a complex of many elements, any of which may be much or little developed, but in one and the same gifted mind equal development of *all* the elements is never to be found.

It is essential to the formation of an artistic genius that the concrete elements of the mind should be prominent and the abstract unmarked ; to the mathematical genius precisely the opposite ; and so to every peculiar shade of genius there must be a peculiar hypertrophy of certain mental elements. It therefor appears to us that *qualitative differences of genius necessitate quantitative differences of mind :* but if so, then the arguments already adduced will show that *mental inequality must prevail* thro'out the society—or, in other words, that in no future society, not even in Utopia itself, can all men be equally gifted. It does not appear to us sufficient to assume that by such general processes as may be exemplified by the individual case of a poet's son marrying a mathematician's daughter, an equable double-sided genius would be produced : no doubt very clever, very talented, offspring would be obtained, but it appears to us that to produce a genius some one mental power must be greatly, pre-eminently, if not, alas! exclusively, developed.[1]

[1] We find our arguments as to the great *variety* of human genius, and also as to the connection between qualitative and quanti-

Moreover, there are very cogent biological reasons rendering it doubtful whether this intellectual unity of level can ever be reached; and whether we may not rather expect that the older grows the world the greater variations will be found in its inhabitants. *Individuality* is probably *far more* marked to-day, and mental divergence from type far greater, than was the case in the Middle Ages, or than obtains now among savages [1] and barbarians.

The slight insight, that we have already obtained into the mechanism and results of heredity, seems to indicate greater chance of variation the further we go; and we should imagine that, could the chances be calculated by a mathematician, infinity were requisite to produce universal uniformity—if even infinity could. Perhaps some might feel inclined to retort upon us that, in far less than infinite time, *some* one or two types are bound to swamp all the others; just as Galton has calculated that, starting with so many different surnames in a confined community, a certain number die out in each generation until, finally, a very small number have obtained universal prevalence. But the problem is really not nearly so simple as this— even putting aside the initial objection that, in the

tative differences, considerably strengthened by Galton's *Enquiry into Human Faculty* and Bain's *On the Study of Character* respectively—two works with which we were not familiar at the time of writing the above. With regard to the (Helvetius) doctrine of the *sameness* of genius—referred to on p. 100—we may direct our readers' attention to Prof. Bain's *Criticism of J. S. Mill (passim)* for animadversions thereupon.

[1] One need not, however, attribute the sheep-like similarity of such (small) communities to their lowly character only: the absence of intermarriage must be taken into account.

struggle for existence among surnames, half the population, *i.e.*, all the women, *are necessarily ignored.*

Let us pause a moment to consider this problem.
What *is* the mechanism of heredity?   So far as our
knowledge goes at present, the *chromatin-threads* in the
nucleus of the reproductive cells are the vehicles of
heredity: now these chromatin-threads contain thousands of ancestral qualities of almost every conceivable
type; and by the composition (whether qualitative or
quantitative, or both) of these chromatin-threads, the
character of the resultant organism will be determined. If
in both the male and the female chromatin-threads there
were contained units of poetical or scientific faculty for
instance; or if there were present in the *two* contribu-
tories *units which, when brought together, resulted in the
production of, e.g., poetic and scientific faculty, tho
neither kind of unit had any such effect alone*—and we do
not know but what this may be the chief and essential
process by which genius is gradually built up [1]—then
we can well understand how these units, re-enforcing one
another, could bring about the—*apparently* spasmodically-
occurrent—*Genius.*   " Well then"—it may be retorted—
"given sufficient intermarriage, an unrestricted *panmixia,*
and the uniformity is certain: for in a comparatively
few generations you get all these *chromatin-threads* so
thoroly mixed up, that every generative nucleus will
contain equal proportions of every kind of 'unit' in

[1] Altho we are still almost entirely in the dark as to the
actual facts, and can only speculate from scanty data, yet the
extraordinary phenomena of the distribution of genius seem to
us very strongly to indicate such a process; but to discuss the
subject would lead us far into biography and heredity.

the community!" But is the actual case anything like so simple as this, and not rather infinitely more complicated? Let us take a simple analogy. Here are a thousand differently colored beads and a million kaleidoscopes, and—to grant the most favorable case to the objector—there are a million individuals of each bead, and a thousand beads in each kaleidoscope. Now, look thro some of the kaleidoscopes: you will find every conceivable variety of *design and color.* Very well, let these million kaleidoscopes with all their differences represent the society of to-day ; and let certain *patterns* or arrangements represent genius, and let a combination of all the thousand differently-colored beads represent a perfectly all-round man with every human faculty. Now, postulate as much time as you like, so as to institute the most perfect panmixia, and we will concede that *at last* you have contrived to get one bead each of every color into each of the million kaleidoscopes ; so that, as regards their *composition,* your kaleidoscopes are all alike. But are you any nearer getting the same kaleidoscopic effects manifested by your kaleidoscopes? Scarcely appreciably so ! for the *pattern, the effect,* depends not upon color only but *upon arrangement,* and you are powerless to condition the arrangement—much less to ensure that, shaking up your million kaleidoscopes in a machine, you will produce a million copies of one and the same pattern ; much less still to restore that or another pattern to all the million after another agitation : and so on. If, therefor, *Genius* be to any extent a *function of pattern or arrangement, as well as of composition*—as we should imagine that most biologists and

8

psychologists will insist that it is—then this kaleidoscope-analogy will help us to perceive how utterly futile it is to expect uniformity of character as a result of however much panmixia.[1]   But the difficulty is really even far greater than this kaleidoscope-analogy suggests, for the generative nuclei with their chromatin-threads are the analogue, not of a kaleidoscope, but of a specially segregated, infinitesimally small, product of the kaleidoscope and its contents, possessing the faculty of developing another kaleidoscope and contents, and affected as to its composition and character by a thousand and one variations in the environment !   Add to all this the yet far greater complication that the living organism, unlike the kaleidoscope, may, under the influence of the exceedingly variable stimuli, both external and internal, produce *not only varieties but sudden sports* which may breed true, which is as tho any of our kaleidoscopes could evolve several new colors at any time, and, consequently, the faculty of forming hundreds of new patterns—and the case seems conclusive !   And note that we are ignoring the possibility of *acquired* mental character being inherited;[2] which possibility with all its corollaries, if granted, would alone annihilate the argument for uniformity.

[1] Of course the difficulty were proportionately lessened if we could suppose that the composition itself was a factor in determining the arrangement after agitation.

[2] The scientific reader will of course have perceived the reference to Weismann's work thro'out this argument.   Any non-biological reader interested in the subject is strongly advised to read Weismann's *Essays on Heredity* and *Germ Plasm.*   With regard to the extraordinary differences of human character, *vide* biographies, etc., generally, and Galton's *Enquiry into Human Faculty* particularly.

On the whole then, it seems fair to sum up by saying that even after infinite time there seems no reason to expect uniformity of mind; and that *à fortiori* therefor there is no ground for supposing that in semi-Utopia or Utopia itself all will be equally gifted;[1] but there is very strong reason for supposing that then, as now, there will exist varying degrees of talent; and in favor of this contention may be quoted the following passage from Weismann :—

"When once individual differences have begun to appear in a species propagated by this process (of sexual reproduction) *uniformity* among its individuals *can never again be reached.* So far from this being the case, the differences must even be increased in the course of generations, not indeed in intensity but in number; for new combinations of the individual character will continually arise."[2]

And here perhaps it is well to point out, what ought however to be already quite clear to the reader, *viz.*, that the Utopia (and the semi-Utopia) with which we are concerned, is no arbitrary invention of one's own brain, which may be constituted exactly as its author's fancy pleases, but, on the contrary, a distant society whose

[1] It is therefor not worth while to follow out this supposition in detail : but supposing that there could possibly exist a society of equally gifted (and equally industrious and moral) men, it is clear that all wages would tend to equality, whether the manual and mental laborers were distinct or not : for any such distinction, if made, could result only from some kind of arbitrary division— as, *e.g.*, by casting lots to decide who should be bricklayer and who physician. Note that the relative agreeableness or disagreeableness of different occupations would however exercise a somewhat disequalising influence.

[2] *Essays in Heredity*, vol. i., p. 282.

characters must be inferred by rigorous argument from the data afforded by Evolutionism and Sociology. The tellers of fairy-tales, and builders of purely imaginary Utopias, might legitimately build entirely according to their own fancies ; and, setting out with the premise that all men should be happy and equal, might arrange their Utopia in such wise as to make them so. But our procedure must be entirely different ; having learned from Biology and Sociology what is possible in the way of human development, and what tendencies are likely to persist, we must endeavor to imagine—arguing from these data—what sort of social state is likely, and what happiness Man may expect there. In fact, the difference is just this—that in the old anthropomorphic fairy-tales the invariable assumption was always made that man was the one and supreme aim of Nature ; consequently that whatever conditions were necessary to ensure his perfect happiness, these conditions must be postulated as a possibility, probability, or certainty, of the Future. The fact that man hates death were a fair warrant for making him immortal in the Utopia of fairy-tale—that he wants to fly, for giving him wings. But we of to-day must take a very different course ; having ascertained, to the best of our ability, the limit of possibilities, our problem is to determine how far man can adapt himself, and how much happiness will ensue. We would therefor insist that our Utopia is no wild dream, but that all our speculations thereupon may have—or at least should have—a rigorous scientific justification.

CHAPTER VIII.

ON FAME, HONOR, AND GLORY.

" What shall I do, to be for ever known,
　And make the age to come mine own ? "

" There was a morning when I longed for Fame ;
There was a noontide when I passed it by ;
There is an evening when I think not shame
Its substance and its being to deny."

" Oh youth, men praise so, holds their praise its worth ?
Blown harshly, keeps the trump its golden cry ?
Tastes sweet the water with such specks of earth ? "

PERHAPS, before passing to other divisions of our subject, it may be worth while here to call attention to one somewhat interesting reflection that offers itself. We remarked above[1] that, in even semi-Utopia perhaps, the effect of paying workers equally for equal hours of labor would be most injurious and would inevitably result in stagnation or rapid retrogression. Perhaps it may have been thought that, in so saying, we were overlooking one potent incentive to thoroness in working, that we were ignoring " that last infirmity of noble minds "—the love of Fame. Now, it is precisely regarding this love of Fame that it seems desirable to say a few words.

[1] See p. 97.

We are very strongly inclined to think that, as mankind approaches perfection, the love of and regard for Fame of any sort, kind or condition will disappear, inasmuch as—essentially—regard for Fame is incompatible with Perfect Love : the more pure therefor grows our love for our fellows, the more distasteful will Fame —anti-Love—become to us. The psychology of Fame-hunger is very peculiar. "Fame is Love disguised," sang Shelley ; and so *in one sense* it is ; but this does not, we think, affect our conclusion. As we have elsewhere pointed out,[1] the essence of Fame-quest is to be sought in the *strife-element* still latent—or rampant—in "civilised" man.

The Love *accorded to* famous men by their fellows may in some cases perhaps be pure : but usually it is probably clouded either by some form of that fear which "Perfect Love casteth out—for in Perfect Love there is no Fear" —or (and this far more probably) by the most natural, scarce avoidable, taint of envy. But however this be— and tho in this sense *Fame* be Love disguised (Fame being here used as equivalent to the homage of man), this is not exactly that wherewith we are concerned : it is not

---

[1] The essay referred to has, however, not yet been published. Shortly after the MS. of this essay had been written out, we had occasion to turn up to an old Commonplace-Book for some references, and came across the following extract from Bacon—made some years previously :—"The delight which men have in popularity, fame, honour, *submission, and subjection of men's minds, wills, and affections*, seemeth to be a thing in itself without contemplation of consequences, grateful and agreeable to the Nature of Man. . . . The best temper of minds desireth good name and true honour ; the lighter, popularity and applause ; the depraved, subjection and tyranny."

with Fame as Homage rendered to another, but with *Fame as sought for oneself*, that we have to do; for it is here that the strife-factor, the *anti-loveliness* of Fame, becomes apparent.

What is the desire for Fame: what but the desire for *Pre-eminence, for distinction beyond one's fellows,* for Victory over others: here truly we have the *strife*-element rampant. Of course one must admit that there are varied degrees of purity in Fame-seeking; from that yearning of the lonely scholar or poet who longs to make his thoughts and projects known to others, and to feel that thousands of his fellows sympathise with him and share his thoughts and aspirations—from this, which is probably the purest, but *not an all-pure*, form of Fame-seeking; thro that form in which Fame of any sort, no matter what, is sought merely to gratify a personal vanity—a vanity which is rejoiced to hear " there goes *that* Demosthenes"; down to the impurest form in which the would-be-famous yearns to be the one unrivalled greatest man of his day—*the Pre-eminent*, intolerant of every neighbor to his throne: and this is the *typical* case, wherein one perceives clearly enough the strife-element, the unsocial, the anti-love-like, character of Fame. We do not deny that, in so far as Fame-seeking be a desire for the love and approbation of our fellows, Fame *is* Love disguised; but we contend that this element is altogether subordinated to and masked by the strife-element, the *desire for pre-eminence and distinction above our fellows.*

With the mutual hatred and jealousy of two suitors to the same woman there is avowedly a very strong love-

element bound up : but who will deny that the rivalry
and jealousy are unlovely, unsocial, and inconsonant
with a high social state ?   Even so it is—but more
markedly—with Fame-seeking: all Fame-seeking involves *rivalry :* there may be a love-element in so far as
we desire the approval of the multitude ; but there is a
strong strife-element, hate-element, in so far as we desire
this as a *distinction* granted to but few—in so far as we
desire pre-eminence both over other aspirants for public
favor, and over the general public who bestow the
favor.   Anyone who doubts that Fame-seeking connotes
rivalry and tacit strife with others, need but ask himself
of what avail were a distinction which everybody
possessed, in order to be answered and convinced.   From
the ancient conqueror, who enslaved a people, and fed
his proud heart with the adulations and entreaties of a
fettered race that trembled before him and acknowledged
his prowess and victory, or from the heathen heroes who
contended as rivals in musical skill—*and the loser was
slain by the victor*—there is a lineal descent to the
highbred cultured civilized European who joys to be
famous as artist, scientist, thinker, or statesman.   In
every case alike, *victory, superiority,* on the one hand,
and defeat, submission, inferiority, on the other, are involved.   We think it is, therefor, scarcely needful to
further enforce our argument that Fame is incompatible
with a perfect social state, and that, as Utopia approaches, the regard for Fame will vanish; while we
may well expect that even in semi-Utopia Fame will be
very distasteful to men who are learning to regard as
bad and tabooed every deed or word that might imply

pain or disquiet to a fellow-man, *or superiority to self.*

This being admitted, however, it is somewhat curious to follow out one or two of the consequent results; since we are thus led to conclusions that would hardly otherwise have occurred to us.

Admitting that Fame-worship will disappear (which implies that not only will men no longer be so unsocial as to seek for Fame, but also that they would be positively pained to wake up and find themselves famous—since this connotes pain, actual or potential, to others—we seem then compelled to infer that in Utopia (if not before) all books that are published, all poetry, all music, all scientific discovery, all research, all painting, will be *anonymous:* for to publish in one's own name a great poem, or a grand discovery, were to seize on Fame and to mark oneself as a man out of the common, a man who is pre-eminent above his fellows. But this were intolerable to an Utopian who will be too loving and gentle to stand upon a pinnacle built up of his fellows' deficiencies. To the Utopian it were more than sufficient reward, it were a chiefest joy, to know that he had been the means of advancing human happiness or human knowledge: he will desire no acclamations in life, neither will he permit undying commemoration after death; for since such individual commemoration is impossible for the majority, why should he seek for, or accept, a distinction that at once assigns him a pre-eminence above his fellows? And, paradoxical tho it at first may seem, this view is probably alone right. Could you object to him that it is unreasonable and ungrateful for the world to forget its

benefactors, he would justly reply that no shadow of
credit attaches to him for having been gifted by Nature
with unusually fine brain-power, and rare talents.   If
any credit belongs anywhere it belongs to far back unknown ancestors who each, little by little, helped to
mould his brain : nay, if he were a thoro Weismannite,
he would rather refer the chief credit to climatic, nutritive, phototactic, and similar, influences, acting on the
primeval protozoa!   But, as for him, what possible
credit can reflect on him for simply using those Nature-
implanted brain-tools, which not to use were arrant sin,
and a functional impossibility besides?   Is any credit
given to the Æolian Harp because it resounds when the
wind sweeps along its strings?

And thus it would seem that in Utopia all intellectual
work will be—so far as possible—anonymous, and will
go down to later ages, not as the poetry of Tennyson,
the music of Chopin, the painting of Turner, the discoveries of Darwin, the thought of Spencer, but as the
collective spoils of humanity.   If this be so, biographical
dictionaries and obituary memoirs will be unknown to
Utopians, who would wonder at the incredible selfishness
of men who could allow their (nature-given) genius to
be commemorated and enshrined in history, while 999
fellowmen in every 1,000 live and die unknown :
Utopians could not tolerate such unsocial, unlovable,
fame. So too statues, portraits, and pictures, as com-
memorations, will lose their value to a race who love all
humanity so much that they would not insult it by
cherishing one individual's name to the exclusion of
thousands of his fellows : and it is open to us to specu-

late whether they will not—on principle—wilfully destroy every shred of biographical information, retaining, of course, the psychological studies tho the actual *names* be lost, and take steps to ensure that the names of all precedent immortals are erased! They will insist that they shall delight not in Shelley's poetry, Chopin's music, Darwin's theories, Berkeley's philosophy, but in the grand stream of knowledge and art that has flowed down to humanity from an older humanity. To such Utopians Positivist calendars will be, indeed, a strange fantasy: and here, the conclusions as to the standpoint of Utopians, to which we have been led by no positivist leanings, but by simply deducing necessary conclusions from—what seem—probable data, approximate very closely to Comte's views on the celebration and worship of *collective humanity*—

"Thus the individual withers; and the world is more and more.'

After this it is but a very small thing to point out that, even long before so advanced a stage as that just depicted is reached, all such minor distinctions as university-degrees, Fellowships of Royal Societies and of Royal Academies, medals and titles, will have been abolished. It is however worth while to bring this category under attention since many will probably accede to the proposition now advanced, and acknowledge its truth so far, who will have been staggered by the more sweeping conclusions just enunciated.

In all probability it will be readily granted that the only value of a degree, an F.R.S., or an R.A., of a medal, or a title, is that it is something *possessed by only a few,* and therefor marks out its possessor as more or less pre-eminent and distinguished above his fellows. If every-body possessed such degrees and distinctions, no one would care a rap to have them : on the contrary one sometimes hears the significant remark that it is a greater distinction *not* to possess a given title than to possess it ; which sufficiently points our moral—that the only value of degrees and titles is due to their monopoly by a few : they are essentially *anti-social,* and *anti-brotherly :* love is *very much disguised*—disguised so thoroly as to be transformed—in such form as this. Clearly this were utterly inconsonant with Utopia.

This speculation will presumably be altogether re-pugnant to—as perhaps unexpected by—many ; and it is easy to imagine indignant protests being uttered against such a levelling view. But one caution may well be taken to heart by all such objectors. If the argument be sound, and this consummation of anonymity be veritably the destined lot for by-and-bye, *then* assuredly it is utterly useless to kick against it, and object, and de-nounce this " cold-blooded dispiriting " prophecy. The question is simply one of fact—of future fact if you like : either this consummation is to be expected, or it is not : if the former, then objection and denunciation and resistance are equally futile, and resignation to. this death-to-glory is as inevitable as resignation to individual dying ; but if the latter, then denunciation is wasted.

To show that we are not exactly alone in indicating this as the probable direction along which society will ad-vance, it is worth while to quote a paragraph from M.

Ribot. Referring, in his *Contemporary English Psychology*,[1] to the necessity for a great mass of detail-work in psychological science, he writes, " In this work of detail, each might share according to his measure and strength. . . . . . . A hundred workers might perhaps wear out themselves over one obscure point. What matter if a result be obtained. *The science will accept their work, and forget their names.*"

Lest it should erroneously be supposed that, because we are arguing for the probability of this development, therefor it is satisfactory and grateful to us, let us frankly avow that such thoughts are apt to send a shudder thro us, and compel a despairing assent to Tennyson's mournful cry—

> " We pass : the path that each man trod
> Is dim,--or will be dim with weeds :
> What fame remains for human deeds ? "

To us personally it has often seemed that his fate was most horrible, whosoever should come upon this earth, live, and die, and yet leave no trace or mark behind him —no " footprints on the sands of time." To live and die, unknown and fameless—that has ever seemed a horrible negation and mockery to us who anticipate no personal hereafter.

But, altho the yearning for lasting commemoration, which prompted Tennyson's lament, and which equally repels us with a shuddering horror from the picture of men laboring at new discoveries and new thoughts, but

[1] English translation, p. 33.

yet for ever unknown and unacknowledged as their author, and from the picture of a dead level of privacy whence tower up no " celebrities," and gleaming with no sparkles of fame-light—altho this be most natural and inborn in each of us, and the consequent resentment and opposition almost as innocent as they are intelligible, *yet* not only, if the picture be truly drawn, is this resentment useless, but we think that deeper reflection must show the (assumed) Utopian state to be, on the whole, the *best possible.* That it is profoundly mournful we do not for a moment deny ; we are in hearty sympathy with— for we ourself have shared in—that passionate anguish aroused by the steady conviction that not even in the sense of fame is there any immortality for the individual ; that ever

" The individual withers and the world is more and more."

We are no whit concerned to prove that this is absolutely good and just—for we deem it to be, like most other worldly institutions, hateful and cruel and accursed: but we do think that it is relatively the *least bad, the least unjust.* People fail to see this simply because they regard the question from the standpoint of the few famous individuals, instead of from the platform occupied by the whole surging world of humanity. The same man who anathematises this prophecy as cold-blooded and cruel, and passionately asserts that ever as now great and good men must and will be famous, forgets that this present system, which is so dear and seems so good to him, is one which condemns to utter oblivion and non-fame more than 999 men in every thousand in the most advanced country: taking the world we might probably say 99,999 in every 100,000 and be far below the mark. Yet this murderous and cold-blooded negation-system is tacitly or avowedly approved as very good: whereas the procedure prophesied for the future, which puts every man on the same level of oblivion with his brotherman, and ordains equal non-fame for the odd 100,000th man—this we are to be told is abominable?

However difficult for us, let us strive to regard this question from the standpoint of a higher wisdom, and transcend the private cares and turmoils of our little life. Is it not on the whole the best—or the least worst—that all men, *having deserved* alike, should share alike ; and that the immortality of fame—no less than the renown of to-day—inexorably denied to the thousands, should equally be denied to the units ? At least then we are all brothers in a common misfortune. The trouble is that we of to-day are trying to judge a more or less Utopian state with very non-Utopian eyes : and our vision is altogether blurred by the motes of selfishness—and we are not using the word with any specially bad connotation, but simply to denote a certain selfward regard that will disappear in the distant future. We must strive to understand that, to a very highly developed man, it would be an intolerable reflection that he was to be elevated—thro no real deserts of his own, or ill deserts of their own—to a pinnacle of glory and fame hopelessly denied to his fellows. In Utopia, it is the quasi-famous men who will insist on abolishing fame : not the mass, jealous and envious of a distinction denied to them—for envy and jealousy are incompatible with Utopia—but the distinguished few who will refuse to accept a distinction that their fellows cannot share.

"But"—comes the indignant rejoinder—"you are ignoring the one salient point of difference. You are ignoring —or rather flatly denying—that there *is* any difference of deserts : whereas it is precisely because they *have* deserved it that our great geniuses should inherit immortal fame."

But this very plausible defence were really quite beside the mark ; for "desert" has a double meaning. In the lax and popular sense, no question but Genius *does* deserve fame ; but we have only to go one step further to see this desert vanish. We have but to ask, "Could Genius, if it would, be not-Genius : and could mediocrity or stupidity, tho it struggled ever so earnestly, be Genius"—to see the inevitable answer. Genius *is* Genius simply in virtue of the possession of certain brains—with the preparation of which Genius had no more to do than had the Man in the Moon : all that Genius does is to use those brains which constitute Genius : not to use which were almost criminal—besides being impossible—for Genius, like Murder, will out : and to use which is a highest pleasure, and in no sense, therefor, morally " creditable "—especially to an Utopian.

It is plain then that whoso approves the present system constructively declares that it is highly desirable, and very just, to confer immortality upon a given man, *because* his parents, grandparents, great-grandparents, and others, have bequeathed to him a most magnificent brain : whilst it is equally just to consign to oblivion both such ancestors and the majority of men whose ancestors have *not* so endowed them. To cut away the last support we will add that the popular definition which declares Genius to be "an infinite capacity for taking pains," however admirable and commendable as a moral maxim, is hopelessly false as a scientific statement. Genius is something inborn, inherent, inherited, and is not, nor ever will be, a product of "painstaking."[1]

If the whole question be regarded from this standpoint, it seems to us that one will be a good deal more reconciled to what is anyhow probably inevitable. As it is necessary so constantly to remark in striving to sketch the outlines of an Utopian society, *one must always choose the lesser evil.*

APPENDIX.

The following passage, which we have hit upon in Galton's *Hereditary Genius,* seems pertinent to this discussion.

"The fact of a person's name being associated with some one striking scientific discovery helps enormously, but often unduly, to prolong his reputation to after-ages. It is notorious that the same discovery is frequently made simultaneously and quite independently by different persons. . . . *It would seem that discoveries are usually made when the time is ripe for them*—that is to say, when the ideas from which they naturally flow are fermenting in the minds of many men. . . . A small accident will often determine the scientific man who shall first make and publish a new discovery. There are many men who have contributed

---

[1] If anybody at this close of the nineteenth century still have doubts on this point, he may be strongly recommended to study a certain golden book entitled *Hereditary Genius,* by Francis Galton.

9

vast numbers of original memoirs, all of them of some, many of great, but none of extraordinary, importance. These men have the capacity of making a striking discovery, *tho they had not the luck to do so. This work is valuable and remains, but the worker is forgotten*" (p. 185). It is an old and true proverb that *Kissing goes by favor.*

Cf. also Shakspeare.

> " By Heaven, methinks, it were an easy leap
>   To pluck bright Honor from the pale-faced moon,
>   Or dive into the bottom of the deep,
>   Where fathomline could never touch the ground,
>   And pluck up drowned Honor by the locks :
>   So he, that doth redeem her hence, might wear
>   *Without co-rival all her dignities.*"

CHAPTER IX

ON CHOOSING THE LEAST EVIL; WITH FURTHER REMARKS UPON LUXURY AND WASTE.

"The whole art of living consists in giving up existence in order to exist."—*Göthe.*

"Love in a cot, with water and a crust,
  Is—Love forgive us—cinders, ashes, dust."—*Is it?*

" Cursed be the social wants that sin against the strength of
    youth ;
  Cursed be the social lies that warp us from the living truth
  Cursed be the hearts that err from honest Nature's kindly
    rule ;
  Cursed be the gold that gilds the straitened forehead of the
    fool."

Now this principle—of choosing the lesser evil—to which we have just referred, is really invaluable when we wish to construct an Utopia that shall be scientifically possible in our " temperate " climate, and that is not a mere unfettered impracticable South-Sea-dream.[1]   The case is simply this : it is given in the definition that in Utopia

---

[1] We take this opportunity to point out that to hypothecate the existence of any general and world-wide semi-Utopia necessarily implies—as it appears to us—the abandonment of a considerable portion of the earth's surface. We entirely dissent from the notion that it is desirable to people every land, and we protest against any population calculations based on the supposition that the humanity-supporting powers of the world may be determined by allotting so many acres per head, and then dividing this number into the acreage of dry land. We assert

all of us are to enjoy the maximum possible happiness:
now happiness is a function of very many factors, of
which Love, Friends, Poetry, Knowledge, Music, Art,
Fine Scenery, Travelling, means of Physical Recreation,
in addition to *comfortable* houses and clothing, and a
sufficiency of plain and palatable food, are the chief.
Most of these factors are again functions of many sub-
factors ; but—not to carry the analysis into tedious detail
—it may suffice to point out that, to any highly-evolved
beings, Happiness depends in very large measure upon

that since Utopia connotes the highest possible happiness and
refinement, and a life of esthetic grace, it is impossible to assign
as dwelling-places for Utopians any parts of the earth's surface
that are so situated as to render refinement and comfort difficult
or impossible : and we are convinced that such places as Iceland,
Siberia, much of Scandinavia, Russia, and Canada, etc., will be
unanimously deserted before semi-Utopia universally obtains.
We defy anyone to reconcile an Utopian life with the prolonged
cold of these regions ; and we feel no doubt that in Utopia a
large part of the earth's surface will be permanently wild and
deserted—except that tourists will visit it in the summer season
—just as many Alpine tracts are deserted, except for a
few months in the year. We even doubt—for our own part—
whether such high latitudes as Scotland will be permanently
inhabited in Utopian times—seeing that the Grecian life of bright
sunshine, open-air living, light clothing, and abundant vegetation,
is probably the physical type of the coming age : but still we
express this opinion only with reservation, since into such prophecies the personal equation must enter largely : and it is
possible that in Utopia many men may enjoy *moderate* cold just
as even now we believe that certain extraordinary people enjoy
a Scotch winter, whilst to ourself the Equator or India seems
to offer a climatically desirable residence. But that such *miserable* districts as Iceland, Orkney and many other Scotch isles—
we speak of them as winter-residences—Siberia, Northern Russia,
etc., etc., will be abandoned, we feel sure ; and, to afford our
readers some notion of what *capabilities* Iceland must possess in
comparison with more temperate climes, we subjoin an extract

the possession of a number of "things," both material and immaterial, which are the products of our complex civilisation : to put it in its briefest then, *Happiness* connotes *comparative wealth* and leisure *for all.*

Now at present some few of us possess most of these appliances to happiness ; most of us possess only some ; and a terribly large proportion possess practically none ; in Utopia all must (equally ?) possess all such appliances : and hence our difficulty in tracing the lines, along which Utopia must be developed, arises from three sources :

(1) Many of the enjoyments, or the means of enjoy-

---

from Mr. Huth's *Marriage of Near Kin* (p. 172). "They eat their food generally cold, often putrid, and always at irregular times. They have no artificial means of warmth, and therefor allow no ventilation in their miserable hovels, which are built of damp earth, and where the whole family remains huddled up, not only at night, but the greater part of the day also, during six months in the year, with their cattle, sheep, dogs, and all the live-stock they may happen to possess. Indeed the air in these dwellings becomes so poisonous from the breath of the inmates, their refuse, and the fuel they use composed of dung, rotten bones, and anything that can be got to burn, etc., etc."

Can any ingenuity fashion such a hell-bound island into a dwelling for Utopians ! On the other hand, here is a lesson for us so civilised Westerns to profit by—Landor says, "I have often noticed how easily affected the Mikado's subjects are by atmospheric and geographical conditions, and how, before settling to do their business, they make a point of finding some pleasant spot where to cast anchor, *thinking more of the amenities of physical existence than of the facilities for successful trade*" ("Hairy Ainu," p. 74). Happy and wise are they !

(Dr. A. Oppel has recently estimated that about 1,700,000 square miles of the earth's surface are uninhabited or ownerless, about 5,000,000 square miles more without settled government, and the remaining 45,000,000 square miles are occupied by definite states—of which the eighteen largest make up 87 per cent. of the whole area [*Nature,* 47/499].)

ment, possessed by the happy ones of to-day, are either obtained at the expense of suffering—not necessarily acute, but *massive*—to the workers, or else are so expensive that their universal possession equally by all men were an utter impossibility; the former condition were evidently incompatible with Utopia; and the second very naturally appears a grave obstacle to Utopia—for how, it will be asked, could any of us be happy without all these pleasure-appliances; whilst evidently mankind at large can never be expected to enjoy them!

(2) *Wealthiness* is a comparative term, and is partly a function of the purchasing power of money: now the man of to-day, possessing £1,000 per year, may be considered enviably comfortable; but his comfort, depending—as it does—on what his £1,000 will buy, really depends ultimately upon the fact that multitudes of workmen are paid only £60-70-80-100 per year—happiness therefor being acquired for the few at the expense of the many. How then can one bring about an Utopia where *all* shall enjoy as much happiness (in so far as happiness be a function of purchasing power) as is at present enjoyed by, *e g.*, the thousandaire?

(3) Utopia connotes not only sufficient wealth, but also abundant leisure, for all: but to make this latter condition is practically—it may be thought—to reduce the wealth-making labor of the world to one-half or one-third of its present amount, thereby rendering the solution of the two previous difficulties exactly twice or thrice as difficult.

Now in reply to these difficulties we have to urge several considerations; and, with regard to number 3, we will forestall its due turn in so far as to at once point out that this diminution will be more or less compensated by the abolition of stupid and useless luxuries, and by the scientifically inspired saving of wealth at present wasted—as we are about to point out in some detail—and also by the drafting off of tens of thousands of at present entirely unproductive consumers into the ranks of the wealth-creators—a consideration which we have already had occasion to emphasise,[1] and must return to again presently. Here it will be sufficient to remark that when the million or so unproductive consumers who are at present *kept* at the expense of the nation, that is to say, of the workers, come to be employed in creating wealth themselves, then the wealth of each worker will be practically increased, in so far as he no longer has to keep, in addition to himself and his own family, one-seventh or more of another man and *his* family,[2] as is at present the case; whilst he will further gain positively to some extent in so far as the labors of these new workers may greatly increase the general national wealth.

To procede, we may perhaps fairly expect that there are yet to come many ingenious inventions which may materially increase the wealth of the world; either positively by creating new and at present unsuspected sources of wealth, or negatively by cheapening the processes already in use, and by utilising the immense amount of wealth that is at present annually *wasted* owing to imperfect processes, etc.: the history of bye-

---

[1] See chapter iii.

[2] See details and statistics in chapter x. : all over twenty are reckoned as workers in this calculation.

products in the chemical trade is a lasting monument to the ability of scientific discovery to save otherwise-squandered wealth.

To take one example—if the present wasteful, dirty, and stupid, practice of burning coal as fuel could be superseded by the use of coke or gas, there would not only be an end to that terrible infliction—the London Fog—but such an annual saving of wealth as will probably astonish our readers.   Mr. Irvine has calculated that the present idiotic system of house-warming pollutes the air of London *daily* with *600 tons of smuts and 2000 tons of tar and other coal products.*   He remarks, " As a chemical manufacturer I sigh when I think of all the valuable material lost to us, either in the form of wasted heat-producers, or valuable chemical products in the shape of *aniline colors, ammonia, burning-oils, paraffin-wax, printing-ink*, etc., which are floating about in the atmosphere, veiling the sweet sunlight, and choking the lungs of both animal and vegetable life.   Of course if we could over-come our sentimental desire for the cheerful tho smoky blaze of the coal fire, and burn carbonised coal [coke] in our grates, these solid liquid and gaseous hydrocarbons *would be saved and made profitable use of.*   In this case our chimneys might become ornaments to our houses, while the products of combustion would pass from them as colorless gases." [1]

With regard to the mere waste of nitrogen, which would otherwise appear as ammonia in the gas retorts and be available for agricultural purposes, the loss is

[1] We strongly recommend Mr. Irvine's admirable paper to the perusal of our readers (*Chemical Industry Journal*, Dec. 1890

enormous; and finally Mr. Irvine quotes Macauley as estimating, in 1888, the amount of coal annually *wasted* in this country as "45,000,000 tons, costing £15,750,000 at the pit's mouth": *this sum is equivalent to over 1 per cent. of the national income*, or, if we add the expense of carriage, *about 2 per cent.* Is not this an appalling testimony to our national wickedness and stupidity in deliberately *wasting* our substance? At present we are simply throwing away in this one form alone a sum *equal to one-third of the Imperial budget.*

As a parallel to this we may take the awful lesson preached by our present sewage-system. That this system—which is partly the expression of our mingled incompetence and stupidity, partly a supposedly "least evil" safeguard against the barbaric uncleanliness of certain classes, and partly the nemesis of our folly and wickedness in crowding several million persons into a few square miles—that this wretched system involves the most appalling *waste* is a commonplace among thinking people; but the extent of the calamity is but little realised. Putting aside the outlay—*i.e.*, waste—of untold millions sterling upon "main-drainage systems" and all their accessories, and putting aside too the ruin of our rivers and the conversion of "silver Thames" into a filthy and stinking drain, let us see what loss is involved to agriculture. Messrs. Rawson and Smithson have recently calculated [1] that the human excreta produced in the United Kingdom would yield 237,500 tons annually of dry solid matter worth no less than

[1] *Chemical Industry Journal*, 12, 997 (Dec. 1893).

£1,068.750.[1] They point out that "in order to compensate for the mineral and nitrogenous matters that are taken from the soil and subsequently washed down our drains or otherwise destroyed, England imports artificial manures to the value of from £2,000,000 to £2,500,000 per annum." They add—"*In China nothing is allowed to go to waste which might be useful to the soil.* Notwithstanding its vast population, China is entirely independent of all other nations, not only for its food-supplies but for the fertilising materials required by the soil. Since England imports immense quantities of wheat and flour and other foodstuffs, if the whole of the excrement were returned to the land, it naturally follows that the soil, instead of becoming impoverished, *would yearly become richer*, without the importation and application of any foreign manure."[2] Similarly too it has been recently contended that "if fæcal matter were saved in France to the extent of only 20 per cent. more than is now the case, that country would not be compelled to import in some years £2,000,000 worth of grain; but would, on the contrary, export nearly £2,000,000 worth per annum."[3]

Thirdly, we have to take into account the fact that,

[1] This assumes that the sewage be presented to the farmer "in the state of a concentrated powdery manure," and is based upon an estimate of the late Dr. Voelcker's.

[2] So that a reformed system would rid us simultaneously of two objectionable features of modern life — *viz.*, sewage and Nitrate-Kings.

[3] C. W. Shepard in *Journal of American Chemical Society*, 1893: abstracted in *Chemical Industry Journal*, 12 1046. See also an admirable paper on "The Conservation of Farm-yard Manure" in *Royal Agricultural Society's Journal*, Dec., 1893.

since as Utopia approaches lunatics and criminals will become scarce, we shall no longer see men bringing into the world families of six [1]—much less eight, ten, or a dozen—children. The normal family will doubtlessly be far smaller than at present; and in any individual case therefor a man will, *ceteris paribus*, be relatively richer then than now, since his expenses will be diminished. Looked at nationally, a given amount of wealth will be shared among fewer consumers. [2]

We may also add here, in addition to what we have just said regarding the prevention of waste by the utilisation of bye-products, and to what we are about to say regarding luxuries in detail, that an enormous amount of wealth must be annually wasted by sheer unthrift or criminal carelessness of little things. Altho highly necessary to salvation, one canon, least of all understood or realised by the community at large, is the *downright wickedness of waste.* Let us take one or two

---

[1] Unless in the case of geniuses whose breed it is desirable to rapidly increase. (See note to p. 52.)

[2] This must not be confused with a different question, *viz.*, that (in countries not overstocked) the more workers there are, the more wealthy becomes the country. The expense of children is incurred during their infancy when they are not workers: when they become of working—*i.e.*, self-supporting—age they pass from our consideration. Taking the state of things at the present day it is clear that, if families were halved, or reduced 2-thirds, all round, every pater-familias would be made relatively considerably richer: his expenses would be lessened; and—far less national wealth being eaten and otherwise used up by these children—there would be a national gain in addition, that is to say, finally, more wealth for distribution to each citizen. (Note that in this calculation a large number of adult women must be included as "children"—the unmarried unemployed quota to wit.)

examples only. How much *paper* is annually burnt or otherwise destroyed as sheer *waste*—as tho it possessed no value at all! So little realised are the canons of social economy that people who—as, *e.g.*, Darwin and Pope—object to waste, and insist on utilising half sheets of paper or backs of envelopes, are either chaffed as crotchety or stigmatised as parsimonious! A few comparatively thrifty people, it is true, make a practice of collecting the waste-paper of the household into sacks, and periodically selling it to the paper-makers; but their number, we fear, is *very small.* The amount of paper that is devoted to *sheer waste*, as *e.g.*, by being "thrown on the fire," must reach a gigantic annual total : and yet—as a thoughtful friend connected with a paper-making firm once said to us—if one con-siders the amount of paper that is annually required for the millions and millions of newspapers alone, one must wonder how the continuous demand is to be supplied. This is only one more example of the *curse* that great wealth may prove to be to an imperfectly moral nation like our own—*in that it encourages waste.* As another example, how many people ever take thought of the enormous waste of wealth and labor involved in our destruction of matchboxes! Many will laugh at us for worrying about such trifles ; but they are ill advised ; for such a laugh merely advertises their own profound ignorance, semi-barbarism, and—we say it advisedly—very imperfect morality. They are probably unaware that the firm of Bryant & May alone manufacture about 500 *million wooden matchboxes annually, not one of which is ever used for matches a second time.* Yet there is no

reason why these boxes should not be used over and over
again, had we only enough sense and morality to institute a simple system of returning them to the makers
or the " hands." This—be it noted—excludes the con-
current waste on boxes for wax vestas—of which we have
no statistics. Again the actual waste both of wood,
and of phosphorus or other chemicals, must be something appalling—simply because to half-moral men
cheapness is a curse: if matches were expensive we
should find no trouble in reducing our use of them to
a fifth or a tenth of the number. As it is, we might
abolish, almost entirely, the waste of the wood by
collecting the "burnt" matches and sending them to
the papermakers as materials for wood-pulp: but we
are content to continue the present wicked "system,"
altho told that Bryant & May alone manufacture about
34,000 *million* wooden matches annually, besides about
4,500,000 "vesuvians:"[1] and that "for the production
of wooden matches, *whole forests are denuded* to supply
the raw material, and Bryant & May are among the
largest timber merchants in the world." Then again,
do any of us realise the waste upon wax matches? The
same firm, we read, manufacture 900 *miles* of these
daily—which involves an annual consumption of "750
tons of wax and over 250 tons of cotton." What the
total waste of wax and cotton, by this means, in the
United Kingdom, may amount to, we do not know; but

---

[1] Some being of course for export: but this deduction must
be far more than counterbalanced by the home-use of matches
made by other firms, English and foreign. As to the latter, it
is said that we spend £400,000 annually upon imported matches.

it is certain that by far the *greater part* of this waste might be avoided. We strike a wax-match to light pipe or lamp, and then throw away practically all the cotton and wax : yet by a simple provision of " waste-" boxes in every house, restaurant, railway carriage, and street, all these used matches might be collected : the wax could be melted out of them and used again, and the cotton, even if useless to the match-maker, would be welcome to the paper-maker. But here, as everywhere else, we all aid in the national amusement of squandering millions annually, and then complain of the chronic burden of pauperism, and lament that Utopia remains a mere dream. No wonder ! Utopia is not likely to be realised by fools and sinners, but only by men with clear heads and sound hearts.[1]   •

Finally, let us consider the wicked waste of *tobacco-ash.* The annual consumption of tobacco in the United Kingdom now amounts to over 62,000,000 lbs. The percentage of potash (K_2O) in this may be taken on a very rough

---

[1] We may point out that, on any theory of government, the Legislature are under a moral obligation to discourage this terrible waste. So far as concerns matchboxes, it could remedy the evil at once by imposing a tax of 1d. or 2d. on each *new* matchbox. As a result, the wasteful manufacture of wooden matchboxes would be immediately discontinued, and their place taken by *tin* ones. For these the consumer would be charged the price of the tax and the cost of manufacture, and allowed an equivalent rebate on returning them : consequently the boxes, like wine-bottles, would do duty over and over again ; and when once a sufficient stock had been made, practically no more would be required.

We have taken no account above of the wanton waste—involved in the use of superfluous matches—of phosphorus that would otherwise be available for agricultural use.

average as 5 per cent., and this gives us an annual *waste* of 3,100,000 lbs of an essential constituent of our crops. Here again it is plain that by the mere provision of ash-boxes in all our houses, hotels, railway-carriages, streets, etc., the whole of this invaluable manure might be collected and saved ;[1] for any appreciable quantities of it the farmers would be willing to pay a fair price ; and, even if they were not, any man with a grain of morality would rather give it to them than let it be wantonly wasted.

Innumerable further examples of this wicked waste, in which we all indulge, might easily be quoted ; but, since our object is not to compile a catalogue, but rather to offer *examples* and hints, we will leave our readers to exercise their brains and consciences for themselves— merely remarking that *one essential element* in promoting the advent of semi-Utopia is the cultivation of *thrift*, both in great things and small ; and that in semi-Utopia there will be in every house a " glory-hole " full of receptacles for every species of " waste," whether paper, matches, tobacco ash, or what not, where this now-wasted wealth may accumulate until there be a sufficient quantity for removal.[2]

---

[1] We commend the hint to railway-employés, who are frequently enthusiastic gardeners.

[2] We have said nothing of the waste of gas, whether in private houses, etc., thro the sheer stupidity of people who won't turn down the gas when leaving the room, or in streets and elsewhere on the occasion of illuminations in honor of some royal parasite or equally worthless person—nor of the waste of various articles consigned to the rubbish-heap On the latter point we will quote again from Messrs. Rawson & Smithson, who tell us

Having thus accounted for a really very considerable portion of the wealth required by Utopia in apparent excess of its supply, we now have to consider how far we may balance the remaining deficit, *i.e.*, increase the Utopians' wealth to any pitch required by the conditions of Utopia —without shortening their leisure. Here it is that we

(*Chemical Industry Journal* 12'998) that in Chelsea, 1000 tons of *refuse* (sifted and picked by boys) have yielded on an average

					Tons.
Coal and coke (pieces over 1½ inches)				...	8
„ „ („ under „ „)				...	799
Rags, paper, string, etc.,			...	...	76
Vegetable matter,	...	...	..		44
Tins, ...	...	...	..	...	7
Iron, ...	...	...	...	...	2
Bones,	...	...	...	..	5
Crockery,	...	...	...	...	5
Glass, ...	...	...	...	...	2
(About 5000 *unbroken* bottles)					———
					948

In other words only 5 per cent. at most of the refuse was true waste! What an awful example of unthrift such facts preach to us. Similarly "London" recently told us that "the bottle exchange, which exists to collect and return bottles to their various owners, recovered no fewer than 391.516 dozen bottles, 12,568 boxes, 3,572 syphons, and 112 casks. Out of that number there came from dustyards, chiefly in London, 233,124 dozen bottles, 318 boxes, and 565 syphons. Previous to the establishment of the exchange almost the whole of this supply from the dustyards was wasted. If it is worth while conducting a system for the collection of bottles, it would certainly be to the advantage of some enterprising person to organise a system for the collection of one or other of the various articles in London's refuse which are as yet practically untouched." We would ask why so much labor should be wasted on the filthy work of picking refuse-heaps, and why every householder should not have his "waste" stored into several bins and removed at intervals. We do not yet understand the *morality of economy in little things.*

must procede to apply our principle of *choosing the least evil.*

Now it is obvious that there are two methods by which a man may become relatively wealthier, *viz.*, (1) By adding to his actual wealth ; (2) by circumscribing his wants. Of two men with equal incomes, families, and necessary house-expenses, etc., clearly that one is decidedly and deservedly the poorer who considers it proper to keep a couple of ridiculous and useless flunkeys, and to drink champagne : the other, relatively to his lunatic neighbor, increases his wealth by discountenancing such extravagant absurdities. Now the question that we have to answer is simply this : how far are our expenses of the present day unnecessarily high owing to our consumption, in one sense or another, of practically *useless luxuries*—luxuries, that is to say, that yield us no appreciable happiness, or even that are distinctly irksome, but yet are ordained by that archfiend *Fashion ?* At the same time we must, in accordance with our principle of choosing the lesser evil, call especial attention to many luxuries that, we do not deny, were very tolerably pleasant in themselves if they could be had for nothing, but are decidedly *not worth the candle* employed in getting them. So far as we can discover any such sources of expense—and they are probably far more numerous than one would *a priori* anticipate—so far may we see our way to relatively increasing our wealth without extra work.

Now, as exemplifying these stupid and unnecessary expenses, the maintenance of large staffs of servants has already been several times alluded to : here is a luxury that—prompted as it is in large measure by a mere vulgar

10

love of pompous display—is doomed to go. Nowadays—
when reasonable people are still exceedingly scarce—it may
be thought only a right and dignified proceeding that a
gentleman, taking riding exercise, should be followed, at
a "respectful" distance, by a groom—not for companionship but for display; or that an old lady, taking an airing
in the Park, should be similarly followed by a gorgeous
flunkey armed with an equally gorgeous staff as tall as
himself; or that the same old lady, proceeding to church
in order to express in the most solemn wording her sense
of humility, her contempt for the pomp and vanity of
the world, and her acknowledgments of human brotherhood, should be similarly escorted in high state by the
flunkey carrying her prayerbook (!); or that another
estimable old lady, retiring to Florence for a few weeks'
rustication, should be accompanied by a retinue of fifty
servants;[1] all such proceedings may indeed be thought
very right and proper now; but in a semi-Utopian age
they would be scorned as contemptible examples of arrant
stupidity and vulgar snobbishness. Here then is one
type of luxury that may be ruthlessly eliminated; but we
have already said so much on the subject of servants
generally that it is unnecessary to go farther into details
now.

In the very forefront of all however we would place the
wicked waste of wealth that is annually swallowed up by
the Augean stomach of mankind: and among the very
first luxuries to go must be the wines and liqueurs, the
ridiculous extravagance of hothouse-fruits, and all the
sickening extent of gorging-material displayed at a big

[1] See Daily Papers, February, 1893, *à propos* of the Queen's visit.

dinner. It seems clear to us that a highly-civilised Utopian society will know as little of such luxuries as do we of *long pig*.

Perhaps however it may be as well, in order to avoid misunderstandings, that we should explain our position as to wine-drinking somewhat more fully. We are in no sense advocating Teetotalism *per se ;* and our argument is addressed to all rational men alike, whether Teetotalers or not. It is true that personally we must rank—tho unchartered, and much against our physical inclinations —among the Teetotalers ; since it seems to us the duty of all *for the present* to range themselves on this side, in order by example and influence to fight against our country's awful curse: but, since before even semi-Utopia be reached, drunkenness will have disappeared, one may incline to doubt whether Teetotalism will prevail then, and to consider it probable that in Utopia all will be *moderate* drinkers—alas for the fanatics! The many esthetic advantages sacrificed by Teetotalers—putting aside the physical gratification—are so clear that we might well hesitate to ascribe Teetotalism, and deny *red wine*, to an arch-esthetic society of too high a moral development to fear drunkenness or any excess. However this be, we will provisionally concede that cheap beer and light wines may be moderately consumed in Utopia, altho the subsequent course of our argument may tend to considerably discredit this assumption: but we wish to understate rather than to overstate our case ; and, if Utopia must after all be ranked as practically Teetotal, then is our farther argument only strengthened. It seems certain however that all—even moderately—expensive wines, all except the mere *vins ordinaires*, will be unknown—as we will now procede to show.

If this declaration raise an angry outcry that Utopia without fine wines would be no Utopia, and that therefor we are diminishing its happiness below that of the present day instead of giving to all Utopians wine of the best, our retort is very simple. We must reiterate that (1) we have nothing to do with an impossible Utopia but only with a strictly feasible one ; and (2) we are depicting the Utopia *not* of a privileged few—a Greek aristocracy supported by a world of slaves—*but of the all ;* and we should greatly like to know *how* our objectors would propose to give every Utopian abundance of expensive wine consistently with any scheme of short work-time, abundant leisure, and general affluence, for all. At present not one man in one hundred drinks choice wines, and yet the total expense of wine-drinking is sufficiently appalling : what will it be if one hundred in one hundred must be supplied ?

The average man never reflects on at all—or in the least understands—the enormous annual loss of wealth entailed by such unproductive consumption. Thanks to our venerable school-system, which instructs boys in athletics, Latin verse, royal divorce-cases, and such-like rubbish, but steadfastly refuses them the rudiments of Political Economy, the nation consists for the most part of men who are absolutely ignorant of the fundamental principles on which society hinges ; whilst—worst perhaps of all—they are usually too pig-headedly and insanely conceited of their own vast superiority, as " men of practical common-sense," to all " mere theorists," to be susceptible of any instruction. Such men are intellectually incapable of understanding that consumption of luxuries is a purely unproductive consumption, and that in wine-drinking they are simply pouring so much wealth—*i.e.*, the product of so much human labor—down their several and respective gullets.[1]

It is sufficient for such men—that is, for the nation generally—that such an industry as wine-making "employs many thousands of people": and they are too ignorant and too stupid to see that, not only is the whole work of these thousands, strictly speaking, *wasted*, but that they are all of them *kept* at the public expense.

When we reflect on the immense area occupied by the vines—*the area in Europe alone being sufficient to raise yearly food enough to support 30,000,000 men for a year* [2]

---

[1] Thro'out we ignore the nutritive value of wine, since the amount of carbo-hydrates present (as alcohol, etc.) can be replaced by bread or fat at a mere fraction of the cost, and with great benefit to the digestion.

[2] According to a report compiled by the French Statistical Bureau, the vineyards of Europe cover 22,973,902 acres. The annual average production of the European vineyards is put at 2,652,300,000 gallons. Spain exports most wine (200,000,000), but it is chiefly common wine, and it is estimated at only £12,000,000; while the value of the 56,000,000 gallons exported from France is put at *nearly as much*. Italy comes third with exports of 45,000,000 gallons, estimated at £2,800,000; while Austria and Hungary exported only 16,500,000 gallons worth £1,720,000. (The annual average production of wine in the whole world during the five years 1886-90 is estimated at 2,811,600,000 gallons.) Again, "the Chamber of Commerce at Rheims has published the statistics of the trade in champagne since 1844. In 1844-5 the value of the trade was £265,000, and in the following year it exceeded £280,000. In 1868-9 it amounted to nearly £640,000, but fell to £360,000 in 1870-1, and then rose in 1871-2 to £800,000. The value in 1872-3 was £880,000,

—and calculate the immense amount of capital and labor so locked up, even now, we shall be forced to conclude that, of the two alternatives, Teetotalism is after all a far more probable habit than costly-wine-drinking in Utopia. Now, if it should still be contended that the loss of champagne, hock, madeira, and port, is a distinct hedonic loss, it must suffice in reply to invoke our principle of *least evil.* It were surely better that all

and it oscillated between this sum and £680,000 until 1889-90, when it became £920,000. The figures were £1,031,000 in 1890-1; £970,000 in 1891-2. The number of bottles used in France rose from 2,225,000 in 1844-5 to 4,558,000 in 1891-2; while the number exported rose during the same period from 4,380,000 to 16,685,000 " (*Nature*, 47/157, 614). If we calculate, by a process of averaging, the value for the 23 years 1845-1868, and then add together *all* the figures, we shall obtain approximately £50 *million* as the value (at *Rheims*—*not* to the final purchasers) of 50 years' champagne. Fifty million pounds for less than fifty years' growth of one wine in one country; how immensely richer, therefor, the world would quickly become if champagne and other such luxuries were discarded and their manufacturers and the land otherwise employed!

Referring back now to the earlier extract, which gives us 23,000,000 acres of vineyards, let us see what this means. To make the calculation as simple as possible we will suppose the whole acreage to be reclaimed from wine-growing and devoted to wheat: then assuming the average English yield of 30 bushels per acre, and that each bushel represents only 40 lbs. of flour, then since 2·5 lbs. of flour per day will form a sufficient diet for a man (less than 2 lbs. yield sufficient carbo-hydrates, but 2·5 is necessary for nitrogenous food) we get this result $\left(\dfrac{23,000,000 \times 30 \times 40}{2\cdot5 \times 360}\right)$—that a population of over *30 million* adults could be entirely supported by the yearly wheat-produce of the present European vineyards. Of course we do not for a moment suppose that it would pay to grow wheat without rotation, or that wheat could be grown on all the vine-soils; but, whatever crops were grown, the result, calculated in terms of wheat, is that a population of 30 million adults could be fed by the acreage at present wasted on this luxury of wine.

should suffer the slight—the very slight—deprivation implied, than that, as now, the indulgence should be continued at so terrible an expense of toil and treasure.

Secondly, we may point out the *very important qualification* that a generation, which had never seen, tasted, or smelt, any alcoholic drinks—or, taking our qualified supposition, anything but *vins ordinaires* and beer—could suffer no possible unhappiness thro the deprivation of a physical pleasure that it had never experienced—any more than our happiness is marred by our inability to obtain nectar and ambrosia.

No doubt, *during the transition*, those, who had been in the habit of drinking such wines, would suffer somewhat: but when the last bottles of champagne and madeira had disappeared from the world, and their last surviving consumers had followed them, *then* all the trouble would be at an end; and semi-Utopia would find its wealth immensely increased—both directly and indirectly—without any payment of unhappiness therefor.[1] Such considerations are—as it seems to us—of great importance to the discussion of the abolition of any similar luxuries.

Thirdly, it is well to bear in mind that the modifications impressed upon a progressively evolving race may not improbably involve a continually lessening regard for the merely sensual pleasures of the palate, concomitantly

[1] There is so little *ideal persistence* in wine that merely to *read* of its pleasures would, we think, excite no craving for it. As to this, see discussion in note on tobacco, p. 171, and compare the experience of reclaimed drunkards—who feel the temptation chiefly when they see or taste wine. But one may also remark that chastity involves physical denial: is it therefor un-Utopian!

with an increasing regard for intellectual and esthetic pleasures. We can see, perhaps, some indications of the same sort even now; for among ourselves aldermen, liverymen, and vestrymen, are notoriously ranked as the most contemptible and hog-like members of society; and it is precisely these men who find their chief happiness and satisfaction in guzzling and gorging—whilst the cultured few regard them with much the same feelings of loathing and disgust as filled Æneas' mind when he beheld the harpies' foul and filthy feasting.[1]   If, therefor, this suggestion be valid, our way is made still smoother.

[1] Readers will of course recall Thackeray's description of a City dinner: and we may perhaps subjoin here a cutting from a recent paper chronicling a few days' City-feeding. (*Star*, Feby. 1st, 1893.)

London gives a little diary of City-company activity within the last fortnight :—

Wednesday, 1st Feb.—A court dinner of the Worshipful Leather-sellers.

Thursday, 2nd—The Blacksmiths' Company dine.

Friday, 3rd.—Dinner of the Committee of the Cooks' Company.

Friday, 3rd.—The Horners' Company dine.

Saturday, 4th.—Clockmakers' Company. Luncheon at Guild-hall Tavern.

Monday, 6th.—The Carmen's Company. Dinner at Guildhall Tavern.

Monday, 6th.—Bakers' Livery met.

Tuesday, 7th.—Merchant Tailors' Company. Meet to admit the Duke of York and dine.

Tuesday, 7th.—Butchers' Company meet and dine.

Tuesday, 7th.—Coopers' Company go a coopering at the Hotel Metropole. Business: "One of those recherché dinners for which the Hotel Metropole proprietary is justly celebrated."

Wednesday, 8th.—Paviors' Company dine together.

Thursday, 9th.—The Worshipful Basket-Makers—none of whom could make a basket—hold a winter banquet.

We may next glance at a few gastronomic luxuries
other than wines : and, in order to safe-guard our
argument, both here and hereafter, from the retort that
of course it is easy enough to sketch an Utopian scheme
giving comfort and wealth to all, if one put the standard
of that wealth and comfort low enough and premise a
Spartan simplicity of life—in order to obviate this
danger, let us state at once that we do *not* look to any
such ideal of Spartan or cynical simplicity. It is true
that one main object of this essay is to advocate an

Again, as another example of this disgusting stomach-worship,
note the provision made for, not feeding but, unnecessarily stuff-
ing, the sons and daughters of Belial (and others) that thronged
to the Imperial Institute conversazione in 1893— " Four hundred
lady attendants will wait upon the guests, 1000 of whom can be
supplied with refreshment every minute. To give some idea of
the provision which has been made for accommodating this great
party, we may mention that there have been prepared 40,000
sandwiches, 130,000 ices, tons of cakes, confectionery, crystallised
fruits, and fruits from Tasmania and South Australia (sent by
the respective Governments), 400 gallons of champagne cup, and
600 gallons of claret cup. It is estimated that 700lb. of coffee
will be consumed, together with 300lb. of tea, 15 cwt. of butter,
and scores and hundreds of apples, pineapples, and every kind of
fruit, a great deal of which has been received from the colonies.
Tons of strawberries and cream have been prepared. To meet
the great demand, there have been laid in 40,000 glasses, 30,000
cups and saucers, and 30,000 plates for sandwiches and ices "
(*Star*, May 17th, 1893). Yet again we are told that 1500
guineas were to be thrown away by the City Corporation on a
déjeuner to the Duke of York, and 2000 on a similar tribute to
the King of Denmark, just as, in 1881, 2000 guineas were thrown
away in fêting the King of Greece (*Star*, July, 1893). But
these items are mere insignificancies when compared with the
gigantic total of *nearly a million sterling* which we are told that
the twelve great City-Companies alone have dissipated in *ten
years* on *Entertainments* and in grants to the Courts of Assist-

earnest and beautiful simplicity of life ; but *our* simplicity is very different from that of Sparta or of the Cynics— as different as is day from night. For us, the Spartan life, with its incessant hardship, rigid discipline, ceaseless governmental interference, and cruel inhumanity, its narrowness, bareness, and unamiability, has none of the attractions which it has offered to some foolish sentimentalists who profess to long for such " wholesome " living: to us Lycurgean Sparta rather suggests devildom [1] let loose on a saturnalia of repression ; whilst the coming

ants (*Star*, Jan. 15th, 1894). The blood boils with indignation to think of the incalculable good that might have been, and should have been, wrought with the wealth that these high priests of sensuality have crammed into their own hog-like stomachs. We ourself have private information of a certain small City-Company that spends four-fifths of its income on two half-yearly banquets—the tickets for which are priced at *two guineas each !*

As one example of the effects of drinking, this item of newspaper intelligence is noteworthy :—

" The Swiss Federal Council recently instituted an inquiry as to the best means to be employed for diminishing the consumption of spirits, in the course of which it was shown that the population of Switzerland, numbering 2,500,000, drink 27,000,000 litres of brandy yearly, the result being that every year the number of men unfit for military service increases ; that 44 per cent. of lunatics have lost their reason by the abuse of spirits ; that of every 100 criminals 45 are given to drink ; that a minimum of 254 deaths per annum are caused by alcohol ; and that the great majority of the suicides—600 a year—are attributed to the same vice."

In addition to the moral and physical evils, what an awful waste of the means to material happiness does this represent !

[1] Presumably the nearest modern parallels to the *spirit* of Spartan life are offered by the Redskin savages, and the public-schoolboy savages, respectively.

life, that we picture, is warm, glowing, bright, *human*,
cultured, refined, beautiful, and unrestrained, beyond
anything that most of us to-day can realise. Yet—tho
inconceivable, without a thousand adjuncts such as only
culture and refinement can give—it is in one sense nobly
simple—simple as devoid of stupid or useless excrescences:
and we do claim the right to provide for its necessary expenses and its necessary leisure by abolishing costly and
more or less stupid luxuries that are most appreciated by
the leas' cultured members of society. Of course we do
not deny that very many luxuries are really very pleasant—if one could have them for nothing. If champagne and madeira, winter-pine-apples and peaches, were
cheap as daisies, mankind would be very absurd not to
enjoy such delicacies; but we do contend that since
these luxuries can be had only at a great expense of toil
and treasure, since the pleasure afforded by them is
essentially fleeting and of the moment—the pleasures of
taste having least of all our pleasures any ideal persistence—since in fact the consumption of such luxuries
means the mere emptying down our gullets of so much
wealth and labor that would otherwise—Proteus-like—
have appeared in the form of esthetic intellectual or
material gains, or prolonged leisure, that since in fact we
have to pay pretty heavily for such luxuries, the game is
most emphatically *not* worth the candle.[1]   But in

---

[1] One of the most disgraceful sides of this stomach-worship is
the malversation of trust-funds and endowments to kitchen-
expenses: see the late review-charges against Oxford University of crippling education by heavy disbursements for the
table.

addition to all these table-luxuries, and many others that
were pleasant enough if they could be had for nothing,
but are not worth one hour per day's extra labor, and can
be dispensed with without any discomfort—in addition
to these there are a multitude of downright *stupid* and
useless luxuries which nobody really wants, but which a
tyrannous *fashion* or a snobbish love of display dictates
as " indispensable to every gentleman's household "—to
which matters we will return anon. In short we contend
that the result of the general worship of luxury and display is to ruin half our happiness—half our lives being
devoted to working for things that we don't want and
that we are none the really happier for obtaining : and
the nett result of this follow-the-bell-wether-like mumbo-
jumbo worship is—what !—

> " That chasing *dreams*, that dreamlike chased,
>   Thro lapse of years our life doth *waste*."

   To conclude our gastronomic survey however—we are
quite ready to admit of course that in semi-Utopia the
daily dinners of *all* will be triumphs of artistic and scientific effort, and—to adopt the cook's jargon — pre-
eminently *recherchés*. But it is a moral certainty that
they will not include a dozen courses, nor be com-
pounded of rare and expensive materials. The lady of
the future—devoting somewhat less time to trumpery
novels and wearisome fashionable lounges—will pride
herself on her skill in devising a dinner fit for a prince
from materials little costlier than now supply the food of
a peasant. In fact, here as everywhere, we must aim at
refined simplicity, at *skilled treatment of simple material*,

and eschew extravagance and vulgar display. For how much frightful and criminal waste is not that detestable custom responsible which, not content with simply enjoying cheap luxuries in their due season, insists on having the same things as dear luxuries in their very anti-season; which scorns strawberries and green peas in summer at a few pence per pound, but insists on them in midwinter at many shillings;[1] and so on thro'out.

This is one of the most indefensible forms of waste, and one that cannot excite too much reprehension: however they be obtained, whether by purchase or by private rearing, the consumption of all such out-of-season fruits is a *sinful waste:* and we may be very sure that the pineries[2] and peacheries of the present are doomed luxuries.

[1] "The vegetables called Peas were exceedingly scarce, and cost 20s. a quart . . . . 'There are 200 quarts of peas,' said the old fellow, winking with bloodshot eyes, and a laugh that was perfectly frightful. And goodness gracious—said I—what can be the meaning of a ceremony so costly, so uncomfortable, so savory, so unwholesome, as this? Who is called upon to pay two or three guineas for my dinner now in this blessed year of 1847? Are there no poor: is there no reason: is this monstrous belly-worship to last for ever?" (Thackeray.)

[2] Mrs. Fawcett put the point very neatly when she wrote (*Political Economy*, p. 28): "If two tons of coals are consumed in producing a pineapple in March, the wealth represented by that coal is *wasted*, or at any rate it produces only the very inadequate return of giving two or three people a pleasant taste in their mouths for a few minutes. If the same coal had been used to smelt iron, or to make gas, it would have had a much more productive result." Perhaps it may be useful to those unversed in economics to point out the difference between the reckless squandering of an individual's fortune and *actual waste:* a man may ruin himself utterly, and yet be guilty of *no waste*; whilst a rich man, living barely up to his income, may yet be

But eating and drinking are far from being the only medium of waste, or the only department where a return to far simpler living is essential : for our national amusements afford ample scope for reform, and imperatively demand some notice here.   Englishmen are wont to pride themselves on their pre-eminence in *sport ;* and, were we polytheists, there can be no doubt that the devilgod of Sport would rank second only—if, indeed, second—to Zeus : but we think that few men have any conception of the frightful *waste* entailed by several of our national pass-times.   We propose here to pass by all the more trifling items, and confine our attention to two divisions only of "le Sport"—*viz.,* hunting and shooting: and we think that the unanimous verdict of all men, who really care for the progressive evolution of Humanity, will be, that in our pleasures as in our feeding we must aim at far greater *simplicity* and far less extravagance. [1]

guilty of frightful waste.   Waste is measured by the amount of labor or wealth that you (directly or indirectly) consume by using luxuries : but *expensiveness* may be a function of rarity also ; and the mere transfer of wealth, or destruction of wealth-symbols, involves no waste—no national loss.   To give £500 for an unique postage-stamp, to lose a fortune at pitch-and-toss, or to light a cigar with a bank-note, may be hopelessly idiotic, but is *not waste :* to give £5 for a bottle of wine is waste—for so much labor has been employed merely to get a pleasant taste in the mouth for a few minutes.

[1] A note may, however, be added with regard to Football— the cult of which game involves (as the Archbishop of Canterbury is reported to have said—we know not on what authority) *an annual cost of £1,000,000.*   The author of an article "On Football" in the *Fortnightly Review* for January, 1894, states that " £200 or £250 per annum has in many cases been paid to some particularly efficient player "; and that " the receipts of a club are very large, perhaps £2,000 or £3,000 a year, but the

With regard to hunting now we will quote the statistics furnished by Lord Yarborough. He states that there are 330 packs of hounds in England, Scotland, and Ireland: assuming the cost of fox-hounds to be £650 for one day per week per year, stag-hounds to cost £550, and harriers £200, keeping up hounds in the United Kingdom causes the expenditure of £114,850; and estimating 100 men hunting with each pack, each man having three horses, that means that 99,000 horses are engaged. Putting the cost of each horse at 15s. per week this comes to considerably over £3,500,000! Therefor, as Lord Yarborough maintains, the cost of keeping hounds and maintaining the hunts in the United Kingdom comes altogether to over four millions (!) independently of the expense of carriage-horses, cover-hacks, travelling-expenses, etc. Making certain allowances[1] it seems fair to reckon, on this presumably good

expenditure is almost always equally great. . . . A high authority on football finance gives the average wage of a professional player at £3 a week in winter, and £2 a week in summer."

We commend this article also to those who wish to realise the social results of this pernicious cult, which finally turns men loose on the world at 30 years of age without any craft or trade. We are also happy to find the writer thoroly at one with ourself as to the *true raison d'être* of football and all other games and recreations.

[1] If we assume hunting to be dropped, it does not follow that a*l* these horses would be set free for other work: but if we assume that each quondam huntsman retained *one* of his three horses for rational use, this would set free two, and save about 2½ millions: adding to this the cost of dogs we get 3 millions; then all the incidental expenses must be added. We presume that the entire cost of human labor wasted in supplying these amusements is included in the above calculations of Lord Yarborough.

authority, that about *3 millions are annually wasted* on
this very selfish and destructive amusement of a very
few : 3 millions yearly—in good sooth here is a doomed
luxury !   It is clear that we may appreciably accelerate
the approach of Utopia by abolishing such wicked waste
as this—a waste the more indefensible in that it involves
cruel sufferings to dumb animals, and keeps vigorously
alive the barbarous instincts of mankind : it stands to
reason that a fox-hunter, still more a harrier, is by many
removes nearer to primitive savagery than is the average
Englishman.[1]

[1] Unhappily, the "sporting" spirit is not only a barrier to
advance but actually a cause of retrogression.   Fox-hunting is
bad enough ; hare-hunting is far worse ; but now we have the
sickening practice of tame-deer-hunting, with all its attendant
brutalities, bitterly defended ; and a recent development has
given us the cockney butchery of rabbit-coursing.   We may take
the opportunity here to protest against the steady training of
certain youngsters in fox-hunting, and the boorish practice of
regarding that occupation as the only serious business of life.
Here again Leech's cartoons show us, beneath all their humorous exaggeration, a very striking picture of English life : and
the knickerbockered urchin who is galloping over ploughed ground
because his second pony is waiting for him : the "old fox-
hunter," *aetat* perhaps ten, who finds Rotten Row rather dull,
having been accustomed to go across country all his life ; the
enthusiast of a similar age who deems it such a bore that school
begins just as one's hunters are in such splendid condition ; no
less than the grown men who get thro a wet day by an imita-
tion steeple-chase in the dining-room, or by playing cat's-cradle
with their cousins, or by functioning as Aunt Sally to have choco-
late thrown into their mouths ; all these instances alike preach
an eloquent lesson against that wealth-wasting, labor-wasting,
life-wasting, worship of Sport—to whose votaries apparently
any kind of intellectual or esthetical occupation is utterly impossible.   *Oh tempora, oh mores !*
   We subjoin, as pertinent to this subject, a letter that recently
appeared in an evening paper.—

So much for hunting. Shooting entails a parallel system of waste—waste of labor to a shocking extent, waste of powder and shot, and waste of land : whilst the moral aspect of it, at least so far as concerns the senseless butchery of the battue, is, if possible, worse than that of hunting—and, indeed, one shudders to think of the sufferings of *merely-wounded* birds, that linger on in pain and die slowly of starvation perhaps. Unfortunately we have no statistics to hand concerning the annual outlay on this form of waste, and can only fall back on the census, which returns (1881) the number of game-

"HARE-HUNTING AT ETON.

"TO THE EDITOR OF THE 'STAR.'

"SIR,—It may interest some of your readers to know that while 'calf-hunting' is in full swing around the royal borough, the youthful scions of aristocracy are being carefully educated in brutality. From the *Eton College Chronicle* of 2 Feb., a paper written by boys for a schoolboy public, it appears that during the week ending 28 Jan. the school Beagles were out no less than four times, four out of the six working days being either half or whole holidays ! We read how a hare, after a run of one hour 20 minutes, 'was so stiff she couldn't go a yard, and was pulled down ;' and again, in another case, 'we then bustled her along into Orkney Cottage garden, where, after being raced round the garden, she was killed in the gateway.' 'While we were breaking her up,' adds the youthful writer, 'another hare was viewed away,' etc.

"Now, sir, I would ask any right-minded person, is it not simply horrible that boys should be thus brought up and encouraged in brutal cruelty by those who are supposed to have charge of their moral welfare? It is well known that hare-hunting is one of the most cruel of all sports, the heart of the victim being often burst by the strain of panic and exertion. The idleness tolerated by our public school system is sufficiently disgraceful, but it is far worse that organised inhumanity should be sanctioned by the school authorities. Does Dr. Warre, so zealous for the 'manly training' of Englishmen, regard this

11

keepers in England and Wales alone as 12,600—an astonishing figure. The whole labor of these 12,000 men is, of course, utterly *wasted:* like so many other luxury-mongers they are simply kept at the public expense, and it is certain that the abolition of the whole 12,000 will be an inevitable item in the preparation for semi-Utopia. Shooting then is also a doomed luxury;[1] and, like hunting, must be replaced by simpler, cheaper, and morally healthier, amusements—by boating, rowing, walking, riding, skating, cricket, and a score other available recreations.

There are countless other devices of fashion and custom for ensuring *waste* by frivolous and stupid expenditure, at which we can only glance. We very greatly doubt

cowardly torture of innocent animals as forming part of that curriculum?'"

The following passage has come under our notice just in time for insertion :—

"It is a result of Teutonic conquest that the landed gentry of Europe are largely descended from this race—Goths, Lombards, Normans, Franks, Saxons, Angles—and they preserve with singular persistency the physical characteristics and the mode of life of their remote ancestors. It is, as an acute writer (Hamerton) has remarked, 'a strange result of the wealth and intelligence of the modern world to give the upper classes the pursuits of the savage, without the necessity which is the excuse for them. They *are barbarians* armed with the complicated appliances of civilisation. Their greatest glory is to have killed a large quantity of big wild beasts. Field-sports are good for keeping up the energy of semi-barbarous aristocracies'" (Taylor: *Origin of the Aryans*, p. 245). With every word of this we most heartily concur.

[1] Just as hunting gives us rabbit-coursing, so, too, shooting gives us the cockney butchery of pigeons, and of larks and other singing birds.

whether the Utopians will tolerate the professional cricketers who turn a splendid recreation into a business; and we are sure that they would scorn the absurdity of sending teams of cricketers all over the world to play international matches, or the parallel absurdity of allowing some scores of " county-cricketers " to devote their whole energies, summer after summer, to *playing* cricket as the business of life.

So, again, with dancing. We suspect that Utopians will greatly prefer the simple quasi-family dances among a score or so of friends to the waste and display of a grand public ball ; and we are sure that they would be aghast equally at the wickedly wasteful expense, and the wearisome stupidity, of fashionable receptions and routs, and of royal drawing-rooms and levées. What Utopia would say to the crassly stupid and servile flunkeyism of people who waste several hundred pounds in temporarily " decorating " — save the mark — the streets thro which a serene highness [1] is to drive, or even in the crowning folly of the annual city-circus in honor of an ungrammatical alderman, can only be surmised ; but it is very certain indeed that Utopia will be far too wise to waste wealth and labor in such fashion, and especially on such tawdry tinsel ! So, too, the coming age of reason will find it scarcely credible that in the civilised and humanised nineteenth century, with poverty and want crying

---

[1] From one of Lyell's early letters it appears that the educational enterprise of Oxford had been seriously crippled by the enormous outlay (reckoned in *thousands*) devoted to the reception of the allied sovereigns at Oxford ! So that funds intended for education were utterly wasted by these lickspittles in their eager cringing before several despicable monarchs.

out on every side, and innumerable schemes of philanthropists, educationalists, and artists, languishing for
want of a few miserable thousands, "sane and sober"
men could waste millions on such childish, ephemeral,
and objectless, extravagances as international exhibitions,
worlds' fairs, Watkin towers, and Antwerpian castles-in-
the-air—the nett result of all which is a vast squandering
of toil and treasure to gain—truly speaking—nothing!
These things are the portentous visible signs of a terrible
and desperate social and moral disease.[1] These are
sights to make the angels weep.

Now, a very great deal of the present waste is due to
that snobbish and servile worship of fashion, and vulgar
love of display, that lead men into so much wrong-doing.
Let us for instance glance at dress. So far as concerns
men there is not in the present day much *waste*, in all
conscience; for men take so great pains to make their
dress hideous and absurd that there is scant room left
for waste; and perhaps the only marked instance of

---

[1] *The first* international exhibition. we doubt not, was productive of great good, material and moral. and especially at a time
when men travelled far less, and were far more *foreign* to each
other than now; but their constant repetition is absolutely in-
excusable. They may benefit certain individuals by increasing
their piles of *filthy* lucre, but they wreak a terrible injury on the
world at large. They may make the rich richer, but, indirectly,
they *must* make the poor yet poorer. It was asserted that the
World's Fair at Chicago cost *seven million sterling*, of which at
least a million sterling was spent in building a *temporary* suburb
of lodging-houses, etc. (*Daily News*, 23rd June, 1893.) It would
be superfluous to point out that all such expense, as well as the
unknown and incalculable expenses of travelling and freight,
involve an *absolute loss* of the world's wealth, however much
certain manufacturers and restaurateurs may have benefited.

wasteful expense in man's dress is that, in deference to an insane fashion, he buys a hard chimney-pot-hat which is hideously ugly, exceedingly uncomfortable, and absurdly inconsequential, instead of—at a tenth of the price—some light cap which were exceedingly comfortable and becoming. At the same time we may express our own strong suspicion that in the esthetic, rational, and economic, atmosphere of semi-Utopia, starched cuffs and collars may entirely disappear, to be replaced by something far more becoming and far less troublesome. We may also point out that, even now, a very appreciable expense might be saved, and a large amount of discomfort and deformity avoided, did not a pigheaded custom absolutely forbid us to go barefooted, no matter how warm the climate or how soft the path. As it is, we are compelled to lace up our feet in hot and heavy boots, endure much discomfort—and pay for our sufferings! Often have we envied the barefooted children of Scotland and Italy; and we are sure that, before very long, children *at least* will invariably go barefooted in the house during mild weather; and we have little doubt that the nearer modern society approaches to the Greek love of beauty, especially the beauty of humanity, the more desirous will it be to save our feet from distortion, and the more imperatively will it insist on everyone minding his own business and leaving others to mind theirs—so that if any find it agreeable to walk about London barefooted, they shall be free to do so without exciting the monkey-grimaces of an ill-bred brainless crowd.

Nothing more painfully evidences the innate intolerance of mankind than the insufferable impertinence and ostentatious consciousness of vast "superiority" which they display towards those who wear an unconventional dress; and no sadder proof could be asked of the rarity, in England anyhow, of good breeding and politeness, than the fact that no one can publicly wear a somewhat unconventional costume without running the gauntlet of barely veiled or overt insults from, not merely ill-mannered servant-girls, street boys, and loose women, but also from "educated" and "respectable" self-styled ladies and gentlemen. Recognising, as one must, that good breeding and courtesy are merely the outward and visible signs of truly *gentle* and noble dispositions—and conversely—one must admit with a heavy heart that primeval clownishness and boorishness are very prevalent beneath a vanishingly thin cover of "manners." The irony of the situation however—and one must admit that this renders it distinctly comic—is that these aggressively supercilious people who are so vastly "superior" to "fads" and "outré" costume, are in reality—could they but be made to realise it—the veritable dregs or scum of society—judged that is by any esthetic and intellectual standard; whilst their butts are, in this aspect, the first approximations to the semi-Utopians.[1]

---

[1] Bain aptly remarks, "The love of Influence, *Interference*, and *Control*, is so extensive and salient as to be a great fact in the constitution of society, a leading cause of social phenomena. It prompts to *Intolerance* and the *Suppression of Individuality*. Many are found willing to submit to restraints themselves, provided they can impose the same upon their unwilling neighbors" (*Mental Science*, p. 259: italics ours). The wearing of

But proceding now to women's dress, we may find luxury and waste galore. It is not so much that the expensiveness is a necessary function of the beauty of the dress, as it is that, from an ill-bred desire for displaying their wealth, or from deference to a tyrannical fashion, or from pure love of expensive fabrics *qua* expensive, they choose the costliest materials. Now so far as concerns the beauty of their dresses, the women of the future will far outshine the average women of to-day: for *then* every woman will wear a dress of purely artistic make— both in shape, set, color, and combination—instead of caricaturing her natural beauty of form by all the incredible and hideous absurdities that some crack-brained milliner in Paris dictates as the next fashion—or instead

stove-pipe hats, black coats, and trousers, is, of course, a case in point—the last mentioned abominations having been, as we surmise, invented by some wooden-legged or spindle-shanked man-milliner who desired to impose on mankind a fashion that would enable *him* to conceal his natural or acquired deformities. Unhappily—so slight is the moral courage of mankind—we could mention artists and philosophers who rail eloquently against all these hideous abominations, and, having done so, conform scrupulously to "fashion," leaving a few other and more courageous rebels, who are neither artists nor philosophers, and are therefor far more exposed to obloquy and far less able to effectually set an example, to practise the true faith which the great men content themselves with preaching! In this connection we may quote an excellent passage from Bagehot, who remarks, "You may talk of the tyranny of Nero and Tiberius; but the real tyranny is the tyranny of your next-door neighbor. What law is so cruel as the law of doing what he does? What yoke is so galling as the necessity of being like him? What espionage of despotism comes to your door so effectually as the eye of the man that lives at your door? Public opinion is a permeating influence, and it exacts obedience to itself: it requires us to think other men's thoughts, to speak other men's words, to

of wearing the sombre and depressing blacks and browns
that mournfully characterise an English assemblage to-
day. Women have yet to learn that the beauty of the
dress (and indirectly therefor of the wearer) depends
almost entirely upon the graceful and flowing draperies,
and upon the artistic combination of colors : given these
two elements, and a dress of serge or cotton will be
beautiful and the wearer winsome ; without these, the
most expensive silks, satins, and brocades, are thrown
away, and afford no pleasure to the beholder. Not that
we anticipate the disappearance of silks and satins and
other beautiful materials in Utopia ; far from it ; but we
do anticipate that far less regard will be paid to the
material of the dress, and far more to the beauty ; and

follow other men's habits. Of course if we do not, no formal
law issues, no corporal pain, no coarse penalty of a barbarous
society, is inflicted on the offender ; but we are called 'ec-
centric' ; there is a gentle murmur of 'most unfortunate ideas,'
'singular young man,' 'well-intentioned, I dare say, but
unsafe, sir, *quite unsafe.* *The prudent of course conform*"
(*Biographical Studies,* p. 4). Doubtless the *prudent* do conform ; but there are higher virtues than worldly prudence.
Had not earnest-minded men and women in all ages scorned the
selfish dictates of worldly prudence, freethought and liberty
had never been achieved, and a parcel of bigoted, ignorant, and
intolerant, old women in trousers—or rather in cassocks and
petticoats—would have stifled progress with their own nasty
clutches ; and here, in our own dear island, the banner of Engli-h
liberty would never have been emblazoned with the imperishable
glory of Oliver Cromwell's name, nor our annals have boasted
the felon's-death of one royal scoundrel, and the ignominious
dismissal of another. All these things, all our liberties hardly
wrung from despots and bigots, we owe to men who *scorned
prudence,* and for the world's sake poured out their lives like
water. "The prudent of course conform"—aye ; but "the
world has need of martyrs."

that all such wickedly wasteful and stupidly expensive absurdities as we now see in *court-dresses*, and in so many ballroom-dresses, as well as in the unnecessary multiplicity of costumes involving *four or five changes* a day, will utterly disappear.[1]

Closely akin to this subject is that of jewelry—which must of course be ranked among the truly *useless*, and very expensive, luxuries. In so far however as the value of jewels is less a function of labor bestowed than of intrinsic rarity-cum-beauty, it may be difficult to surmise whether or no they will be sought after or worked in semi-Utopia: but that any one individual's wealth of jewelry will be almost incommensurable with many ladies' jewel-accumulations of to-day, goes without saying. No Utopian could understand either the selfishness or the stupidity which are involved in the possession of many thousand pounds' worth of jewelry by a single person; and his only verdict on a burglary which carried off the whole collection at one fell swoop would be— *Serve her right!* In speculating on the jewelry of Utopia we must therefor remember that there is already an enormous quantity of jewels in the world; were these equally divided, probably everyone would possess as many jewels as he or she could reasonably desire or find use for: therefor, since jewels are practically immortal, and since the various natural processes so frequently alluded to already will probably tend to bring about a distribution of such jewels among the commonalty, it seems a

---

[1] To read an account of the dresses and jewels at a royal drawing-room, or a description of a royal trousseau, is simply heartbreaking to a sociologist.

tenable supposition that, even were the search for new
jewels to be entirely abandoned very soon, the world
would have sufficient to meet all its reasonable requirements.[1]

Anyhow it is certain that at the present day there is
a great and unnecessary waste of wealth and labor on
jewelry generally: and, were it not for the vulgar love
of display and ostentation, each one of us might save
him or her self considerable unnecessary expense (and in
the aggregate appreciably lighten the currency problem)
by substituting silver for gold in articles of necessary
jewelry. Almost the only such really necessary articles
of jewelry are watches and chains; and—given equally
good timekeeping—a silver watch is every whit as good,[2]
vanity and display excepted, as a gold one: whilst to
almost everyone a silver chain should be as acceptable as a
golden. So too for rings, bracelets, brooches, pencil-cases,
and the like, silver might perfectly well replace gold; a
vast amount of expense would be saved and the currency
benefited, and at the cost only of mortifying vanity and
vulgar ostentation. It is worth while remembering that
silver has a higher *esthetic* value than has gold; and this
intrinsic difference is accentuated by the extrinsic consideration that silver jewelry is *pure*, whereas gold jewelry is always, and necessarily, largely alloyed.

[1] To say nothing of the probability that chemists will soon be
able to manufacture jewels to any extent in their laboratories;
whether these will be as much prized when plentiful and cheap
is quite another thing; but probably diamonds will always be
valued.

[2] If silver watches, of the *best* timekeeping qualities, were generally demanded, they would be made.

One reform which we should greatly like to see—regarding it as a symptom of a healthier public feeling—would be the abolition of that despicably servile practice of heaping up gold bracelets, gold caskets,[1] gold all-

[1] Ouida asserts that these are currently understood to be turned into hard cash at once by their recipients. See her scathing article on the " Sins of Society " (in *Fortnightly Review* for December, 1892), with much of which we cordially coincide, altho we must take serious exception to one or two passages. In this connection too we may remind our readers of the fulsome toadyism displayed by the nation at large on the recent marriage of the Duke of York, when not only the wealthy, but ragged schoolchildren, sailors, and soldiers, were all robbed to swell the wealth of a young man who had no single tittle of a claim on his countrymen's gratitude, and who, by encouraging this miserable system, demonstrated nothing so convincingly as his kinship to the other royal " guinea-pigs," and his absolute unfitness for the post of " first *gentleman* " in the kingdom. It is the sight of such wealth-squandering on unworthy recipients that converts men to Socialism in thousands and prompts such speeches as those of Mr. Keir Hardie, who is reported to have said : " It was a disgrace when poverty was so rampant that men should make a parade of their pomp and their wealth. Recently an appeal was made to the nation on behalf of the poor widows and orphans who suffered by the failing of the Liberator Building Society. The sum of £100,000 was asked for, but it was never raised. But when an appeal was made for wedding gifts to Princess May and the Duke of York, the toadyism of the nation responded to the extent of £250,000."

We subjoin one or two other extracts from the daily papers on these topics.

" PRESENTS TO PRINCESS MAY.

" Yesterday afternoon a deputation waited upon the Princess May at White Lodge to present to her a very handsome revolving bookcase containing the works of Kingsley, Scott, Byron, Dickens, George Eliot, Lamb, Charlotte Brontë, Macaulay, and other authors, the gift of the children attending some of the elementary schools of London. The Duke and Duchess of Teck and Princess May received the deputation in the drawing-room, and Princess May expressed her warm thanks for such a handsome gift."

manner-of-absurdities, upon the idle royalties who set so
evil an example of waste and extravagance to society.
When corporations and committees cease to fawn on

"THE CITY AND ROYALTY.

"A Collective View of the Corporate Generosity to the Royal
Family.

"Here is the City's expenditure on the Royal Family during
the present reign :—

JUBILEE—
  Her Majesty £5,000

WEDDING GIFTS—
  Princess of Wales £10,000
  Duchess of Edinburgh   3,150
  Princess May   2,625
                                          ————— 15,775

GOLD BOXES (sometimes wedding gifts)—
  Prince of Wales   275
  Duke of Clarence   250
  Prince Consort, Alfred, Leopold, Arthur,
    George of Wales, Duke of Fife, Prin-
    cess Louise of Wales, Duke of Cam-
    bridge (100 guineas each)   840
                                          ————— 1,365

MEMORIALS, &c.—
  Prince Consort   644
  Princess of Wales (Imperial Institute model)   525
  Duke of Cambridge (sword, 1857).......................   218
                                        —————
                                        £23,527

"This does not take into account moneys expended by the members of the Corporation upon themselves in connection with
royal events. Thus, on the occasion of each of these presentations, there was a civic gorge, and when it is realised that the
sum of £1,500 is to be expended upon a mere midday lunch
when the Duke of York and the Princess May come to receive
their gift, it will be understood that a considerable sum should
be added to that just mentioned in order to cover the total expenditure. No account is here taken of presentations to foreign
notables, such as Kaiser, Tsar, Sultan, and Shah, nor does this
statement, which we have compiled from Corporation documents,
bear any reference to moneys expended by individual guilds,
such as the Saddlers' which presented its freedom to the Duke of
Connaught on Monday."

these expensive excrescences with the adulation at present fashionable, moral progress will be evidenced.

Whilst speaking of these matters we had better include all that need be said of the precious metals in manufactured form generally; and, therefor, we will point out that all such luxuries as silver serviette-rings, silver teapots and coffeepots, silver milk-jugs, silver toast-racks, silver candlesticks, silver salvers, silver cups, and, in short, silver plate generally, are mere expensive frivolities and wasteful excrescences of modern life that will probably disappear presently. People will become too sensible, and too averse to display, to waste their labors on acquiring what can be perfectly replaced by good china at a fraction of the cost.[1] In conclusion, we may note as significant for the present day that the less plate one owns, the less temptation is there to burglars, and the freer from anxiety is the householder.

If now it be asked how much *waste* is caused nationally by this over-indulgence in jewelry, we must point out that since jewelry is not—like wine—consumed in the use, and since all the gold, at least, that is now worked up into jewelry, would otherwise be snapped up by the mint, the best measure of such waste must be found in the amount of labor absorbed in the work. Now the census-returns (for 1881) number the workers in precious stones and jewelry at 23,622 [2]—besides 6,010 women.

[1] Emphatically we have *not* included in this account silver spoons and forks, which belong to another category entirely—to that, *viz.*, of useful and necessary domestic furniture. Above all things we would have that *lying* practice of plating abolihed—to say nothing of the fact that it is dearer in the long run.

[2] It is not clear how many of these may be also shopkeepers —*i.e.*, sellers of jewelry, nor whether watchmakers are included.

Disregarding [1] the latter, we have as a result that the luxury of jewels and silverplate costs the nation annually (*a*) the keep of 23,600 men, and (*b*) the wealth which might otherwise be created by such men. If their wages be reckoned to *average* only £2 per week thro'out we get (23,622 × 2 × 52) close on *two and a half millions* as the direct cost of this luxury, besides the loss of wealth (to be valued considerably higher than this figure) which these men would otherwise create if employed in productive work; at this rate the national charge for the luxury of jewels might very well reach at least *seven or eight millions* apparently! Now, if we take into account all the quite unnecessary jewel-like luxuries that have just been indicated, it will seem a very reasonable supposition that this large class of unproductive workers may be *reduced* by certainly 15 or 18 thousand—thus effecting an *annual saving*—according to our calculation —of *five or six millions.* Calculations of this sort—however necessarily rough and approximate only—are yet very useful in assisting us to realise what a terribly large proportion of our national work-time, that is of *Life,* is frittered away upon useless luxuries——

> " So chasing *dreams,* so dream-like chased,
>   Thro lapse of years our life doth *waste*."

—but things will be far otherwise in Utopia. [2]

[1] The reason for consistently disregarding the women in these calculations is the assumption that in semi-Utopia women will be sufficiently occupied in household work and childward care— and, therefor, must not be regarded as wage-earners.

[2] In a recent article in the *Fortnightly Review* we read—" The fact that there are in India 400,000 jewellers, and only 300,000 smiths, is eloquent as to *one* cause of poverty." So say we.

Before passing on to our next heading—or rather perhaps as a transition from jewelry thereto—we may instance, as exemplifying in a comparatively trifling way the general spirit of wastefulness which pervades Society, the thousand and one more or less useless and absurd gimcracks of every description that may be found in "fancy"-shops and bazaars, especially in the West-end of London. It would be an interesting thing to catalogue the contents of a few shop-fronts, with their prices, and then determine how small a percentage would be really missed were a general massacre of these trifles carried out. How much labor is annually wasted on amassing useless bits of (supposedly ornamental) crockeryware that are of no imaginable service for any purpose and do nothing but lumber up a house, and innumerable other such trifles—all of which absurdities may be bought, either by *noncompotes* for themselves, or by people generally when called upon to make wedding or birthday presents.[1] But in Utopia common-sense will be less uncommon.

And now as a closing instance of wasteful luxury *in excelsis* we may point to house-" decoration " and house-furnishing generally—a waste the more unpardonable in that the costly effects are often enough so hideously inartistic ; for " decoration " and beautifying are very far indeed from being synonymous terms. Ruskin has an excellent passage in one of his works deprecating the opinion that a small house cannot be—architecturally—beautiful : we wish that men generally could be made to

[1] It is very regretable that in making such presents so many people prefer to choose some absolutely useless and cumbersome article (of crockeryware for instance) that only puzzles the unfortunate recipient to dispose of it.

understand that mere size—size for the sake of ostentation and display—is the very last thing to aim at; and
that similarly in decorating and furnishing the interiors
it is necessary to start by absolutely ignoring all the
traditions of decorators, upholsterers, and other vulgar
and pigheaded human shams, and to make a clean sweep
of all their proposals.   The *waste* of work and money
annually entailed by the absurd and tyrannous traditions,
that Mrs. Grundy expects everybody to observe, is
something painful to contemplate : and while "decoration" is still laid on by housepainters and their like at
the cost of *several hundred pounds for a single room*, and
the "decorated" room is then handed over to the purveyors of vulgar upholstery for furnishing on a similar
scale—so long is social improvement yet very far to
seek.   All this will be altered in semi-Utopia ; *there*, the
decorations will consist in, not vulgar stucco and gilt, but
beautiful pictures and flowing draperies ; and tho perchance many houses there might boast true decorations
that we should think cheaply bought at hundreds of
pounds, that will be only because, year after year, loving
hands have labored joyfully at frescos and carving, to
beautify in their leisure their own home—their own, and
not a stranger-landlord's, house.   But at present we
are stupidly dominated by the Grundy-upholsterer-de-
corator league, and waste our money on the lying
vulgarisms of gilt picture-frames, gilt cornices, gilt
mirror-frames, on troublesome lustres, on *ornamental* but
never-to-be-used fireirons, on expensively and uncomfort-
ably upholstered chairs, impossible candlesticks,[1] in-

[1] Perhaps carefully covered up under glass shades ! !

credible vases, shelves of old china, and china plates, cups and saucers to be hung up as ornaments on the walls but of course never used (!), and a multitude of similar absurdities ; simply because it is thought fashionable and proper and respectable so to waste one's money on these fooleries ; whilst any self-willed sensible man who should insist on substituting wooden-framed mirrors and wooden picture-frames for their present gilded representatives, and on abolishing gilt cornices and all the other absurdities we have noticed, would be considered a *very odd man, quite outside society don't you know.* The standards of common sense, independence, and estheticism, are so terribly low that probably ninety-nine people in a hundred would prefer gilt cornices and gilt mirrors to a houseful of beautiful pictures—were they offered the choice of either exclusively. [1]

But we need not linger longer on this topic : enough has been said to show that here again is another department of useless expense that may be considerably curtailed with advantage : it were superfluous to follow the subject into further details ; suffice it again to indicate the lines along which reform may travel. [2]

---

[1] We may remark that here again we have had the pleasure of finding Mr. Morris' views on house-decoration and its reforms strikingly concordant with our own : we may especially recommend his lecture on " Making the best of it" (*Hopes and Fears for Art*) as affording abundant details of reforms that might be adopted : but we dissent entirely from his dislike to gas.

[2] In connection with these expenses, one should take count of all the stupid and wasteful expenditure that is lavished on the fittings and " decorations " of ocean-steamers, of traines-de-luxe, and especially of theatres ; this last expense being particularly cruel since the result is to increase the prices of admission, *i.e.*, to render it more difficult for many to enjoy an esthetic gratifica-

Lastly, as a set-off to all the foregoing economies of expense and wealth, it must not be forgotten that in *other* directions the Utopians' expenses will outstrip ours:

tion: hence it is—tho the extravagant sums paid by Englishmen and Americans to operatic and dramatic artists represent another factor in the expense—that men who have lived abroad justly complain that, not the necessities but, the *amusements* of life are so ruinously expensive in London ; and tell us that in Dresden, *e.g.*, they can enjoy for two or three shillings what costs them eight or ten in London. We must be pardoned for adding that, great as may be the services rendered by Henry Irving to the English drama, we cannot but deem his influence ruinously disastrous in that he has educated theatregoers to a ruinous extravagance of altogether superfluous stage-scenery, stage-dress, and meretricious glitter, that, while enormously increasing the expense, have not one iota of value in increasing the artistic illusion, but can only—so far as they are effectual at all—distract the attention from the acting. We had scarcely expected to see *Henry VIII.* converted into a series of circus-pageants suggesting nothing so much as a vulgar Lord Mayor's Show—and at the cost too of excising a large portion of the play and rendering the conclusion logically meaningless—and, tho it be somewhat invidious to draw comparisons, we could not avoid contrasting the comparatively simple settings of *Hamlet* at the Haymarket and *Twelfth Night* at Daly's theatre—where there were sufficient scenic effects to complete the illusion and afford graceful stagepictures, but without such extravagance of glittering "sup rs"—with the recognised style of the Lyceum.

As other examples of this wicked cult of sheer waste we may mention the practice of issuing editions *de luxe*, and distributing the type when 250 or 125 copies are printed—as if human toil and human wealth were valueless as water—in order that a few unprincipled persons may enjoy the selfish and stupid luxury *of possessing something that hardly anyone else has.* That the same fatal disease is sapping every branch of social life is evidenced by such trifling phenomena as the absurd extravagance with which barbers' shops are fitted up, and by the preposterous luxuries provided on the steamers which now perform fortnightly cruises to Norway and other parts—the effect of which is of course to double the expense and prevent thousands from enjoying such cruises !

while despising so many of our stupid and sensual luxuries, they will require far far more than we do of esthetic luxuries. Pictures, music, statues, aye and such minor esthetic properties as scent, flowers, draperies, and the like, will be far more necessary to Utopians than to ourselves.[1] What a happy and gracious halcyon-life will theirs be!

---

[1] It may be matter of surprise that in condemning these luxuries we have said nothing of tobacco - on which, excluding cigars, in 1892, 16½ millions were expended in the United Kingdom alone : surely this is a luxury as much as wine, and equally, here is unproductive consumption. Some years ago we had denounced tobacco as being as useless and needless as wine : but we are wiser now. Then we were without the pale : now we worship at the shrine of "oure gracious ladye Nicotine." Seriously, however, there is a great difference between smoking and wine-drinking. In the first place, of the 16½ millions expended no less than about 9½ were duty—Government tax, thus leaving only 7 millions as actually spent on tobacco—whilst, as every economist knows, this sum would again be enormously reduced but for the various middlemen's profits on the amount of the duty which is levied on the imports : as a matter of fact the declared value of the tobacco at the customhouse was *under 2 millions.*

Cigars however we regard as exactly upon a level with expensive wines ; while tobacco answers to beer and clarets. Now just as we defended the drinking of beer and claret *in Utopia*, so now far more strongly do we defend smoking, both in Utopia and here. Of course economically smoking is waste, but so is everything—including all esthetic properties—that is not necessary to life-sustentation ! But the true *moral* criterion can be obtained only by comparing amount and character of pleasure with amount and character of expense. Now if we consider how much real *happiness* may be obtained from smoking, and that supposing a man to smoke 4 ounces a week—which were tolerably heavy smoking,—the expense (minus duty) would be only 30s. *a year* to him, it seems to us that the charge of wastefulness falls utterly to the ground !

It may be retorted that, according to our own showing in the

We must once more emphatically protest against the selfish objection so apt to be raised against such speculations as these, that (grumblingly) " *we* want servants and wines, expensive dresses and big dinners, to make *us* happy : of what use is it to prove that they are wasteful ;

case of wine, if a coming generation had never tasted the pleasure, they would be none the less happy, since smoking is, like drinking, a mere passing physical pleasure, with no ideal persistence, so that even reading of it would produce no regrets in a tobacco-less race.   But here there are several errors ; smoking, we think, *has* a strong ideal persistence, and is capable of being ideally represented in such wise as to induce desire for it : the pre-eminently dreamy character of smoking should be remembered also. With regard to this marked ideal-representability of smoking, and its ability to impress the imagination, we are able to speak somewhat from our own experience.   Every one is familiar with such *novel* phrases as " knocking the ashes out of his pipe "— " reflectively filling and lighting his pipe "—" drawing at his pipe with an expression of deep satisfaction "—" wreathed in a cloud of smoke " etc., etc.—in fact with all the innumerable pictures of tobaccaceous content and happiness that our novelists have painted for us.   Now an abiding result of these word-paintings (strengthened no doubt by the daily sight of scores of actualities corresponding thereto) may be to call up frequent ideal representations in the mental picture-galleries of those even who have never yet experienced the pleasure of smoking.   Long before we had commenced smoking, and at a time when we rather objected to the practice than otherwise, yet if we were day-dreaming and amusing ourself by painting a mental picture of mankind under various imaginary circumstances, the tobacco *would* crop up and claim to be included in the picture : the ideal persistence of the well-known weed was strong : and if finally we refused to include it, the picture was apt to look unfinished to our mental eye, and perhaps in *visualising* it the pipe or cigar *would enter* the mouth whether we desired it or not.   No doubt, thousands could bear out our experience in this direction, and this indicates that an age which had never smelt or tasted tobacco might yet experience a strong *desire* for the pleasure which is incidentally portrayed so frequently in our light literature.   *But* you can't prove that they are not *very pleasant.*" Now against all this it is sufficient to reply that we do not deny that they *are very pleasant :* but the question is whether those who enjoy these luxuries would propose to

we have observed little or no such ideal persistence with regard to wine.

Again there is unmistakably a distinct *physical craving* for some such employment of the mouth as smoking affords. Dogs perhaps satisfy the same craving by gnawing bones : certainly children (and to a less extent probably women) experience a similar craving which they satisfy by chewing sweetmeats or pen-holders : and in our own experience—and we have heard a similar declaration from others—in pre-smoking days of manhood there was a constant craving for employing the mouth somehow. This fact, of the physical craving of the mouth for some such employment as smoking affords—in addition to the strong *nervous* appreciation of some species of narcotic, as testified by the prevalence of betel-chewing and many similar practices in parts where tobacco is not used, and by the disgusting practice of snuff-taking among many who do not smoke—seems to us one that should by no means be neglected in any discussion upon the ethics of tobacco. That smoking is an incomparably better solution of the difficulty than incessant eating goes without saying ; and we may point out the special advantage of smoking in that it may be so long continued : smoking can in no sense be described as a *passing* pleasure ; and herein consists another marked distinction between smoking and drinking—which latter is decidedly momentary. A man may be steadily smoking for many hours at a stretch, and experiencing *massive* pleasure all the while : whereas such persistence in drinking were clearly impossible.

Whether or no smoking be injurious to health, is another question altogether, and one that must be left to the experts. If sufficient proof could be obtained of its injurious influence, *that* might be a sufficient reason for giving up tobacco ; but it is well to remember the—too often forgotten—truth that health itself is valuable only as a *means* to the end of happiness ; and some might think ill health and happiness preferable to tobaccoless health minus happiness.

retain them at the cost of discomfort, suffering, and poverty, to the many : or whether they can muster sufficient unselfishness to admit that a social state in which all are comfortably rich is incomparably superior to one in which a few are rolling in wealth, and many are heart-hungry, soul-hungry, even body-hungry, very poor. *It is very pleasant* to be waited on by a dozen slaves ; but will it be asserted that to deny this pleasure to Utopians is to deny them happiness? We admit—freely —that to achieve Utopia we *must* forgo many pleasures and luxuries of to-day ; but is not the loss many times over counterbalanced by the gain? Over and over again we have—as our only course we *have*—to choose the lesser evil ; and an Utopia for which a few must sacrifice luxuries is far superior to our present miserable social state in which a few have luxuries—and many nothing ! To give up slaves may doubtlessly be painful to the slaveowner : but what about the hedonistic gain of the slaves ; are we to neglect that? We must strive— however difficult it be—to view all these things unselfishly, to "legislate" not for our few selves, but for all our brethren, when we deliberate upon Utopia. The selfish complaint, " Oh, *I* don't want an Utopia in which *I* shall have to do so and so " must disappear.

Now many, perchance, may feel inclined to ask ; how far are these reforms a matter for by-and-bye, and how far for the present : are they merely prophesied, or in addition preached for present use : assuming these speculations on the ultimate disappearance of many luxuries to be correct, what *ought* a man to do now in this present social state ; ought he to forgo—however rich—expensive

wines, expensive houses, expensive " decorations," a large
retinue of servants, and in fact expensive living generally;
or may he continue his present state undisturbed, leaving
Utopia to bring about Utopian conditions? Before
definitely answering this question we must make two
provisos.   Firstly, in using the word *ought*, in the present
connexion, we do *not* use it in the sense of the *categorical
imperative*, implying that to disregard it is a distinct
breach of duty; but rather in the milder and popular
sense of what is highly advisable, desirable, or to be
recommended as " good deeds."   We make this reservation for reasons that we cannot explain without going
into a fundamental ethical discussion that would be out
of place here, and we must content ourselves, for the
present therefor, with simply stating this reservation.
Secondly, we are by no means oblivious of what Spencer
has emphasized—that an ideal life is impossible except
in an ideal state; this, however, is very far from saying
that one should fold one's hands and be content with
the actual present; but, nevertheless, we have intimated
that many of these luxuries will be abolished willy nilly
by the natural processes of economics, *viz.*, by the increasing price of labor rendering their cost prohibitive.

   Granting, however, their full importance to these
reservations, we do think it urgently necessary that a
reform should be set going *at once*, instead of waiting
contentedly for time to unfold his own developments;
and, since men might so immensely expedite the advent
of Utopia if they would, we *do* hold that men, however
rich, emphatically *ought* to cease indulging in numberless
wasteful luxuries such as we have specified, and set an

example to their fellows of living *simply* and moderately. "However rich"—yes; and the richer, or the higher in social standing, the better; for then by so much more would their example be effectual. It cannot be too often reiterated that what we primarily want is a *simpler and healthier individual social life:* and we may point out one inestimable advantage that would at once accrue to every young man—(and to the young we must mainly look for reform)—who would adopt this ideal of simple, unwasteful, unluxurious, life. It cannot be doubted that both physically, morally, and emotionally, it is *bad* for man to live alone; and that compulsory celibacy is a deadly social disease responsible for cruel sufferings : but, nevertheless, thousands of men are compelled to defer their marriage thro weary years until—life's first flush and romance, alas, now vanished for ever !—they can afford the expenses of a married life. Now, that we are deadly opponents of *improvident* marriage, that is to say, chiefly, of improvident child-bearing, has already been made sufficiently clear; but—putting aside the preposterous superstitions usually prevalent—children need never be born until they can be afforded ; for the rest, any man and woman, who are willing to adopt the simple ideal of refined but non-luxurious and non-conventional life that we have set forth, might probably marry with assurance at twenty-three on an income of £150—and wait a few years before bringing children into the world—instead of, as at present, starving their hearts for years in pining isolation. In this sense *Love in a cot* is a true, real, and practicable, ideal of life !

CHAPTER X.

> " The World's great age begins anew,
>   The golden years return :
>   The Earth doth, like a snake, renew
>   Her winter weeds outworn :
>   Heaven smiles, and faiths and empires gleam
>   Like wrecks of a dissolving dream."

In connection with the discussion of the luxuries that we
may expect to disappear, and of the new forms of social
life that will appear, in Utopia, it is very well worth
while to consider how many of the various typical trades
we may expect to die out—to the promotion of *general*
happiness and at the expense of no real desideranda.

First of all, it has been already pointed out that
soldiers, policemen, law officials, and numbers of other
functionaries, will nearly or quite disappear in semi-
Utopia : but it has not yet been remarked that the
abolition of these occupations will entail the co-relative
disappearance of many trades which at present use up an
enormous amount of wealth, and the concomitant setting-
free of another large body of laborers who, at the pre-

177

sent time, are (directly or indirectly) *kept* by the community : here again, as has been so repeatedly urged already, the community at large will gain, not only by being freed from the burden of keeping these men, but also by the fresh wealth that will be created when they become productive workers.

Now, for instance, the abolition of soldiers will put an end to the trades of the sword-and-bayonet-maker, the rifle-maker, the cannon-founder, and in large measure the powder-and-bullet-maker. All the labor employed in Government and private factories in manufacturing *wealth-wasting* contrivances—in practically making the nation so much poorer—will then be diverted into useful channels. Further, all the great administrative staff, at present required for the organisation of army, navy, and police, will likewise be liberated : and all the labor employed in tent-making and barrack-building will further swell the record. So too it is clear that the millions annually spent in building and in maintaining war vessels will be left clear for our mercantile marine : that is to say, that, for the same annual national expenditure as at present, we should have at our disposal a largely increased number of fully-equipped ocean-going steamers ; or, if not so many be required, we should annually save several millions sterling.

If we again take the trade of wine-making and enquire how much labor would be set free by abolishing the greater part of this trade, we should probably get an appalling result. Since, however, wine is not made in England, and since, on the hypothesis, we have provisionally retained beer and *vins ordinaires* as Utopian drinks, we cannot here avail ourselves much of this argument. But it is clearly relevant to include in our estimate the majority of the wine-merchants and their clerks and servants who are at present employed in the distribution of the wine : and also—since it is clear that semi-Utopians who drink beer will not drink it in pot-houses—we may include the publicans, barmen, and barmaids, employed in the majority of public-houses, and in all the gin-palaces, as among the at-present-useless laborers. It may startle some to learn that the total number of publicans (*i.e.*, landlords alone) in the United Kingdom in 1881 was 12,855 (besides 3,728 female ditto), there being no fewer than about 4,000 included in the London directory alone: whilst the census-returns farther show (in England and Wales) 5,758 cellarmen and 7,467 wine-merchants and agents : we might add that, altho, ex-hypothesi, beer, like light wine, is accorded to our Utopians, yet the excessive beer-drinking of to-day will certainly be diminished, and therefor the census-returns of 24,196 brewers and 9,473 maltsters (England and Wales) must be very largely in excess of the country's real requirements. When it is considered that many of these figures must be multiplied by several so as to include, *e.g.*, the barmen and barmaids, and also the wine-merchants' clerks, it will be seen that the total amount of labor locked up here is very considerable indeed.

One more instance. Among the commercial tendencies of the present day a strong one is that which sets towards the abolition of middlemen and agents. More and more the wholesale dealers or producers seem inclined to deal

directly with the consumer, thus supplanting the inter
mediary.   In spite of the indignation thus excited in the
middleman, and the suffering often perhaps inflicted upon
him, it can scarcely be doubted that, so far as workable,
this tendency is eminently beneficial, saving loss to both
producer and consumer, and setting free so much more
labor.   Anyone who will calculate the number of agents,
merchants, and other middlemen, in the London directory,
and then multiply by several to estimate the clerks, and
then add in similar estimates for all the other large business-
towns in the kingdom, will perhaps be somewhat astonished to find how much labor is locked up in this one
kind of middleman-work alone.   Add thereto all the
retail shopkeepers and their assistants, and then sum the
total ! [1]   Now of course it is not for one moment contended that *all* this vast array of middlemen is likely to
be supplanted : but it is contended that there is an immense superfluity of such workers for the work to be
done ; and that it would be in every way a healthy
symptom could one see a considerable thinning of their
ranks.   To take but one class—the insane desire of almost
everyone in the lower middleclass near London to get his
sons into a city-office where they will slave at an unhealthy occupation for bad pay, instead of teaching them
a handicraft or emigrating them—this insane procedure,
we say, makes it every year more difficult for London
agents, brokers, and such like middlemen (whose ranks
are steadily swollen by this stream of recruits) to obtain
a living ; and leads to the cut-throat-competition that we
all know of.   It is vital to remember that, altho the more

[1] See *infra*, p. 187.

manual laborers and other productive workers that there are, the richer grows the nation, and the more wealth there is to be distributed among them, yet almost the inverse holds with regard to the middlemen. For *these* create no iota of wealth, but merely assist in its distribution. Obviously there *can* be only a certain grand total available as wages for their work; and clearly this total must be a function of the total wealth created, and of the difference that is possible between the cost of producing it, and the price that the consumer is willing to pay. Clearly, therefor, the more middlemen that there are anxious to obtain a share of the "middlemen's wage-fund," the less will there be for every individual: whilst as to the obvious remedy, *viz.*, to increase this total "wage-fund" by raising the price to the consumer—the possibility of this is negatived by the very eagerness of competition among the middlemen.

Now it is obvious that, however necessary middlemen may be, the nation would be so much the richer if it were possible to get the same distribution without them; for then there would be so much extra labor set free for wealth-creating, and so many the fewer to be *kept* by the nation. Probably, however, in a large measure, this is not possible; and middlemen are to some extent indispensable; but clearly every additional superfluous middleman represents a twofold loss to the nation. Now it is probable that, were the competition less furious, a city-broker would earn £100 a year as easily as (*i.e.*, with no more labor than) he now earns £50. If this be so, the inference seems clear that when, as now, owing to the superfluity of middlemen, this £100 is divided among

eight men at £50 each, there is a very large waste of
labor that ought to be employed in wealth-producing or
in research—with concomitant want and discomfort to all.
A precisely similar calculation may be applied to the
shops.   Whether shops will ever be superseded by some
better mode of distribution it is difficult to say; but we
may take it as a safe inference that they are indispensable
to such a state of society as ours.   Granting this however
it must be admitted that there is a ridiculous superfluity
of shops at present.   Just as in the city, so too here,
wherever it seems possible for a fourth man to snatch a
living by proportionately diminishing the profits of three
established shopkeepers, we find a fresh shop opened.   In
the same road, often within a few doors of one another,
we may find two or three butchers, bakers, fruiterers,
grocers, and so on : whereas it is quite certain that one
of each trade would fully suffice to the wants of the
neighborhood, and with a far greater profit to the shopkeepers.   Let anyone who cares to follow up this argument
make a census of all the shops in his own village or town
of so many thousand inhabitants; and then calculate
whether even a third of them are necessary—even tho
he leave two or three of each trade so as to ensure *healthy*
competition, and to preclude inattention, overcharging,
and incivility.   Here again if we multiply by the number
of towns in the kingdom we shall find a truly considerable
quantity of labor that may be set free for wealth-
producing.[1]

[1] There is often a ridiculous denunciation of the middleman,
qua middleman, as a rapacious fiend who robs the producer of
his profits. Clearly there is no moral question necessarily in-

If now all the supplantable trades and occupations referred to be considered, and the numbers employed in each estimated, it will be found that a truly gigantic total is obtained—and all these men are at present truly being *kept* by the nation generally: regarded thus, how gigantic a tax do we not labor under! Now if the keep of these men were simply taken off our hands, the relative wealth of each one of us would be very greatly increased; but when we reflect that the majority of this great body of workers would also become *wealth-creators,* we shall see how much increase were then added to the national wealth: whilst by the work of the remainder, set free for teaching, for scientific research, and for art-production, a vast indirect increase would be (eventually) made to the national wealth, and a great immediate increase to the national happiness.

And now let us endeavor to sum up the results that we have obtained with reference to the numbers of the various *useless-and-unproductive*[1] classes, in order to ascertain how many of the nation are kept at the expense of the workers, when they ought to be working at wealth-creating themselves. It seems almost superfluous to remark that these results will be exceedingly rough and approximate only—even more so of course than the figures on which they are based—and can make no kind of pretension to any statistical accuracy. Were we

volved. So long as no better machinery of distribution be invented, the middleman is a necessity—and must have his profits. Find a better method of distribution, and he disappears.

[1] An *unproductive* worker may be more useful than 100 productive workers—if he be an intellectual or artistic genius: we speak of the useless non-producers.

engaged on a professedly statistical investigation this
would amount to a confession of unpardonable inac-
curacy : but since our business is not with a *quantitative*
statistical enquiry into the actual facts of to-day, but
rather with a *qualitative* enquiry into the feasibility of
an improved social state—into which enquiry we have
introduced these present-day approximate statistics only ·
to show that we have a good general basis for our
general calculations ; to indicate the *kind* of procedure
which, as it seems to us, should be adopted in speculations on the advent of Utopia ; and to render our argument less vague and more real to the reader ; since
finally many of our figures are necessarily ten years
behind date, whilst the rapidly increasing population
must introduce continual errors into not only the absolute
numbers, but, probably into *the proportions also*—it seems
to us that the probability of introducing errors of even,
for instance, 20 per cent. into the results, need not deter
us from summing up our estimates in this preliminary
and te tative enquiry.

Let us procede then with our figures. We first, evidently,
knock off the whole of the army, which we will take to
be represented by 105,000 [1] men from England and Wales;

[1] To make these estimates correctly, without details of which
we are not in possession, is a matter of difficulty. The census-
returns for 1881 report, for the army, 87,000 men actually in
England and Wales at that time ; but this figure seems to include certain non-effectives. On the other hand, Whittaker
states the total effective force of the British army (1886), *including drafts abroad and in the colonies* (but excluding the Indian
regular establishment), at 141,000. Now, since the men—wherever stationed—are drawn from, and paid for by, Britain, it seems
clear that this latter figure is the proper basis for our calculations.

and the navy, which will be similarly represented by
53,000 men. The police-force is returned (1881) at
32,500 (besides female detectives, etc.): if we retain
the odd 2,500 for municipal organising-purposes, etc.,
this represents a balance of 30,000 men wasted. Then
we have the "irregular police" of ticket-clerks, ticket-
collectors, omnibus-conductors, etc., whom we have already estimated at about 50,000: to this—for the
reasons already explained [1]—we may add perhaps half of
the present cabmen, or 15,000 men.

Next, with regard to the absurd excess of merely wasteful
servants, we find 72,000 *domestic* grooms and coachmen,
74,000 domestic gardeners, and 56,000 "indoor-male-
servants"—that is, we suppose, flunkies. Now, it seems
to us that if we knock off, as merely wasteful excrescences, 50,000 of the first, 55,000 of the second, and
50,000 of the third, we are dealing very gently with
these non-producers: [2] to these we must, of course, add
the complete tale of 12,600 gamekeepers.

But then the army is recruited from England, Scotland, and
Ireland, whilst—for simplicity—we are at present estimating
only for England and Wales: this being so, the army-figures
should be *reduced* in order to correspond with the population of
England and Wales only. This reduction we have made in the
ratio of the respective populations, thus obtaining as the result
for England and Wales about 105,000 men. By a similar
process we have reduced the navy-figures from 70,000 to 53,000.
That, anyhow, our estimates in this case err by understatement
rather than by overstatement is plain if we take into account the
large number of militia, etc., whose time is partly occupied—*i.e.,*
wasted—by their annual turn of soldiering. Probably, to do our
argument full justice, we should need to add several thousands to
this estimate of 158,000 soldiers and sailors.

[1] P. 18.

[2] Of the million and a quarter women-servants we take no
13

We next come to the class of men engaged in the manufacture and sale of alcoholic drinks. Since wine is not made—or rather not grown—in England, of course we are unaffected by what would become an immense item in a parallel French or Italian calculation: and since we have provisionally admitted beer and light wines into Utopia, we cannot knock off *all* the brewers and wine-merchants; but we can, nevertheless, very considerably diminish their numbers. If we admit that at least three or four times as much beer is drunk as should be (which is probably very much understating it), and that semi-Utopians will not sit in a pot-house to drink any beer that they may require, we may fairly reckon that out of the 9,500 maltsters, and 24,200 brewers, at least 6,000 and 16,000 respectively may be eliminated in company with the whole 13,000 male-beersellers.[1] Then as to the 7,500 wine-merchants, and 5,700 cellarmen, these may probably be reduced to say 2,500, and 1,700 respectively, thus yielding us 8,000 more superfluities. We must specially point out, however, that, for various reasons, these intoxicant-estimates absurdly understate the real strength of our argument; for we have no means of estimating, for instance, the large number of carmen and others engaged in the conveyance of drink: whilst, if after all it should be concluded that Utopia will be

count for the present: and we also leave the hotel-servants, male and female, entirely alone: which is a very generous and self-denying proceeding on our part.

[1] Of course, this figure ought to be very much increased to take count of potmen and other assistants; but we have no data. In addition to these 13,000, there are a large number of women returned as beersellers, who, of course, equally require potmen.

entirely teetotal, our figures must be increased proportionately. In obvious connection, however, with these drink-estimates, we must add on the enormous total of 180,000[1] in-door paupers to the list of superfluities.

Next as regards the disposal of middlemen. The census (1881) returns 30,700 brokers and agents, 175,000 clerks, etc., besides 35,470 commercial travellers; and, on the principles that we have already explained, we propose to knock off certainly two-thirds of these figures, *viz.*, 20,000 and 115,000 respectively; while with regard to the *travellers*, since we are quite sure that in a healthier, less greedy, and better informed, social state these men will be in a twofold sense unnecessary, we propose to eliminate practically all of them—*i.e.*, 30,000. As to the shops, we are in a considerable difficulty, owing to the want of data. The census returns the *general or in definite* shopkeepers at 29,500 (besides 17,000 women), but this is only one item, and we are no nearer to the mark. We have, however, been favored with a private calculation which puts down the shopkeepers in a certain town as *two per cent. of the population.* If we assume only half of these to be men, and that for the country at large the proportion shall be 1 man in 150, this would give us for England and Wales a total of 160,000 shopmen. Considering, however, that the census returns 80,000 butchers and meat-salesmen alone, this calculation would appear to be absurdly below the mark. We must, however, take it, such as it is, and if the similar propor-

---

[1] This includes an unknown number of pauper-children in schools · but this error must be more than balanced by the 600,000 out-door paupers who are partly kept by the nation.

tion of two-thirds be eliminated hence also—which seems a very mild estimate—we get a saving of 107,000 men. To this we may add the 16,000 jewellers already referred to, and obviously 7,000 at least out of the 7,522 gunsmiths : whilst equally clearly we may add the whole 29,500 costermongers and streetsellers,[1] who earn a precarious existence in a society where they are "kept" to no sufficient purpose.

Besides these main groups there must be an immense number more of non-producers distributed in larger or smaller proportions among a multitude of trades and occupations from which it would be impossible to disinter them ;[2] *e.g.*, the builders, "decorators," painters, etc., etc., employed on useless or wasteful work, but who cannot be disentangled from the general assemblage of such workers ; we can, therefor, only entreat our readers to bear in mind that our total estimates, large as they may appear, must be ridiculously *below* their legitimate figure. As a concluding item we will put on 25,000 for the rich unemployed who have to be *kept* by the community, and do no adequate intellectual, esthetic, or philanthropic, work in return.

Now let us tabulate these figures :—

Labor wasted in the	Army	in England	105,000
	Navy	,,	53,000
	Police	,,	30,000
	Cabmen and Ticket-collectors, etc.	,,	65,000
	Grooms and Coachmen	,,	50,000

[1] There were, in 1881, 17,000 women similarly engaged also.
[2] Besides many small groups such as the 700 artificial-flower-makers—an utterly useless class of anti-esthetic purveyors.

Gardeners	,,	55,000
Flunkies	,,	50,000
Gamekeepers	,,	12,600
Wine and Beer Trade	,,	43,000
Indoor Paupers	,,	180,000
Commercial (wholesale)	,,	165,000
Shops, etc.	,,	130,000
Street-sellers	,,	29,500
"Upper 10 Thousand"	,,	25,000
		993,000

In round numbers then, it would seem that somewhere about *one million men, with their wives and children,* have to be kept by the community in order that they may be employed in police work, in producing or purveying wasteful and unnecessary luxuries, in functioning as superfluous middlemen, in ministering to the selfish and wasteful amusements of a few, or in doing nothing. Now what proportion do these million "drones" bear to the workers —the wealth-creators at large? We presume that agriculturalists, industrialists, railway employés and carters, with fishermen and sailors, may be taken as a fairly exhaustive account of them. The figures for the last two classes are not in our possession, but they must be comparatively small when placed alongside of the other items, which are 1,318,344, 4,795,178, and something like 500,000[1] respectively, giving us, therefor, a total of

[1] The census-figures for the last item were (1881) as follows:—
Conveyance of men, goods, and messages—

Railways	...	...	138,760
Roads	...	...	165,854
Water	...	...	183,034
Storage	...	...	27,847
Messages and porterage	...	136,775
			652,000

about 6,613,000 *men* [1] engaged in the creation of material wealth. At this rate, then, every worker has to keep not only himself and his family but also one-sixth-and-a-half of another man and his family—that is to say that about one hour and a half per day of his work goes to supporting useless non-producers. But really there are two (fortunately opposing) disturbing elements to be taken into account: firstly, that in addition to the men there are over one and a half million women engaged in industrial pursuits, and 64,000 in agricultural—which fact not only increases the workers to over 8 millions, but entirely disarranges our method of calculating by men as representing families: secondly, however, *an immense proportion of these workers,* both agricultural and industrial, *are engaged in the production of luxuries* of one sort or another *that are destined to be unproductively and wastefully consumed: these men clearly are really in the same category as the wine-growers, gardeners, jewellers, and other superfluities whom we have struck out:* they do not permanently increase the national wealth, but are *ultimately* kept at the expense of the nation just as are their confrères. Now, to introduce this correction would not only *enormously* diminish the 8,000,000 true " workers " (*i.e.,* wealth-creators), but would equally increase the 1,000,000

The item *on water* would include some, but only some, of the mercantile marine. These figures are, however, in every case, far too high for the purpose of our calculation, which requires the actual *wealth-creating accessories only:* therefor we have taken 500,000 at hazard.

[1] According to a very recent calculation the total workers of the *United Kingdom,* including women and children, number 13,200,000.

superfluities. so that *the ratio would be doubly affected.* Unfortunately it is utterly impossible for us to make any, however approximate, estimate even of the result that would thus be obtained : but as a *mere guess*—to which, of course, no objective value whatever attaches—we should think it highly possible that the ratio might become 7 : 2, or even 6 : 3, in which latter case every worker (*i.e.*, every wealth-creator) *spends a third of his working time* in supporting useless or superfluous other people ! How vital is the bearing of such enquiries upon the promotion of Utopia becomes very evident : for, assuming an 8 hours' day to suffice as an average working-day now, it could be replaced by a 5½ hours' day ! [1]

But really, however, we have so far been concerned with only *one* of several components ; for we have shown merely that these million superfluities entail an increase of X hours on the general working-day to supply their keep : their simple removal would lighten the working-day by X hours ; but there is more to account for. First, if they became direct wealth-creators themselves, the national wealth would be increased 12 per cent. at once ; secondly, if the unknown Y number of the 8,000,000 workers, who are at present making luxuries only, were similarly told off for useful work there would be an annual increase of 2Y per cent. more wealth ; thirdly, in addition to the labor at present wasted on producing luxuries, there is a huge waste of *material wealth*—as coal, iron, manures,

---

[1] It is *very much* to be desired that some competent statistician, with the data at his command, would undertake an exact quantitative investigation of this character . his results would be invaluable to sociologists.

etc., etc.—and of land ; this being saved would represent
another Z per cent. more added (*i.e.,* saved) to the
national wealth. We thus get at this rate an annual
wealth-increase of $12 + 2Y + Z$ per cent. more than at
present—where Y and Z cannot be exceedingly small
figures : but since the increase of wealth is cumulative,
and waste would be greatly circumscribed, the nation
would *tend* to double its wealth at short intervals.

"But"—will probably be the retort—"what is to be the
good of hoarding up and continually increasing the
national wealth if it must not be wasted on luxuries?
You would presently be overburdened by your wealth and
have no use for it." Exactly so—if the nation were to
keep on steadily increasing its wealth at so much per
cent. per year ; *but it would not*—in a semi-Utopia. Altho
necessarily emphasising this *tendency* of wealth to accumulate, under the conditions postulated, we do not
anticipate that play would be allowed to such tendency,
but rather that it would be taken advantage of to decrease the working-day *until wealth no longer tended to
accumulate—until the annual increment of wealth exactly
balanced the annual consumption,* given a definite scale of
expense. Such margin of wealth measures the possibility
of reducing the length of work-time ; or, in other words,
the abbreviation of the general working-day must be a
function of the difference between the total wealth that
would annually accrue at the present time with the
present working-day (supposing all idlers and all *useless*
non-producers or producers of wasteful luxuries to be
engaged in productive work) *and* the total wealth that
would be annually required for the expenses of such

simple and refined living as we have already pointed to —populations being supposed numerically identical and new inventions of labor-economising machinery being ignored.[1]

To render this quite clear we will take a supposititious concrete example of the simplest character. Let us hypothecate a nation whose annual increment of wealth may be valued at 2,000 millions sterling, created by the labors of 6 million adult workers employed for 8 hours net per day, and supporting, in addition to themselves and their families, 2 million idlers, *useless* non-producers, and luxury-mongers, and *their* families ; and let us farther suppose that the total annual wealth-increment of the nation, if equally divided and all carefully applied, would *more than* suffice for all the wants of a simple semi-Utopian life. Now, supposing that the 2 million idlers and useless workers are diverted to useful and productive work, and that they create on the average the same amount of wealth as any other 2 million of their countrymen, then it is clear that the total annual increment of wealth becomes raised from 2,000 millions to 2,666[2] millions odd. But in consonance with our hypothesis we must furthermore remember that indulgence in waste and luxury involves a great loss of *material wealth*—a consumption of material wealth—as well as a waste of labor :[3] this amount we will put down as represented by a sixth of the annual wealth-income, *viz.*, by 333

[1] Clearly any such inventions would additionally shorten the working-day.

[2] Six millions raise £2000 millions; therefor, 2 raise $\frac{2000}{3}$ millions.

[3] *E.g.*, the loss of coal and iron in manufacturing luxuries and war-material, etc.

millions odd. We arrive, then, at this result: the annual wealth-income under present conditions is taken at 2,000 millions, of which a sixth is wasted—the remainder being sufficient, if equally divided, to maintain the given population in a state of semi-Utopian comfort: by the labor of the 2 million fresh productive workers the wealth-income is further increased from 2,000 to 2,666 millions. Now since a general 8-hours-day is given as producing in this reformed state 2,666 millions, and since 1,667 (2,000—333) millions are sufficient for the wants of the population, it is clear that the working-day may be reduced in this proportion, *viz.*, from 8-hours to 5 hours! This very crude and hypothetical example may suffice to show the kind of reasoning upon which speculations concerning such social amelioration should—as it seems to us—procede. Whatever new inventions or discoveries may be made, whatever fresh sources [1] of wealth laid open—

[1] In England the average total yearly income of each member of the nation is said to be £33 (*Fortnightly*, Aug., 1893). Assuming an average family to consist of five persons, this would give an average yearly income of £165 per family. Assuming all the economies proposed in the text, the elimination of the million or two useless and unproductive drones or workers—with the consequent great increase of wealth—it seems very far from impossible to raise this average income within a very reasonable time from £165 to a satisfactory Utopian minimum—could we only render the *average* and every *actual* the same. According to Mr. Giffen the annual savings of the United Kingdom are about 16 per cent. of the annual income of the nation now: it seems to us that, were the millions wasted on drink and other useless luxuries and frivolities alone, added to our savings, these would be perhaps doubled at once—and *that* would be sufficient to raise the *average wages* of *every worker* in the United Kingdom from £48 to £66. It is stated that 135 millions are annually spent on drink in the United Kingdom. This item alone would nearly supply the doubling required.

by so much may the advent of a minimum working-day be expedited : but without any other *machinery* than we already possess, we can thus clearly perceive the feasibility of an approximation toward semi-Utopia—*if* only men would be moderately unselfish, unwasteful, and reasonable.[1] *It is mainly human nature that has to be changed.*

But here, returning from our supposititious state to England, a difficulty at least must be conceded that, no doubt, the thoughtful reader sighted many chapters ago : how far it may be satisfactorily met is now to be considered. We have accounted for at least a million living superfluities who are kept at the general expense of the workers ; and we have dwelt upon the great increase that would be made in the national wealth were only all these men to become wealth-producers likewise : but we may be met by the retort that to turn these men into the labor-market would be to inflict a cruel injury, and not a benefit, upon the workers—that already every craft or trade is overcrowded, and everywhere men are crying out for employment—

"Every gate is thronged with suitors ; all the markets overflow."

---

[1] It may not be superfluous to utter a warning against the fallacies into which one is very apt to fall in such speculations—unless one be very careful to avoid confusion between the properties of wealth and wealth-symbols—*i.e.*, money—and also to avoid arguing by mere multiplication—the *fallacy of composition*—from one man to a nation and a world. Perhaps we may be allowed to point out by the way how the labors of one generation may render possible a permanent diminution of labor for future generations—we mean by the construction of railways, docks, etc., by works of irrigation and reclamation, and, in short, by the execution of practically indestructible works.

—so that to turn a million more loose would make confusion worse confounded; that, therefor, altho our
present social practice of employing superfluous servants,
etc., be very wasteful, yet—looking at the *individuals*—
it offers a method of *distributing* national wealth rather
less unevenly than would otherwise be the case: and,
finally, that our assumptions implicitly involve the
fallacy that the more men, the richer the nation, whereas
a population may easily outgrow its means of subsistence.

Now in reply to these objections we have first of all,
of course, to fully admit—as everyone since Malthus has
necessarily admitted—that a population may very well
increase beyond its means of subsistence—in a wide
sense; that, therefor, conceivably there might, perhaps,
be a limiting case found when it would be of no benefit
to the national wealth to make its idlers work—but we
deny that England has reached this stage: and we also
admit that the difficulty is complicated by the fact that
our social ideal is *not* the mere increase of the total
national wealth, but its more equal distribution.   If
everybody were ideally unselfish, and if the " Laws " of
Supply and Demand, Competition, etc., did not exist,
then to double the number of the workers by knocking
off an equivalent number of idlers would—in a society
where wealth had reached its maximum annual yield—
simply halve the working-days of all: but in our society
of the present it would also at first—one might think—
halve the wages too, and benefit only the capitalists and
millionaires: but, nevertheless, altho conceding these
difficulties, we must set off several considerations against
them.

Firstly, to be merely rid of so many drones, whom they at present have to keep, would be a great gain to the workers, even were there no room for a single extra workman ; for this would render possible—as will appear in a moment—the ultimate raising of their wages.

Secondly, even if our own country afforded no more scope for increasing the annual output of wealth, yet it were still possible to colonise with great profit many— at present—unoccupied or insufficiently occupied portions of the earth's surface: the wealth that is annually wasted on, *e.g.*, useless servants, would more than suffice for their emigration-expenses ; and the wealth created by them in their new land would enable them to repay their expenses, and would, of course, react beneficially upon trade at home.[1]

But, thirdly, neglecting the possibility of emigration, and supposing *that a demand for luxuries and extravagances no longer exists,* and that their former ministrants are to be distributed among the ranks of the workers with the intention of lessening the day's work for the output of so much total national wealth, is it so certain that wages must be generally lowered in accordance with the usual processes formulated by economics? The assumptions upon which we are proceeding must not be forgotten. Let us take now a group of men with £500 a year each, who at present spend £300 sensibly, £100 wastefully, and save £100: now, under the new régime, the

---

[1] We are not assuming any system of State-aided emigration, but simply that the wealth, which capitalists at present waste upon luxuries, would enable them to assist the emigration of the ex-luxury-producers to a colony—*as a commercial speculation.*

only thing they can do with their formerly wasted £100 is to save it. But the sum of all these savings constitutes the *wages-fund* or capital of the country; and, if that be so much increased, the wages of the laborers can be afforded an increase, or the same wages can be continued to an increased number of laborers working a shorter day and producing only the original total wealth. But it may be retorted that our friends will be quite content now to earn only £400 a year, and will, therefor, shorten their own day's-work by a fifth: or that by saving £200 a year they will be enabled to retire from work and live on their investments so much the earlier. True—and in so far the sum total of happiness will be increased, and an approximation made by so much to an Utopian state —but are these £500-a-year-men supposed to be wealth-creators themselves or professional men, merchants, and what not? If the former, then as every one of them retires there is room for an ex-superfluity to take his place as wealth-creator: but if the latter, then his working more or less does not affect the national wealth but merely the distribution:[1] we must beware of that prime fallacy of confusing wealth and wealth-symbols.

But, indeed, fourthly and lastly, we may point out that the causes to whose efficacy we have all along attri-

---

[1] Really all these questions are very complicated, in that each interweaves with several others: it is, however, vital to remember what assumptions one is arguing from and to admit no fresh assumptions that are contradictory to them: if we start from a postulate of semi-Utopian general morality we cannot allow later assumptions of motives, such as greediness, etc., incompatible with semi-Utopian morals. This caution emphatically applies to the discussion now in hand.

buted the future disappearance of waste-mongers and the shortening of the working day, partly by means of the influx of fresh workers, *are themselves incompatible with this alleged difficulty* of preventing a corresponding grand fall in wages. For, firstly, we have prophesied a gradual abandonment of luxuries in that the rising wages of labor will render them too expensive; in which case clearly the assumed tendency of wages to a steady rise will cover the wages of the fresh workers: and, secondly, we have appealed to men, as a matter of ethics, to give up these wasteful and stupid luxuries; now self-evidently, if a class of men have sufficient love for social good and human welfare to give up their luxuries, they are not the men to cut down their employés' wages along with their working-hours. So that after all, however we look at it, this difficulty of employing ex-waste-suppliers really vanishes if we conceive the somewhat complicated problem clearly and distinctly—above all avoiding the fatal fallacy of assuming contradictory premises and crediting a semi-Utopian state with anti-Utopian attributes. As we have already said, *Utopianism is always consistent with Utopia.* For the rest—without doubt the great master-key to all these problems is a vivid realisation of the truth that a *demand for commodities is* NOT *a demand for labor.*[1]

---

[1] Altho we have not followed up the emigration-question farther, it is of course clear that, in any country, the greatest prosperity and happiness will result from a definite population, any increase or decrease of which would be injurious to happiness. For instance (with a fixed maximum possible output of wealth already attained) the more workers the less for each to do; but if each is to be clothed, fed, housed, etc., in the same

But now, to take a new departure, it may have appeared strange to the reader that in summing up all the wasted labor such as that of grooms, flunkies, soldiers, etc., we omitted to add in the lawyers and parsons. This omission was, however, quite intentional, since we assume that these men—or rather the really intellectual members of the profession,[1] together with other intellectual men whom it is convenient to represent, as to numbers, by the remaining lawyers and parsons,—will in a semi-Utopian state be represented by an army of headworkers. As we have already pointed out, the abolition of such time-wasting, Utopianly-useless, labors, as those of the parson and lawyer, will enable an immense accession to be made to the ranks of the plastic artists, actors, and musicians—thus securing largely increased means of enjoyment for the community—and also to the number of teachers and of professional scientific researchers and philosophers, whose work will not only enormously increase the happiness of a cultured and intellectual race, but may indirectly react vastly on their material gains.

Now by way of a concluding concrete instance we will consider the effect on teaching. There are at present 44,000 men (beside several thousand women) wasting their time and keep on preaching an obsolete, discredited, and partly immoral, theology; whilst there are an equal

style, the more workers, the more work to be done. The desiderandum is to find where these two lines intersect—and *then act upon Malthusian principles, without which there is no possible social salvation.* (See, however, pp. 52-54.)

[1] We do not for a moment mean to imply anything so absurd as that the parsons as a class are a gifted or intellectual set of men; but it is convenient to take the *numbers* afforded by a census of the "learned" professions.

number employed, as barristers, solicitors, and lawyers'
clerks, in the work of making the worse appear the better
cause, or of defending us against our neighbors' aggres-
sions: clearly both these occupations are incompatible
with Utopia. Besides lawyers and parsons, however,
we have over 26,000 doctors: this large number is probably a good deal in excess of the real demand, whilst in
a healthier and better informed social state one may
fairly expect illness to be far rarer, and therefor doctors
fewer. If we grant Utopian England 15-16,000 doctors
we set free 10-12,000 men who are, most of all, strikingly
fitted for the work of scientific research. If we further
add the odd 18-19,000 lawyers and parsons to the ranks
of the artists—this being equivalent to increasing them
by 50 per cent. of their present numbers—we have a
residuum of 70,000 men left to increase the ranks of the
teachers: and, seeing that the male teachers in England
at present number only 47,000, some idea may be formed
of the prodigious impetus that would thus be given to
intellectual training.

Since—within certain limits—the fewer boys in a class
the more does each one learn in a given time—the more
chance he has, that is, of being *taught* and not scamped
—it is clear that to so largely increase the number of
(well-trained and capable) teachers would be to grandly
invigorate the intellectual life of the nation.[1]

[1] According to the census (1881) there are about 12,000,000
persons under twenty years of age, of whom we may reckon perhaps 9,000,000 as the student portion in an Utopian state where
all learn. Now we have already explained in a previous work
(*Cry of the Children*, p. 98) that probably women will more and
more encroach upon the sphere of men as teachers of *youngsters*,
and that probably, up to about fourteen, boys and girls will be

And here we must close this discussion that has already carried the chapter far beyond the limits that we had originally anticipated for it, noting that in the foregoing calculations we have not made any estimate of the vast amount of wealth annually *wasted* through unthrift, incapacity, or carelessness with regard to petty trifles.[1]

taught by private governesses in groups of six or eight. Now if we reckon 4,500,000 of our students to be of this class, and the remainder of the University and High School class, what results do we get?

The census returns 124,000 female teachers—whereas to supply the governesses at the rate of one to eight children we should require about four and a half times as many; this, however, need not disturb us, since a sphere of work for otherwise idle women is thus opened out. We then find the total force of 48,000 male teachers left for distribution among 4,500,000 students, boys and girls, above the age of fourteen—a ratio of 1 to 93 or 94! Adding on, however, our additional force of 70,000 derived from the abolition of lawyers and parsons, we get the classes reduced within something like reasonable limits. Of course, at the present time, only a small proportion of the nation is really educated: this calculation shows us that the whole nation might be thoroly educated up to the age of twenty at no more cost to the nation than is now incurred by paying and keeping parsons and lawyers and the existing staff of teachers.

[1] We had hoped to supplement our rough estimate of the useless workers by a parallel estimate of the wasted wealth; but this latter design is impracticable. We know for instance that £136,000,000 are annually spent on drink by the United Kingdom; over six and a quarter millions on the administration of Law and Justice *plus* all the private expenses of solicitors and advocates; something between perhaps seven and ten millions on the maintenance of theological performances; £14,500,000 on paupers in England and Wales; £200,000,000 on the armies of Europe; and so on; but we do not know how much of this is, in final resort, absolutely wasted, and how much goes towards sustaining, clothing, and housing, the economically useless laborers, their wives and children, and so on thro'out. Therefor to estimate the annual literal waste of wealth is impossible without other data than we possess.

CHAPTER XI.

" Whilst the plowman, near at hand,
  Whistles o'er the furrowed land ;
  And the milkmaid singeth blithe ;
  And the mower whets his scythe ;
  And every shepherd tells his tale
  Under the hawthorn in the dale.
  Straight mine eye hath caught new pleasures,
  Whilst the landscape round it measures."

" But as for hazarding the main results
  By striving to anticipate one-half
  Of th' intermediate process—No, my friends."

WE will now turn to consider some other trades and
from a somewhat different standpoint; from that, *viz.*,
indicated at the commencement of Chapter IV., when we
spoke of the happiness or unhappiness inherent in certain occupations. On that occasion the problem was thus
stated : "The trouble is that, while such occupations
seem necessary to the comfort of the public, or of large
classes thereof, they are undeniably unpleasant to the
workers; and moreover, with the growing refinement
of evolving society, and the raising of the general
minimum or threshold of such refinement, these occupa-

tions may be expected to become more and more distasto-
ful to the workers. How then shall we reconcile this
opposition—since evidently there should be no actualiy
unpleasant occupations in even an approximate Utopia?"

It is now proposed to rapidly pass in review some
dozen or so typical trades, in order to note how many of
them are really necessarily distasteful or injurious to
health : and, of these, whether any may be dispensed
with.   To take now as our first example the occupation
of the scavenger, to which we have already alluded, we
will first of all observe, by way of a practical suggestion
for the present day, that if long-handled brooms were
substituted for the present ridiculous brushes, the
scavenger's lot would be ameliorated, not only by the abolition of that terribly *back-aching* work, but also by the
concomitant diminution of personal uncleanliness.   Since
this, however, is admittedly only a slight modification, we
will go a good deal further : and if the need should arise—
as, *e.g.*, owing to a scavengers' strike—we will undertake by
the assistance of the simplest possible (quasi-) mechanical
device, plus a little deodoriser, to abolish for ever the
necessity for scavengers and their accessories and allies :
nay more, to keep by this means a country lane as well
scavenged as Piccadilly.

We should take warning from this unsavory but
necessary example how we conclude that any occupation
is indispensable to a complex civilisation, since so very
many reforms are made directly we are compelled to discover them.   It is superfluous to point out how, once
more, we achieve an hedonic and economic gain by
abolishing scavengers : a quantity of labor is set free for

more productive work, the rates are reduced, and the scavengers find a less unpleasant occupation.

All work at present carried on with regard to the disposal of sewage—and equally the agriculturists' work so far as concerns carting and depositing farmyard-manure —is emphatically *beastly* work : but nobody supposes that a future race of comparatively rational men will make so pitiable an exhibition of incapacity as we of this generation have as regards the sewage problem[1] : as to the farmyard-manure, it is probable that a race, with more refined noses than our present agriculturists possess, will avail themselves of certain simple expedients to make a farmer's work as unobjectionable as it is glorious.

Taking another miserable occupation, that of the sweeps, we may safely predict here that semi-Utopia will solve the problem by abolishing the need for these men : our present wasteful and clumsy system of chimneys can hardly be tolerated much longer *here*—far less there.

And with regard to such *dirty* occupations in general we may well take a lesson of hope and trust from the result of the great gas-strike of 1891. The life of the gas-stoker, quâ stoker, can hardly have been—one would think—other than a lugubrious one : but nobody ever troubled to find a remedy—urged by mere eudaemonistic motives only. One first result of the strike, however, was the invention of gas-stoking machinery—a true labor-saving appliance. We are hopefully inclined to think that many of our philanthropic puzzles and perplexities will be solved by the introduction of labor-saving

---

[1] We have already referred to the awful *waste* entailed.

appliances to do the dirty work for us—given only a sufficient motive to inventiveness. Now the work in certain chemical factories, *e.g.*, white lead and phosphorus works, and in arsenic-works, is in the long run fatal: is this terrible fate of slow poisoning to be allotted to a proportion of semi-Utopia's inhabitants? Here we may very legitimately anticipate that the present processes will be superseded by others by which the worker is not endangered, or else that, failing this, it will be deemed a *lesser evil* to go without the product than to retain it at such a price of suffering. For instance an enormous quantity of the arsenic prepared is required for use in paintmaking : surely it would be no great deprivation to sacrifice our arsenical-green paints, if thereby we rescued annually so many young girls from death.[1] And, in like manner, one of the daily papers, commenting recently upon the horrible results entailed on the workers by the "enamel-plate"-working process, very aptly remarked that surely men might do without these plates if they be obtainable only at the cost of such suffering.

Take again as an example of another class of occupations that of the butcher—horrible calling: what can we say of this? Since now all the men of even semi-Utopia will be as refined and sensitive as the noblest ladies of to-day, how is it possible to imagine them making a trade of killing our four-footed brethren ; and then furthermore going thro the horrible business of cutting them up? We are willing to confess freely that this question has seemed to us *one of the most* perplexing:

---

[1] *I.e.* assuming that life were pleasant and desirable for them; as it would be in semi-Utopia ; as it probably would not be here.

for, granting our premise of hyper-refinement and hyper-gentleness, a butcher's occupation would seem impossible for semi-Utopians Of course our vegetarian friends would solve the difficulty by cutting this Gordian knot : but we are unwilling to posit vegetarianism as a necessity for Utopians, since the case for vegetable diet can not be considered to be made out yet anyhow. At the same time we are not blind to the possibility that vegetarianism *may* be the practice of the future ; and it is also specially incumbent upon us to remember that, seeing how huge strides Chemistry has made during this last half-century, it is competent to no one to deny the possibility that the artificial synthesis of proteids may one day revolutionise all of our present notions with regard to the food supply.[1] But even were we to grant the contention of the vegetarian, we should not have disposed of the whole difficulty : for, unless our friend can find an efficient substitute for boots and all other leathern goods, men will still find it necessary to kill and flay animals : and if 100—as well 1,000 or 10,000—so far as concerns the shock to the operator's feelings. Of course we may fully admit that, by the invention of far more refined and humane methods, the actual killing of the animal will be effected without much chance of sickening the bystander : but it is difficult to imagine how such operations as flaying could be performed merely by machinery. It is well also to bear in mind the fact that, since doctors will remain a necessity to the end of time, whilst *everyone* in a less preposterous age will go thro a course of instruction in zoology—in practical

[1] *See* Appendix at end of chapter.

zoology—it is evident that the actual handling and dissection of dead bodies will remain a necessity probably even in Utopia itself. And with regard to all such dilemmas we must repeat that the Utopia of science is not the most perfect *imaginable* world, but the most perfect *possible :* not one in which unhappiness is unknown, but one in which it is kept at a minimum. Should anyone object to the assignment of unhappiness to Utopians he may be invited to repeat, for good and all, Hercules' exploit, and **to** *vanquish Death :* but, while that grim fiend is able to strike down our joy even in the citadel of Utopia, it were somewhat futile to object to any speculation, that it credited a trace of discomfort to Utopia.

Another trade somewhat similarly intractable is that of the compositor: this is notoriously an unhealthy and trying occupation : but since a civilisation without books is now inconceivable to us, and since we can see no present improvement upon printing, we can only surmise that with far shorter hours of labor, abundant ventilation, and generally brighter surroundings, the lot of this indispensable mechanic will be improved.[1]   "With brighter surroundings:" yes; why not? Why is it that, however fastidious as to cheerful and artistic adjuncts in our home, we all think it "unbusinesslike" to have any thing more than gaunt bare walls and sombre effects in our offices and workrooms? We take it that one modification, which will render the occupations of compositors and of all

---

[1] To say nothing of his work being entirely remodelled by devices of which the Linotype composing-machine is possibly a sample.

factory-hands so far less intolerable than now—apart from the benefit derived from shorter hours—will be the introduction of light and color, pictures and flowers, wherever possible, into the workrooms. We do not mean to assert that a blacksmith's shop were a suitable place for such additions : but surely, in numberless workrooms, where the work is cleanly and dust not superabundant, we might let some sunshine into the workers' daily toil-life by introducing pictures and flowers that would carry their thoughts beyond the factory far away to breezy mountain, shimmering river, and heaving sea.

Admittedly this must be reckoned a very small mite to the discussion of how far one can reconcile a factory-worker's life with any approximately Utopian scheme. We take it that among the chief hardships of a factory-hand's life must be reckoned (*a*) the commencement of work at five or six a.m. at the summons of the remorseless factory-bell, winter or summer—winter, when the day has not yet broken, when all is chill, bleak, forbidding, and cold, and the body yearns for two hours more of blissful slumber ; summer, when the sun is blazing in all his glory, the air is fresh and redolent of dawn, and all earth seems shouting a glad view-hallo ! of field and wood and sea ; when the day's work should be preceded by a long ramble thro the dewy grass, and a plunge into the sparkling stream—did not the factory-bell forbid : (*b*) the monotonous work in close, ill-ventilated, cheerless, workrooms : (*c*) the enforced residence in crowded streets of a closely packed city, and consequent deprivation of country joys.

These seem to us the three main drawbacks, putting

aside entirely the overworking of children and bad wages, both of which, *ex hypothesi*, are non-existent in semi-Utopia. Now, with regard to the first—that is already by implication disposed of; for the hours of work in the time-to-come will be probably 4 or 5 and not 10—and with abundant holidays.[1] The second trouble we have just referred to; while as to the third—that is of course the problem of great cities, and is no peculiar grievance of factory-workers. We can hardly doubt that a more rational and happier age will not only find some adequate remedy for our present terrible centralisation, and some contrivance for drawing off inhabitants from town to country and distributing population somewhat less un-equally, but furthermore that, as opportunity offers, a

---

[1] The wretched superstition so long prevalent, and responsible for so much misery and degradation, that the longer a work-man's day the more work he necessarily performed—as if the human body were a nerveless machine incapable of fatigue—has happily of late received many hard knocks; and at last even Philistines are beginning to realise that as much work is done in 8 hours as in 10. Mr. John Rae remarks (*Contemporary Review,* June, 1893) :—" The surprising thing about these experiments —and indeed about a large proportion of other 8-hour experiments also—is that the same staff of men have done *more* work in the 48 hours a week than they did before in the 54 hours *together with the overtime then habitual.* . . . . In Mr. Beaufoy's vinegar-works the same staff do in 8 hours a day more work than they did before in 9¾ hours with two months' overtime into the bargain. . . . . The hours in the S. Yorks coalmines were re-duced from 12 to 8 in 1858, and the miners sent *out more coals in the day after the reduction than they did before it.*" All this is very encouraging but not remarkably " surprising " to a physi-ologist : it indicates, however, that if the hours were reduced from 10 to 7 the wealth-production would probably be unaffected. At this rate, *with the economics advocated in the text,* a 4 or 5 hours' day ceases to be a wild dream.

slightly less idiotic scheme of building will be introduced, and every town be surrounded by concentric belts of country.[1]   An additional factor in the problem must not, however, be forgotten : Mr. Ruskin, and those of his way of thinking, would probably urge, as the ready solution of the difficulty, that these abominated factories will disappear altogether.   That the present staring, brick-built, long-chimnied, depressingly ugly, factory will in course of time disappear and be replaced by artistic buildings, we have no doubt at all—*in time :* but that in any other than this literal sense the factory will disappear seems to us an exceedingly rash and unwarranted assumption.   No doubt *some*, possibly many, of the industries at present carried on in large factory-workrooms, might be sent out for execution in cottage-homes ; some few experiments [2] have already been made in this direction, and we may fairly anticipate that the feasibility of the scheme will increase *with the intelligence and trustworthiness of the workers ;* and so far as such decentralisa-

---

[1] This rational scheme, which was propounded in a pamphlet by the late Edward Ellis, Esq., has really—we understand—been adopted to some extent in Australia.

[2] We would refer our readers to the *Echo* for Dec. 7, 1885, for a long account of the noble efforts made by Mrs. Ernest Hart to revive the cottage industries in Donegal.   These efforts were crowned with such success that " the peasant women produced hosiery that could compete with that made by machinery in price, and was much superior to it in quality and durability, and tweeds, serges, and friezes, that were not to be surpassed in any market."

Want of space alone prevents us from quoting almost the entire article—to which once more we heartily refer any readers interested in the true philanthropy of helping the poor to do without help.

tion is possible, no doubt it would be a gain in every way, affording, as it does, a solution to so many troublous problems. But it would seem that the extensibility of such a scheme must always be limited: wherever the work involves machinery of any but the simplest form, there must be centralisation in factories; and, tho it is possible that machinery of a not very complicated order might be distributed over *country-side sub-factories*, there would seem always to be required larger factories for the expensive machinery. We would, however, point out that, so far as the nature of the business and the means of transport will admit of such country-side small factory-settlements, we should have here an admirable solution of the multitudinous difficulties connected with over-crowding and city populations. It is also, of course, a very legitimate speculation that greatly improved means of transport may render possible a considerable drafting-off of factories from town to country.

With regard to the wider question, raised by certain writers, of the existence of factories and machinery in any form, we certainly cannot subscribe to the doctrine that machine-labor is, *ipso facto*, accursed, and that in a better future we shall revert to the hand-labor of the "good old days." One must of course admit that, owing both to the consequent extreme specialisation, and to the mere fact that machine-labor *is* machine-labor, a worker's task is far more monotonous, and, if you like, calls for less skill and intelligence, and excites but a languid interest. But have we not here a lesser evil again? For if such machine-labor be far more econom-ical—as who will doubt—this means that, in the long run, the nation generally will have to work fewer hours daily for the same result : that is to say, that, by retaining this uninteresting machine-labor instead of the more interesting but less efficient hand-labor, we shall have a good many more hours daily to indulge in the pre-eminently *most* interesting occupation of art, science, and recreation. It were surely better to work four to five hours daily at a very monotonous and uninteresting task, and to have long leisure for *true living*, than to work eight to ten hours at a more interesting task—but still *a task* and a hard one—and then to have very little leisure afterwards for true living. What we have to devise for Utopia is such organisation that there may be executed with the least possible expenditure of time all such work [1] as may suffice to afford us the wealth neces-

---

[1] It will be observed that, thro'out, we are looking upon this daily *work* as so much work that *must be done*—in order to provide mankind with food, clothing, shelter, and all the essential requisites of a refined and cultured life—independently of any hedonic value that it may intrinsically possess ; but which should be done at the least possible expense of time and energy in order to leave free so much of our life as possible for *real living*—for the *Greek life of refined and cultured leisure.* If however our daily work possess in any degree an hedonic value of its own, if it be so agreeable that even were no *work* at all necessary we should yet devote a part of our day to this occupation, then clearly there is a very great hedonic gain : a man who works six hours daily at an employment to which, for the love of such employment, he, would be willing to devote, say, two hours daily, may then be considered to *work* only about four hours per day. Now, as everybody knows, Herbert Spencer has argued (*Data of Ethics*) that in a perfect social state everyone will experience a real love for his *work*, and will thoroly enjoy the toil by which he gains a living. That much can be said for this contention is of course, even superficially, apparent ; and the artist, the musician, the author, and we may add—as a repre

sary to an Utopian existence; and then we can truly *live* and taste the zest of life in our long leisure and long holidays.

Factories suggest mines—and here we must confess to a difficulty that is almost too strong for us at present. We may without much trouble see our way—even now—

sentative of a class at present small but destined to presently attain far greater numerical proportions—the scientific "researcher," may appear striking examples of a consummation already attained. Whether, however, *all* workers, including miners, bakers, grooms, factory-hands, and *id omne genus*, will one day come to regard their daily toil with enthusiasm and love, as a source of lively pleasure in itself, and as a pursuit to be desired even as artistic creation,—is quite another thing. That use reconciles men—or *at least the present-day lethargic half-living men*—to many things, so that finally a certain affection is developed for most-prosaic occupations; that in a brighter social state, with far shorter hours of labor, with happy homes and genial surroundings, with high health and exuberant spirits, the daily toil, even tho laborious and uninteresting, may be undertaken without much repugnance, and got thro without distress, or even with a certain amount of pleasurable feeling; all this we can quite understand: but that any race, especially a race generally endowed with deep scientific and artistic culture, and far more sensitive in every respect than is the present average man, should find in the ordinary avocations any pleasure comparable with that of the artist, author, or scientist; or should regard with anything but, at the best, toleration, as necessary evils, many indispensable departments of labor; is quite another thing. It is one thing to anticipate that in Utopia, with short hours of labor and frequent holidays, the necessary work will be cheerfully and willingly performed; but quite another to assume that all such work will afford a distinct and permanent glow of pleasure to the workers in the same sense as does art-work or research. The peculiar *differentia* of esthetic and scientific employments must not be forgotten: and, merely because it so happens that these may afford the secondary advantages of a marketable commodity, it seems doubtful how far they should be classified, for purposes of argument, with the ordinary breadwinning pursuits

to reconcile a factory-hand's employment with Utopia; but what of the miner? Can we possibly imagine such qualifications as would render a miner's occupation not unpleasant to a refined Utopian—to work in the dark, deprived of the blessed light, in cramped and suffocating attitudes, in constant danger of a horrible death, and

—most of which *would never have been undertaken at all by any-one except with a view to supplying material wants.* Were we supplied by Nature gratuitously with all our material wants, there would yet be artists and scientists, but scarcely miners or plowmen or factory-hands. Moreover, with regard to Spencer's remark, *apropos* of this question, that, *intrinsically, rowing a boat is no more pleasurable than reaping;* and while acknowledging the support he derives from such phenomena as those afforded by the enthusiasm of amateur gardeners, amateur carpenters, amateur blacksmiths, *et id omne genus;* we may point out two quali-fications : (1) that the special example adduced by Spencer is not a particularly happy one ; because, by rowing, one obtains the *pleasure of motion,* of gliding over the water, of passing in review a long stretch of scenery, of enjoying cool airs, and so forth, whilst avoiding the back-aching and monotony of reaping: whilst, that there *is* an *intrinsic difference of a very marked degree* is shown by the fact that thousands turn keenly to boating as a recreation, whilst no one is found to amuse himself by reap-ing, altho the opportunities for reaping are far and away more numerous than for boating : (2) that even boating, were one compelled to engage in it several hours a day, for most days in the year, would quickly lose much of its hedonic value and pall upon one ; the comparative infrequency thereof, and the fact that it is sought as a recreation from the work of breadwinning, and that it is usually enjoyed in the company of a bevy of friends, combine to give to amateur boating a zest which would necessarily be wanting in the daily routine. Without, however, further dis-cussing Spencer's canon—for which we admit, of course, that a pretty strong case can be made out—we may suggest (1) that the higher becomes our race, esthetically and intellectually, and the more that it learns to value irredeemable time, the more im-patient and intolerant will it become of time-consuming labors which, however unobjectionable hedonically, are yet performed

above all perennially soiled, befouled, begrimed, with
black coal dust! Yes, this is one of the worst of our
problems, and we will frankly confess to our inability to
see a solution; unless—and it is no such very wild con-
jecture—unless coal as a source of energy be characteris-
tic only of our vexed and troublous transition-state,
while the electric machine of the future will be driven

simply *because* they are necessary to material comfort : and (2)
that, if Weismann's doctrines should finally carry the day, *then* the
education of the race into enjoyment of necessary toils must be
—as of course Spencer recognises—far far slower than he antici
pated when writing the *Data of Ethics ;* for in that case all must
be done by a slow selection and nothing by inherited habits.
Under such conditions, indeed, one may well doubt whether the
Spencerian consummation would ever be attained. Now, it is
certainly singular and striking that, turning from the ideal of a
scientist and Individualist to that of an artist and Socialist, we
find the same thing aimed at : William Morris, no less than Herbert Spencer, insisting that our daily work shall become to us a
source (if not indeed the chief source) of happiness. Since then
Morris' declarations regarding *work* seem to clash strongly with
our own as expressed in the text, it is desirable to say a few
words on the subject ; and the more so since otherwise we have
found Mr. Morris' views and our own coincide in so many respects.
On page 201-202 of his *Hopes and Fears for Art,* he criticises the
dictum, "No man would work if it were not that by working he
hoped to earn leisure," and his remarks thereupon run very counter to our own advice to reduce work to a minimum, and then *live.*
A very little examination and reflection, however, will show that
the opposition is far less than it superficially appears, and is
greatly owing to an unfortunate ambiguity in Mr. Morris' use of
the word *work :* this is clear when he procedes to translate the
dictum into "what a man does in his leisure is not work," and
then to traverse this statement. If, however, one defines work
—which we do—as *wage-earning,* then the contradiction in large
measure disappears : but Mr. Morris' remarks on page 203 are
worth reading. since their confession as to the " weariness " of life
without some daily work curiously suggests that he has overlooked
the lifelong employment that study alone may give.

by the power of tho ocean—now wasted utterly! Any such solution as this would indeed be magnificent, and would effectually dispose of one perplexity: but we should still have to reckon with the iron mines, and the—certainly far less troublesome—copper and tin mines, etc.

Then we come to a varied category of trades, which it is necessary to but very briefly glance at : there are the bootmaker and tailor, the blacksmith, the brickmaker, tho navvy, the shepherd, the farm-labourer, tho builder, the carpenter, the engine-driver, and so on. Now our object in quoting these occupations is to point out that—putting a-side the trouble of roughening and staining the hands, which, we admit, is a *bona fide* sore trouble to us—putting aside this, however, there is really nothing in any of these trades that any one of *us* ought to be horrified at for ourselves—once we get over the ridiculous and immoral prejudice that there is something menial, servile, or dis-honourable, in manual work. Any such occupation as we have mentioned might have to be plied by any one of us or of our sons if living in a new colony ; and would be performed without any the least feeling of false shame *there*, and with the most beneficial results to health. Then why not likewise here ? Any one of us will do—and enjoy it—a hard spell of very manual work in our own houses and gardens[1]—yet we should deem professional manual work dishonorable. We have yet

---

[1] During the dockers' strike of 1890 we heard a good deal of "gentlemen black legs :" and during the Irish railway strike a small number of young gentlemen volunteered to do porter's or shunter's work for the *pure fun of the thing.*

to learn that wielding a spade is as honorable as driving a pen—and far more healthy.

"But,"—comes the impatient retort—"all this, however true, is absurd and inconsequential: for whatever we may think, rightly or wrongly, of manual work, our reasons for not adopting it are not that we despise it, but that we can get better paid for head-labor — and prefer this. Of what use then is it to lecture us on the necessity of reconciling ourselves to manual work?"

Now to this retort we have very little to object, in so far as it looks to *the present day only :* but we are looking forward. As will have been already gathered, we anticipate a time when various social developments will have concurred to largely augment the ranks of manual workers at the expense of the non-productive classes on the one hand, and to notably elevate the culture and social standing of the workers on the other. Now our socialist friends, who are nothing if not hasty and enthusiastic, are very fond of denouncing without discrimination the whole category of middlemen and of other wealth-distributers, and of insisting that the future is for the manual worker only : in all of which indiscrimination perhaps they will pardon us for thinking them very foolish : but there is abundant kernel of truth in their declamations nevertheless.

Now when the fully middle-aged, aldermanic, and rather apoplectic, city-gentleman—gifted with no very violent zeal for humanity, and with even less capacity for sociological study, or even for any other form of intellectual exercitation—when this worthy hears our socialist friends so declaiming, he generally mops his forehead, gasps like a dying fish, and breaking out into a cold perspiration, cries, " *Good God!* do you mean to say that *I* am to be set to work building a wall or stoking a furnace : oh, what rascals, what idiots, these socialists are :" and away he trots, as fast as may be, to vote Tory !

Now all this is very absurd : nobody, except some very violent enthusiast of the latter-day-saint type of character, anticipates any such sudden change—a change impossible unless brought about by *very* artificial methods, and then disastrous : we have to do with the *evolution* of society and of social machinery, and with the progressive modifications so entailed. It is only in the vision of some wild dreamer that our respectable city friend—whose consternation we can hardly avoid somewhat pitying in spite of his arrant selfishness— would be suddenly transplanted from an occupation in which he is of *some* use to another in which he would be utterly useless, besides being physically unfit for it. To contemplate the possibility of such rapid changes is to cherish most wasteful and uneconomical desires. There is no question of the old gentleman being turned into a manual labourer ; and, so far therefor, it may be said that his consternation or his assent were equally valueless : *but* there is some possibility of its being very advisable that his grandson or great-grandson should devote himself to some species of " mechanic " work— especially if he be no more liberally gifted in the way of grey brain-matter than is his elderly and respectable progenitor. Now, this being so, we would ask our socialist friends—Is it necessary, is it not rather ex-

tremely unwise, thus to consternate and agitate elderly
citizens of the non-featherweight build ; would it not
be wiser to conciliate their votes and interest by showing
them that in the first place this dreaded reform cannot
possibly occur in their time (a sop for the Cerberus
of *self*), and that, in the second place, it is not after all
so dreadful when it does come—nay, rather pleasant
than otherwise for those who have been suitably trained ?
For even our elderly citizen will tell you that city-life
is vile, and that his dream is to retire into the country,
when—— ! so that after all he may be got to admit
that, if his grandson or great-grandson, instead of being
sent into the smoky city at 15, to arrive, only after long
years of drudgery at a desk, at a moderate income, were,
instead of this, kept at school and university until 20 or
21, and then taught carpentering, *e.g.*, and made as
good an annual income by that in a few years as our
friend after 20 years' drudgery, and with shorter hours
and a far healthier life to boot—why then this so
dreaded millennium might be tolerable after all !

Nor is this all : the Socialists, like other enthusiasts,
are too apt to forget that the new régime *can* succede and
flourish healthily and prosperously *only if* it be a natural
growth indigenous to the people : conceivably it might
be imposed by foreign conquerors or by mob law—but
then alas, *vae victis! vae civitati victae!* No : may
England's fate forbid any so terrible calamity : the new
régime (whether the Socialists be right in their painting
of it or the Individualists in theirs) can only be prosper-
ous and lasting *if* it be a natural growth.   But how do
any changes come to naturally occur ; what is the fore-

runner and cause of every social or constitutional reform: what else but a previous movement of thought and feeling? The reform was made a certainty at that moment when, in the majority of the people, there was implanted a perception of its necessity, or a strong impulse towards the change [1]: always and everywhere the *first necessity then is to revolutionise the thoughts* and to render a given *idea* familiar and agreeable. Now up come the Socialists; and, by way of reconciling the British Philistine to a radical social change which is timed to arrive perhaps several or many generations hence, they fire off at the astonished and scandalised old gentleman a shower of red-hot new doctrines, none of which he understands, and for none of which he is prepared. Now we contend that the proper thing is to take this somewhat dense old citizen into our confidence, and after having convinced him that we have no explosives about us, and that nothing is likely to "go off" in *his* neighborhood anyhow, we should bring him to see how very pleasant such developments are to contemplate, and in fact we should "warm up" the doctrines gradually before him: then perhaps we may make some headway. [2] And this is precisely what we have been aiming at thro'out this essay.

1 "Every institution as it actually exists, no matter what its name or pretences may be, is the effect of public opinion far more than its cause; and it will avail nothing to attack the institution unless you first change the opinion" (Buckle: *History of Civilisation*, III., p. 83).

2 We hope that all this will not be misunderstood as an advocacy of socialistic doctrines: for, altho it appears to us that the *final* social state contemplated by ourself is not very vitally different from that which the Socialists aim at, yet our respective prescriptions for arriving at such state, and for maintaining it

Now—applying the moral of this long digression—we hope that our purpose in emphasising the comparatively pleasurable character of much manual work (at least when subject to certain very feasible reforms) will be perceived.

It is—we think—highly desirable that we should, *beforehand*, reconcile ourselves to the idea of manual labor supplanting—in great measure—"office work," "shop work," and "professional work." Once get rid of that preposterous notion that manual work is degrading; and then—given equivalent wages—surely we must admit that brickmaking or building, altho not an intellectual or intrinsically interesting pursuit perhaps, is at least no worse in this respect than book-keeping or collecting insurance-fees; and that carpentering, with all its beautiful precision, is intellectually somewhat above bank-clerking. An engine-driver may be thought to have a hard life, but—putting aside those engaged in the underground-railway, whose lot in its terrible monotony is too horrible to contemplate, and putting aside also certain suburban-drivers—we would even to-day vastly prefer the engine-driver's life, hour for hour, to the lawyer's-clerk's or the shop-assistant's — tho the one wear a white jacket and be a "mechanic," while the other wear a black coat (odious appanage) and be a "gentleman" (save the mark). Oh! is there not some-

when arrived at, are *fundamentally different.* Of course the Socialists may be quite right, and we may be quite wrong : we are fully open to conviction ; but meanwhile we decidedly object to being misunderstood as an exponent of regimental Socialism— whereas our present convictions are dead against it.

thing grandly romantic in an engine-driver's life : in the summer, for instance, steaming out of London in the early morn while the air is fresh and keen, quickly leaving the throbbing metropolis behind, bursting rapidly in upon—say— the Surrey heaths, dashing thro all the fair summer-wealth of heather and bracken, whirling across the Hampshire and Wiltshire downs with their chalk escarpments, and at last breaking in upon the glories of Devon ; and so, after winding round hill and combe, ending by the side of the surging ocean ! Or perhaps a night journey—a fiery, gleaming, swishing, rush thro the darkness—oh a romantic life and a fine life truly : what can the pallid, smoke-ridden, black-coated, City clerk set off against this ! Again, people—to-day—stupidly scoff at shoemakers and tailors: but an hour's sojourn in an Italian cobbler's shop—necessitated by the effect of a pedestrian tour upon a solely-available pair of boots— taught us how much of interest and skill the art of cobbling enshrined : whilst anyone not blinded by stupid caste-born prejudice would readily perceive that in its beautiful neatness, symmetry, and skill, tailoring is far superior (in intellectual interest) to writing invoices or attending " change," and far more honorable than gambling in stocks or concocting *lies* for newspapers. Shepherds and farmers and fishermen have all the year round that healthy open-air-life which Londoners look to as making their brief fortnight the chief happiness of the year : and even the sailor's life, tho it be hard and dangerous, is so much the ideal of, at least, us sea-girt Englishmen, that it were almost superfluous to adduce any arguments to reconcile us to *that* : we may well anticipate that, when wages have sufficiently gone up, and the workmen's pay be more nearly equal in all trades, then the sailor's life will exercise an irresistible fascination upon our British youth, and the difficulty will be, not to man our marine but, to ship our mariners.[1] It thus appears to us that—so far as concerns social developments—our future is full of hopefulness; and the outlook, as compared with our present surrounding social wilderness, is fair indeed; and surely the efforts of all of us should be especially centred *upon so educating public feeling* and inducing so healthy and truly democratic a frame of mind—to the eternal annihilation of *caste*—as to render it possible, socially possible we mean, for our sons, or at least for our grandsons—unless their abilities clearly designate them as fitted for a truly learned profession—to earn their livelihood by some species of mechanical work rather than by desk-drudgery or supererogatory "middlemanning." At the same time such reflections as the foregoing immensely help us to reconcile semi-Utopian happiness with the existence of numberless mechanics such as are clearly necessary to any society.

[1] We fear that the suggestion will be drowned by peals of Homeric laughter, yet we have small doubt that, in a more refined society, sailors, like many other craftsmen, will wear *gloves* whilst engaged in dirty working; and will *not* consider it a point of honor to have tarry hands. White hands are dear to us; and we cannot easily reconcile ourself to the notion of 80 per cent. being spoiled in Utopia.

APPENDIX.

SINGULARLY enough, about an hour after writing the foregoing discussion on vegetarianism, we found in the current number of the *Nineteenth Century* (April, 1892) a vegetarian pronunciamento by Lady Paget. We read the article with, naturally, much interest: and, altho the authoress had permitted herself to indite—as we were sorry to observe—several glaring absurdities, and once or twice betrayed a comical nescience of physiology; still, after reading and reflecting on the article, we began to see our way thro this difficulty a little more clearly, and to think that perhaps we had, in our remarks above, somewhat exaggerated the difficulties of Utopia's diet.

Lady Paget, in stating her case for vegetarianism, laid great stress on the *esthetic* side of the question, referring for instance to the loathsome spectacle afforded by a butcher's shop, and especially to the reflex effect on the butcher. All this is, of course, thoroly consonant with the views that we have already expressed; and, when Lady Paget procedes to refer to her individual constitutional repugnance to meat-eating, we can farther assure her that our own experience has been very congruous to hers. With all that Lady Paget writes regarding the far more *esthetic* character of a vegetable diet we are thoroly in accord, and emphatically with her objection to condemning so many fellow-men to the degrading trade of *butchery;* and *of course* with her womanly plea for the dumb animals that suffer such hideous cruelties on the route to the slaughterer's; indeed we can hardly trust ourself to think upon this part of the subject. But now, admitting all these arguments to the full, the old question remains, *will vegetarianism work?* Well, Lady Paget's article naturally did not convince us of what has been a moot point—if *even a moot point*—for many years, and seems moreover very clearly repugnant to man's normal alimentary instincts,—which are by no means to be ignored as guides;[1] but, thinking over the subject,

---

[1] We must remark, however, that the majority of the monkeys are normally vegetarian; but, presumably in correlation with this diet, they have frequently hideously prominent abdomens; the potato-eating Irish are well known to be similarly affected. Mr Long—to whose article, in the *Fortnightly* for August, 1893, we may refer our readers for various data as to food-consumption, etc.—remarks that 2 lbs. of flour and 4 oz. of pulse per day constitute the total food of a Hindoo. Obviously it were absurd to argue without reserve from the easy conditions of a tropical climate to the far severer conditions of Northern Europe, to say nothing of the asserted corporal weakness and

and especially regarding it from the esthetic and humanitarian standpoint, we came to the conclusion that, if it should be found feasible to maintain a thoroly satisfactory bodily condition on --not a vegetarian but—a " pythagorean " diet of *fish* and " vegetables," the problem would be practically solved.

The *esthetic* and humanitarian advantages of fish over butcher's meat are so obvious as to need no pointing : the killing of the fish is accompanied by nothing comparable to the horrors of the shambles, the stage of previous suffering is wanting, any kind of prescience or nervous apprehension is absolutely absent, the moral deadening of the fisherman's sentiments is in no way comparable with that of the butcher's—both because there is no bloodshed, and no actual *killing*, and because, the farther removed from humanity is any animal, the less repulsive, both naturally and logically,[1] is its killing—and finally a fish-shop—altho Lady Paget expressly disagrees with us here—is not esthetically objectionable, or at least, comparably with a butcher's.[2]

feebleness of the Hindoos, which will not unnaturally be ascribed to their bad food, tho he adds that their mes-engers will go fifty miles a day for twenty and thirty days without intermission ('); but we would ask our read-rs' attention to a passage in *Forster's Travels* (ii. 142) as quoted by Mill (*History of India*, i., p. 412.) " Having witnessed the robust activity of the people of Northern Persia and Afghanistan, I am induced to think that the human body may sustain the most laborious services without the aid of animal food. The Afghan, whose sole aliment is bread, curdled milk, and water, inhabiting a climate which often produces in one day extreme heat and cold, shall undergo as much fatigue, and exert as much strength, as the porter of London who copiously feeds on flesh-meat and ale ; nor is he subject to the like acute and obstinate disorders. It is a well-known fact that the Arabs of the shore of the Red Sea, who live, with little exception, on dates and lemons, carry burdens of such an extraordinary weight, that its specific mention to an European ear would seem romance."

[1] *Naturally*, because the death of any animal that can reciprocate our human feelings and intelligence—*e.g.*, a dog, horse, or monkey—possesses a peculiar pathos for us ; it is analogous to the death of a man ; and *logically* because the further removed from us is an animal, the cruder is its nervous system and the less capable of suffering pain is it.

[2] " I do not think that anyone has a right to indulge in tastes which oblige others to follow a brutalising occupation which morally degrades the man who earns his bread by it. To call a man a *butcher* means that he is fond of bloodshed " (p. 582, April, 1892). In this connection we may call our readers' attention to a significant statement that appeared in the *Star* (August, 1893), to the effect that a police constable was converted *tout-à-coup* to vegetarianism by a duty-visit that he paid to a slaughter-house. His account of his experience is worth reading. Mrs. Edmonds in her *Fair Athens* (p. 148-9) has some plaintive reflections on the fate of thousands of lambs at Easter, and seems to have had her happiness considerably marred thereby. Mrs. Edmonds, apparently, is no vegetarian.

Well the upshot of our reflections was a determination to make
a loyal experiment upon this " pythagorean " diet, of fish, eggs,
and vegetable food, only—excluding poultry and game as much
as butcher's meat. An opportunity soon offered itself for com-
mencing the experiment, and we can now report (February,
1894) that after eighteen months' abstention from meat we feel
none the worse for it: almost the only differences that we have
observed are (1) that apparently at first we suffered less from
indigestion after dinner, and (2) that the mouth and teeth are in
a decidedly more agreeable condition than they were wont to be
in the days of the normal diet: this latter change was very
marked at once. We may furthermore add that after three weeks
in Scotland, spent partly on board ship and partly on pedestrian
tours—during which time we lived *almost* entirely on this diet
—we returned several pounds heavier than we had ever known
ourself before. At the same time we are fully open to the remarks (1) that some years' trial may be by no means so satisfactory
as eighteen months'—time alone can decide that ; and (2) that it
is considerably more difficult to obtain a palatable variety of
food under this than under the normal *régime.* However that
may be, the general effect upon our speculations has been to bias
us strongly to the conclusion that butchers' shops will disappear
from the semi-Utopia of this latitude anyhow : whether the
poulterer's will remain is another question. It has, however,
been objected by a sceptical friend, against either pure vegetarianism or our own " Pythagoreanism," that to abolish " butchery "
would entail the loss of wool and milk also, since these could
profitably be grown only as *bye-products*, not as the main or
sole products. To this, however, we retort (1) that wool *is so
grown* in Australia, and apparently also by the breeders of the
merino sheep—whose bodies are dwarfed and the wool luxuriant ;
(2) that even in England sheep can get more or less of a living
on bare hillsides where the land is unfit for cultivation, and
pasturage costs nothing ; (3)—and this is very important —that
all the great expenses of fattening would obviously be saved, so
that the expenses of sheep-owners and cattle-owners would be
far less than now ; (4) that even if the prices of wool and milk
be raised (which we doubt), yet since a fish diet—when the cultivation of fish shall have been systematically and scientifically
undertaken —will be far less expensive than a meat-diet, it is
clear that higher prices could be afforded for wool and milk ;
besides which, it seems clear that if we keep our sheep alive for

their natural term, instead of slaughtering thousands monthly, our national supply of wool will be enormously increased. With regard to other and favourite objections of our friend's, we may also at least *suggest* possible solutions : we are asked, What can be done with the oxen if they be no longer eaten ; and how are the dead sheep and oxen to be disposed of ? To these questions we submit (1) that the oxen may well be used for draft-purposes as they are on the Continent—a procedure which would greatly economise our horse-power, and practically therefor increase our supply of horses : besides which, moreover, it is highly probable that the advance of biological science will enable us to practically determine the ratio of bullcalves to cowcalves in accordance with our requirements ; and (2) as to the disposal of dead cattle and sheep, the *same objection might be made in regard to our horses :* whether the dead animals be returned to mother earth, or utilised in fish-culture, the esthetic trouble is far less than that involved in butchery. Finally, as regards the pigs, we must confess that, *personally*, whether we remain " Pythagorean " or not, we would gladly see the Gadarene process applied to every pig in Britain to-morrow. These few suggestions as to the economics of live-stock we commend to our vegetarian friends, whose business it really is, rather than ours, to solve such problems. We hope that they will be duly grateful to us for fighting their battles, altho not acknowledging their suzerainty and only doubtfully their alliance even ! As a matter of fact it is really *their* business to arrange all these things ; and we may point out to them that until they can find a complete substitute for *leather*, or otherwise solve that leather problem, there must necessarily remain an unmanageable lion in their own and our esthetic paths !

CHAPTER XII.

ON CO-OPERATION.

" Le sense commun est le génie de l'humanité."

" A threefold cord is not quickly broken."

THERE are a number of detached observations with regard to social evolution, and bearing especially (in all probability) upon the not very remote future, that we may here record before closing the present discussion.

Among the many forms of social activity, for which one may anticipate far greater development in the future, is that of *co-operation*. It has often seemed to us, when reflecting on social development, that men in the future will live far less than at present by making profits, and far more by diminishing expenses—which diminution can only be brought about by co-operation. Of course this statement can very easily be caricatured into mere nonsense; but we think that there is a very solid core of truth in it : one or two examples from familiar things will render the matter plain.

Take first our daily expenditure on the necessities of life—coals—food—clothes—tools—and so on. Now in buying all of these things we are paying, not only the labourer's wages and the manufacturer's profit, but also the profits of probably two (at least) intermediary dealers

—the wholesale dealer and the shopkeeper. Now if we could buy direct from the manufacturer at the wholesale prices we should save largely : but it were clearly absurd to suppose that we could do this without buying a large quantity at a time—for which large quantity we have no use. The least reflection will suffice to show that in nineteen cases out of twenty some kind of middleman-distributing-agency is absolutely essential : and if so, clearly such middlemen must be paid—must make their profits. Now in this dilemma, many years ago, some few people, unusually endowed with "common" sense, perceived that they might attain the desired end by banding themselves together, buying the goods whole-sale, and then retailing them among themselves. In fact *Co-operative Stores* were invented. Now it is clear that, when rationally carried out, this system of Co-oper-ative Stores is emphatically *the* most economical way of diminishing household expenses, and of reducing to the lowest possible minimum the number of middlemen and the consequent costs of distribution. The whole assem-blage of shops in any one village might be superseded by one large co-operative store—employing the minimum possible staff of distributers—and to the general advantage.

But the system of Co-operative Stores—so called—as we know them at the present day, is the most insane and ghastly parody of Co-operation conceivable—having as . much real co-operation in it as there is moss on a rolling stone. By what mysterious process of brain-bewilder-ment anybody can have persuaded himself that "co-operation" of distribution consisted in X people forming a limited liability company for the sale of miscellanies at subnormal rates, both to themselves and to anybody who liked to subscribe 2s. 6d. or 5s. annually for the privilege, and in then dividing the enormous [1] profit to the share-holders in *proportion to their shares and not to their pur-chases*, this the Demons of confusion alone know. Yet this caricature passes for "Co-operation!" The absur-dity is really so glaring, the fallacy so palpable, that it almost seems superfluous to explain that there can be no Co-operation of distribution in its true sense unless (1) the ability to purchase is confined exclusively to the shareholders, and (2) the profits are annually distributed among the members in the *precise ratio of their purchases, but not to them as shareholders.* Or in other words, the aim should be to sell at cost-price plus management-price; and the profits, as such, should be zero. The only question is, whether it be better to sell the goods at a zero profit in each case; or to sell them at normal or subnormal prices, and then annually divide the profits to each member in the ratio of his purchases. The former plan is of course the simpler *prima facie*; but the latter is preferred by most economists; not only because it is difficult to calculate the managerial and other expenses so exactly as to be able to sell, *e.g.*, a pound of soap at zero-profit-price, but also because it is usually considered that thrift is far more promoted, and extravagance and

---

[1] An original £1 share in the Army and Navy Stores is now worth £15. How heavy a loss is entailed upon the consumer by our present machinery of distribution is evidenced by this fact no less than by the huge proportion to which the *trade discount* sometimes attains: we understand that in certain trades it may be as high as 75 per cent.—or even higher.

frivolous expenditure less induced, if a tangible lump return be made annually.[1]

Another development of co-operation, which we may expect to find in the *very near* future, is in its application to hotels and similar establishments: and one knows not whether to attribute it to national brainlessness, or to national apathy, that this reform has not been introduced years ago. At present, any one visiting a fairly good hotel in anything like a favourite watering-place is charged at—often—the most extortionate rates: so far as it is possible to anyhow check the charges, the landlord seems to make several hundred per cent. profit. But tho this has been a standing grievance for many years, and tho everybody, *more patriae*, grumbles and growls, and declares such charges to be scandalous, and perhaps shortens a holiday, or denies himself the pleasure of visiting a favourite watering-place in consequence, yet the thing ends here : and hotel charges continue to rise, to the general annoyance, and the profit of no one— except the unconscionable landlord.   And yet the remedy is so very simple: there requires only some public-spirited man with some influence to set the movement on foot, and then the difficulty were solved.[2]

There must be at least some tens of thousands of Londoners alone who annually visit one or another of say

---

[1] The qualification usually made that the co-operation is not extended to the shopmen, etc., employed seems to us no more valid than an objection to a bird that it can't swim.   In the very nature of things the co-operation in distribution can only benefit the distributers, and *qua* distributers.

[2] Note also, however, the suggestions *supra* p. 55 on joint households, and temporary exchanges.

a score favourite seaside resorts : now all that is necessary
is to induce—well perhaps a thousand would be sufficient
to start with—to form a limited co-operation company,
with say £5 shares, in order to buy up an hotel in some
town to be fixed by the majority-vote. This hotel then
would be worked on co-operative principles exactly like
a *true* co-operative store ; it would be kept exclusively for
the use of members, who would be charged the minimum
possible tariff, and any profits made would annually be
distributed pro rata, *not according to shares but to hotel
bills.* But, it will be exclaimed, this is only one town :
people do not want to visit the same town every year.
True : but, once the experiment were successfully started,
there would be a rush for membership. The original
company (of 1000) should be so constituted as to permit
of unlimited addition to their numbers : and for every
fresh 1000 shareholders, a fresh hotel should be taken
on. Thus, in probably one or two seasons, hotels would
be acquired in every fair-sized watering-place. The
economy would obviously be immense ; whilst the gain
in comfort would be very great indeed, since hotels, be-
longing in this way to a company of hotel-visitors, would
be quickly made far more home-like and generally snug
than they at present are. That the general public, even
without co-operating, would benefit by this reform is
obvious : since the co-operation would so thoroly scare
the hotel-keeping fraternity as to bring down their prices
with a rush.[1] It is clear too that this scheme need not

[1] We look upon this as a *most practicable* reform which might
well be introduced at once : and there is no reason why a
company so formed should not procede to buy up, *e.g.*, Swiss
hotels also where the prices are steadily rising.

16

be confined to hotel-visitors alone, but that it might most beneficially include provision for buying up blocks of houses for the benefit of those whom it better suits to take apartments.[1]   In fact all of this is nothing else but the application of Club-principles on a larger scale.   Just similarly—to descend to a still more prosaic subject— may we look to such a scheme for buying up City-restaurants and dining-rooms.   It has long been a source of grumbling and complaint that City-clerks—on whom more especially the hardship falls—cannot get a dinner for a reasonable sum.   The remedy is very simple—*viz.*, for some hundreds of them to combine, buy up a restaurant, put a manager in it, and then dine cheaply

---

[1] It is strange that on a small scale this has not long ago been applied by a group of families buying up a cottage by the sea and using it in turn.   So too if our countrymen had the merest soupçon of energy and "common" sense, or the slightest notion of helping themselves, instead of paying the exorbitant sums demanded for berths in the various yachting steamers, a hundred of them would club together, charter a steamer on their own account, appoint a catering committee and stewards, and in fine have all the real enjoyment of the cruise for about a third or half of the sum usually demanded.   It is true that a "club" thus catering for themselves would probably not charter a steamer whereof the woodwork was entirely hidden by velvet and gilt mirrors, nor would they spend as much on the wasteful extravagances of a single dinner as would pay for four reasonable dinners ; but we venture to say that they would be none the worse for these limitations—but rather the better.   The modern curse of object-less luxury has invaded and already half-ruined our ships now, and threatens—at the present rate of increase—soon to render it impossible for any men with "moderate" incomes to afford the expense of the "cheapest form of carriage."

It seems to be, nowadays, considered essential to render a steamship a floating *maison dorée*—which proceeding we beg leave to characterise as a lubberly mistake singularly disgraceful to an island-nation.

at co-operative rates. Here again everyone will profit, for the frightened restaurateurs will bring down their prices. [1]

We are by no means sure either that similar associations will not be formed to buy up theatres and concert-halls; so that we may get our recreations also at co-operative rates. Compulsory co-operation is already applied—rightly or wrongly—in many towns, in the form of municipal gasworks, etc.; and a consideration of the very wide range that co-operation may be made to cover will satisfy us that we have here another of those *natural processes*—the tendency of which is concomitantly to increase the average citizen's wealth, and to render the accumulation of large fortunes rarer and more difficult.

---

[1] A highly desirable—and yearly more necessary—social development is the formation of an *Anti-Blackmail-league*; the object of which shall be to *compel* certain classes, hotel-keepers and restaurateurs pre-eminently, to pay their own servants and waiters themselves, instead of dishonestly leaving them to live by blackmailing their customers for tips. Such reform can only be effected by an organisation so powerful as to embrace the majority of their customers. This evil system is becoming simply intolerable now, and is poisoning trade after trade. It is well known that, in many City-restaurants, the waiters are paid *nothing*, but, on the contrary, pay the proprietor several pounds weekly for their berths, recouping themselves by tips! The utter absurdity of the system is evidenced not alone by this, but also by the fact that, in many City-grillrooms, a man lunching on a steak and bread—price 1/1—is expected to tip 1d. each to waiter, griller, and *money-taker!*

CHAPTER XIII.

GOD THE ALMIGHTY DOLLAR.

> " The World is too much with us : late and soon
> *Getting and spending* we lay waste our powers :
> Little we see in Nature that is ours ;
> We have *given our hearts away*, a sordid boon."

> " Oppressed
> To think that now our life is only dressed
> *For show :* mean handywork of craftsman, cook,
> Or groom ! We must run glittering like a brook
> In th' open sunshine, or we are unblest.
> The wealthiest man among us is the best.
> No grandeur now in nature or in book
> Delights us. *Rapine, avarice, expense,*
> *This is idolatry ; and these we adore :*
> *Plain living* and high thinking are no more."

AND now, in conclusion, let us repeat once more, that in depicting Utopia it is the *general good*, the *general happiness*, that we are regarding, and not the selfish affluence of a few. It is hardly necessary to point out that the whole drift of this essay implies as much—that again and again the sundry reforms denoted really connote—more or less immediately—a progressive levelling of income, status, and culture. For instance, early in this essay we pointed out that the comparative extinction of lawyers would inevitably accompany the introduction of a high standard of general honesty ; and, no doubt, many

readers will have been horrified at such a suggestion—
exclaiming against a reform, however generally beneficial,
that should deprive a Russell or a Lockwood of the
opportunity of amassing a fortune by his eloquence and
address.[1]   But—putting aside the fact that all these
men (however indispensable at present) are simply a
measure of our imperfect civilisation and our uncertain
honesty—we contend that the very fact of so many
fortunes the less being made were in itself a source of
great gratulation.   Since the national wealth is a limited
amount, every fortune amassed *by a non-producer* entails
the inevitable correlative that so many of his fellows are
the poorer: that a lawyer has an annual income of £5000
implies that, for instance, fifty of his fellows are losing
£100 a year; and, whereas to increase a rich man's income by £1000 is to give him comparatively very little
increase of happiness, yet, on the other hand, to diminish
a poor man's income by £100 is to injure him cruelly.
In every case—it is a simplest deduction of economics—
a large fortune for a non-producer *must* mean poverty for
a number of others: but, in this case, that the rich man's
gain is the average man's loss is peculiarly palpable; for
the exchange is brought about, not by any indirect and
occult social processes, but by a very direct payment:
the lawyer's fortune is made out of his clients' fees; and
so much wealth for him means so much loss for them.

We repeat, then, that large fortunes are not [2] a source
of national gratulation—that, on the contrary, they are

[1] *Cf.* too, note to pp. 95-96.

[2] The obvious retort to this is that without abundance of great
capitalists, what is to become of the Wages Fund—how is In-

a cause for great anxiety and regret. That the unproductive rich become continually richer must generally
imply that the poor become poorer; whilst the more
uncommon become large fortunes, the more reason have
we to rejoice—taking this as an indication that levelling
is going on. So much has been incidentally said—or
implied—already in deprecation of any eagerness for
amassing large fortunes—the *main* object of which is to
enable the "successful" man to squander his wealth in
every kind of wasteful luxury and useless extravagance,
against the practice of which this work, from beginning
to end, is principally levelled—that it is scarcely necessary to enter into any formal discussion of plutotheism
here : but, nevertheless, we must once more express our
most earnest and emphatic opposition to this universal
dollar-worship. We know of no more unhealthy and
dangerous social symptom of the present day than this
grovelling adoration of the dollar; and worst of all is
it that the largest fortunes seem for the most part to fall
to the least useful and unworthiest members of society.[1]
If this dollar-worshipping passion for millionaire-manu-
facture, which so unhealthily characterises our time,
could but be quenched; if we could scourge out of men's
minds the evil covetousness which would heap Ossa on

dustry to be supported? But we think the difficulty is more
than met if we concede sufficient well-to-do men. Again, there
may be no merchant-princes to present a gallery of art worth
£250,000 to the nation ; but there will be millions to subscribe
their guineas for such a purpose. *It is well to remember how
rapidly the French raised the German milliards.*

[1] The record of Public Company rogueries during the past few
years is a terrible testimony to the poisonous infection of this
dollar-worshipping, soul-killing, disease.

Pelion to gain the Olympic gold—mainly in order to squander it on luxuries and dissipations which make the sociologist and philanthropist stand aghast with horror and despair—then, indeed, we should be making progress.[1]

[1] When we hear that Vanderbilt is to build himself a palace at a cost of *four hundred thousand pounds*, and that the Duke of Westminster spent—how much?—on the building of his; that Woburn Abbey was built by the Duke of Bedford at a cost of £80,000, and that the grounds are cut up by *60 miles* of walks and drives, and were laid out at a cost of £40,000; that Lord Burton settled £10,000 a year on his daughter—who, as is reported, will inherit £80,000 a year on his death—besides paying off £250,000 incumbrances on his son-in-law's estate; that " money poured into the pockets " of that drunken and dissolute rowdy, the late Abingdon Baird, " at the rate of £120,000 a year," and that " the money he misused in the eleven years since, as a young man of twenty, he took to sport and pleasure, would aggregate to *appalling* figures "; that a successful shopkeeper lately paid £3,000 for a necklace, and that a famous prima donna travels in a special car containing *a bath of solid silver;* that the household salaries of an aged lady, who happens, by a series of accidents of birth and death, to occupy the English throne, involve an annual outlay of £136,260, the " expenses " of her household a similar outlay of £172,500, besides an expenditure of £60,000 for her privy purse; that a well-known millionaire spent £12,000 on a ball at a London hotel; that the cigars supplied to H. R. H. " the first gentleman " of England and very perfect pattern to society, and to a celebrated Jew stock-jobber, are said to cost them *half a guinea each;* that a certain young Vaughan of North-country repute, by dint of spending £40,000 on a billiard-room, £20 each on spittoons, and £1,500 on a bedstead, contrived to run thro a fortune of half-a-million in eleven years; that Princess Beatrice's wedding cost £5,000; that, in short, on every side, wealth is being squandered in the most reckless, *stupid*, and even hedonically unprofitable, waste— wealth wrung from Nature by the painful and lifelong toil of our fellows whose cloud-capped lives are never gladdened by a gleam of sunny interlude — whilst all around thousands are in abject destitution and noble educational or

Now sundry evils of this millionaire-system are patent
to everybody whose heart is not encased in triple brass

philanthropical schemes are languishing or stillborn for want
of a few miserable thousands, such as these fortunati squander
in a day, and social would-be reformers are eating their
hearts in enforced apathy—then we cannot but ask ourselves
whether these self-bound millionaires be really men and women,
or—what? Can such heartless, crassly selfish, luxury-culture be
paralleled in other ages or other climes? Yes: the historian
recalls with a heavy heart the annals of Roman decadence, and
remembers that in the most bedevilled age of Rome, when the
Nemesis of ruin was impending over her, precisely such dollar-
worship and such wasteful luxury were rampant. A few extracts from Roman history may perhaps be permissible in order
to emphasise the analogy. For instance :—" Lucullus had so
regulated his house that he could always bring three of his
friends to supper with him, and, without any previous notice,
set before them a banquet of which the expense was reckoned at
about £650. Even those men of the aristocracy who, like
Cicero, had neither any particular taste for expense, nor any
extraordinary facilities for indulging it, *were obliged to make an
absurd display of luxury for the sake of appearances:* would they
invite their friends to table, they must at least possess a proper
table . . . . yet even Pliny regards it as incredible that Cicero
should have paid £650 for such a table " (Lardner's *History of
Rome*, I., 354, 355). " A table of thuja-root, with a claw of
silver or ivory, marked the man of correct breeding: he whose
table was of beech or oak could have no admittance to good
society ! In the same manner cookery and plate were matters
of great moment : sea-fish could be served up to a man of rank
only on golden dishes set with precious stones ; and his banquet-
ing halls were filled with troops of attendants. . . . *The facility
of life which had existed in former times was gone.* Everyone
who aimed at the distinctions of society must be prepared with
the means of satisfying certain artificial wants, and of following
certain artificial fashions" (*Ibid.*, II., 162, 163). " Philotas declares himself to have seen, and ascertained from Antony's
cook, that a scandalous and useless expense was regularly incurred in order that the table might be instantly served at any
time " (*Ibid.*, II., 77). " As money was the master-key to every
sort of enjoyment, it became the sole object of pursuit . . . .

of selfish lust ; and another less patent objection has just
been pointed out : but there is yet a third and still less

unfortunately the spirit of traffic *took that direction in those times
which it takes at this day*, so far as it deals in stockjobbing and
agiotage, and in joint-stock undertakings of delusive remoteness
and extent" (*Ibid.*, II., 87). "Vitellius' table alone swallowed
up sums so immense that Josephus doubts if the whole Roman
Empire would in the long run have been rich enough to bear the
load of the emperor's table-expenses" (*Ibid.*, II., 130).

Passing by the similarly heartless and riotous luxury of a
privileged few which heralded the break-up of monarchical
France, and which was reflected in other courts, as, for instance,
the Saxon, of which we are told that altho the country had been
impoverished and well-nigh depopulated by the Thirty Years
War, "the Elector George remodelled his court on a scale of
splendor which for a time rivalled that of Versailles, so that
by his expenditure on guards, attendants, parties, banquets,
regattas, etc., he exhausted the electoral treasury, and at last reduced the nation to bankruptcy ;" and again, "A gipsy-party at
Mühlberg cost *three million dollars*, of which five thousand were
expended for porcelain vessels for the bedchambers of the
Elector and his guests"—passing by these almost incredibly
wicked excesses, of which this is a single example only, indulged
in in bygone days, we will cite two or three final instances
from the annals of contemporary modern decay—our authorities
for which are the London daily papers : here they are :—

"The King of Siam has just had a pavilion of glass built for
himself by a Chinese architect. Walls, floors, and ceiling, are
formed of slabs of different sorts and thicknesses of glass joined
by impermeable cement. By one door only can the King enter,
and this closes hermetically when he comes in, and ventilator
valves in tall pipes in the roof open, as does also a sluice beside
a large reservoir in which the glass house stands. The transparent edifice then becomes submerged, and the King thus finds
himself in a cool and perfectly dry habitation, where he passes
the time singing, smoking, eating, and drinking."

"The yearly expenses of the Sultan of Turkey have been
estimated at no less a sum than six millions sterling. Of this, a
million and a half alone is spent on the clothing of the women,
and £80,000 on the Sultan's own wardrobe. Nearly another

obvious mode in which the million-maker (indirectly) *actually lowers* the national wealth; actually brings it about that, to make his colossal fortune, not only are so

million and a half is swallowed up by presents, a million goes for pocket-money, and still another million for the table. It seems incredible that so much money can possibly be spent in a year by one man, but when it is remembered that some fifteen hundred people live within the palace walls, and live luxuriously and dress expensively at the cost of the Civil List, it appears a little more comprehensible."

" Much interest and curiosity have been excited in Bombay by the arrival in the harbor of Mr. Vanderbilt's yacht *The Valiant.* She is manned by a *crew of seventy-eight*, and carried *nine passengers*, including Mr. and Mrs. Vanderbilt. *The Valiant* was built at Birkenhead, and is said to have cost considerably over £100,000. Her length is about 300 feet, the tonnage 2,400, and the horse-power 4,500. The drawing-room is described as occupying the whole breadth of the ship, and is panelled in white and gold in the Louis XIV. style; the furniture, most of it old, being upholstered in red velvet. There is a library lined with polished walnut, and having a fireplace with a richly-carved mantelpiece. Mrs. Vanderbilt's bedroom is adorned with white lacquered panels set in frames of gold and ivory, and the curtains and coverings are of Louis XIV. old rose silk. Her sitting-room is furnished with mahogany of old English make, with green velvet hangings. Two or three other apartments, decorated in the Empire fashion in two shades of blue, open out of the larger rooms; and there is a bath, all the appointments of which are of silver-plated metal. Every bit of metal work, even to the hinges of the doors on the lower deck, is indeed either of silver or silver-plate. Mr. Vanderbilt, adds this account, has his own suite of cabins fitted with even greater splendor and luxury than those of his wife, and in his bedroom, where solid marble has been freely used, are found all sorts of automatic and electrical appliances to save trouble and increase comfort. She has since sailed for Calcutta and other Indian ports."

So that our many English and American wealth-squanderers fall into the same category with dissolute Romans of the decadence, and with Eastern barbarians : and the reflection is anything but consolatory to the sociologist and philanthropist.

many hundreds somewhat poorer, but the *national sum-total* of wealth—which had not so far been affected—is prevented from increasing so much as it otherwise would, or is even actually diminished. To make this plain it is necessary to point out that millionaires may be either producers or non-producers : if the former, if for instance a millionaire's wealth has been made by inventing new machinery, new processes of manufacture, by building or designing railways, or in any other such way, *then* is he not only no malefactor, but in truth a benefactor to the community : for in such case his own fortune is but a proportion of all the immense extra wealth that he has created.

But if he have made his fortune as a *non-producer*, then this additional stricture becomes well deserved. Suppose, for example, that the millionaire be a great *advertiser*—as so many are : and we will admit, first of all, that the wares which he advertises are decently useful and not mere quackery. But what does his very advertising imply ? When we learn that Messrs. Pears spend £100,000 annually in advertisements, whilst thousands of other firms adopt the procedure on a smaller scale, we are simply being informed in other words, that, in order (not to *create* wealth but) to *transfer* so much wealth from other persons' pockets to those of the millionaire, a distinct proportion of national wealth has been *wasted*[1]—rendered practically non-existent, and a still larger increment of new wealth inhibited. For how is the advertisement effected ? By metallic, wooden, or paper, affixes to railway stations, omnibuses, hoardings, etc., and

---

[1] And sometimes a magnificent mountain-landscape ruined by the accursed advertisement-monger !

by printed advertisements. However effected, an immense amount of labor is devoted to printing and otherwise preparing these advertisements—all of which labor might else have been used in producing new wealth. When, in addition to this, the very considerable value of the metals now used so extensively, and of the various other material media employed, and also the gradual destruction of wealth by the wear and tear of printers' type, are noted—in fact when we sum up all that is involved in the expense of advertising, we must admit that the non-producing, self-made, million-heaper (however honest and worthy personally) is literally a noxious parasite living and swelling on the blood of the nation. All the enormous staff of billposters and advertisement-mongers are, indirectly and in final resort, just as much *kept* by the nation, are just as much a *drain* upon every worker's resources, as are the lawyers and police. So that the sum-total of wealth-loss entailed upon the nation by this pernicious, mammon-worshipping, almighty-dollar-adoring, practice of the non-producing millionaire is a matter for grave anxiety : and there is a crying need for reforming away this cancerous disease, that is daily eating more fatally into the moral fibre of the nation. We had long felt—as indeed any reflective man must—that this incessant advertising, of even the most useful articles, was symptomatic of an unhealthy and *restless* age ; and that a distinct social advance would be characterised by a subsidence thereof : but, not until we sat down to write out these speculations, did we fully realise the enormous wealth-loss entailed by our gigantic advertising system.[1] It is probable that in

[1] And if furthermore the articles advertised be not genuine, but

a more healthy social state men would regard the passion for amassing an immense fortune in much the same light as we should regard a would-be-feudal baron to-day ; and indeed it will become progressively more and more difficult—except perhaps for great discoverers and other such wealth-producers—to make such fortunes ; but the present type of millionaire who makes his fortune by advertising,[1] by claiming as his own the national mineral wealth, simply because the mines are beneath his land, or by gambling or cheating in stocks and shares—such types as these will probably become extinct—if only for the same reason that would render impossible for a fish existence without water.[2]

We cannot—nowadays—too constantly or earnestly remind ourselves that this *greed and lust of money*, and this *worship of extravagance and waste* ordained by "fashion," are the deep-seated social diseases, uncured of which no nation can be safe or healthy : however ridiculously and preposterously caricatured by crack-brained

some miserable lying quackery, then in addition to all this loss we have an enormous actual waste of wealth in producing material lies.

[1] Often quackeries.

[2] We have vainly endeavored to obtain some statistics as to the expenditure on railway-station advertisements, etc. : but we may commend the subjoined extract to our readers' reflection. We should greatly like to have had the flavoring of that dinner. "A dinner which is probably as yet unique in its character has been arranged to take place. It will consist of principals of the chief advertising firms, and will be presided over by Mr. T. J. Barratt, managing director of Messrs. Pears & Co., supported in the vice-chair by Mr. Beecham, of St. Helen's. *The little party will it is believed represent an advertising expenditure to the extent of something like one million sterling.*" (*Daily News*, June 23, 1893.)

ascetics of all times, yet there is profound truth in the apostolic injunction that the love of money is *a root of all kinds of evils.* As we have insisted over and over again in the foregoing pages, and as one cannot too constantly or too emphatically reiterate, the *one indispensable reform* that *must precede* any development of a markedly higher social state, is the adoption of a *simpler life*—the abolition of that many-headed, but brainless and heartless, monster, "fashionable society," with all its follies, wickedness, and extravagances. But we must confess to having but faint hopes of any immediate reform when we note that the worst examples of arrant waste, luxury, and extravagance, have their fountainhead in the throne itself;[1] that the heir-apparent to the

[1] The Queen's annual journeys to and from Scotland are *said* to involve an annual expense of £6,000—enough to keep, at least, twenty families in ease and comfort ! We subjoin extracts from an account given of the royal train in the *Daily News* (May, 1893), that our readers may judge what sort of an example in simple living is set to her subjects by the "Mother of the People" :—"The train consisted of an engine and fifteen carriages, its total length being five hundred and thirty-three feet. The Queen's saloons, a very handsomely-equipped drawing-room and sleeping car, were coupled in the middle of the train. Both carriages were panelled externally in claret, white, and gold, adorned with the Royal Arms, and surrounded by a carved floral border of roses, thistles, and shamrocks, the ornamental glass in the side windows being engraved with devices representing the orders of the Garter, Bath, and Thistle. The drawing-room car was upholstered with variegated woods and blue-watered silk, and lighted by lamps depending from the ceiling, the gilt cornice of which was centred by a handsome clock. Cerulean shaded reading-lamps, supported by richly-chased ormolu brackets, were placed upon a console table for the use of the Queen. The sleeping car was divided into two apartments, that next the drawing-room being panelled with crimson

English Crown consorts, not with the leaders of thought and culture, but with stockjobbers and "sportsmen"; and that his influence is typified, not by a radiation of pure tone and healthy life, but by the introduction of baccarat-gambling into private houses. We do not now expect, or even relish, a genius for government in our kings; but, tho political cyphers, they may exert a potent influence for good or ill on the whole tone of society:[1] and if they do not the former—if, worst of all, they do the latter—their "subjects" may well inquire of what service they be: why cumber they the ground? When one thinks of the immense social good that a king or prince—tho politically a cypher—*might* yet effect as the acknowledged head of society; of the wickednesses and follies and extravagances that he *might* discountenance; and of the pure and healthy tone that he *migh'* infuse; one cannot but be appalled by the thought of how vast a responsibility for wrong done and good not done must rest upon the shoulders of Royalty. Perhaps one day—if Royalty last so long and be not first superseded by a Republic—our successors may find a queen who can live on less than £340,000 per year, and can go out of town without a suite of fifty servants; who can use "drawing-rooms" not for the subservice of frivolity

tinted material and provided with small brass bedsteads having mattresses covered with green silk: while the Royal boudoir was neatly fitted with Hungarian ash and brown upholstery."

1 It must be a matter of deep regret to every true patriot that the Prince Consort died thirty years ago. But probably it never strikes H.R.H. that his life of omissions and commissions excites the most unspeakable contempt in the minds of those who think life a serious matter, and moral progress something more than an empty catchword.

and waste, but for the promotion of simplicity and refinement, by refusing an entrée to trains, feathers, and
jewels: perhaps they may see a prince living with
marked simplicity as a private gentleman might, and
setting to society an example of teetotalism, simple
cookery, pure taste, and healthy life—a prince, too,
proud to be known as the companion of philosophers,
scientists, poets, artists, and philanthropists, but treat-
ing with ineffable scorn the great herd of empty-headed
"dudes," rapacious stockjobbers, reckless gamblers, and
"sporting" blackguards. *Perhaps* that may be reserved
as an experience for the future—stranger things have
happened—but to count on all this is to point a long
long way ahead; and we of to-day are hardly upon the
Pisgah-platform.   Yet if everyone of us would but mould
his own life, in some tolerable degree, approximately to
the social ideal here roughly outlined, how vastly quick-
ened would Utopia's advent be! It is impossible too
emphatically to insist upon this truth—that the one indispensable preliminary to such a change is a change in
the feelings, aspirations, and thoughts, of men.   And here
it is precisely that we of to-day, we collectively, might
do so much good—*viz.*, by right truly educating our
children. The whole public opinion must be educated,
and radically reformed : how so effectively as by rightly
training, from the first, the rising generation ? Thro'out
—be it observed—we are looking to a natural process of
social evolution for the working of all reforms : and to
no arbitrary artificial enactment of a colossally ignorant,
criminally reckless, and partly dishonest, governmental
organisation that, with insane conceit, supposes itself

able to mould human nature and human institutions by
Acts of Parliament. No; no; the whole change to be
healthy, and to be effectual, must be a naturally evolved
product: but we may vastly assist the one half of the
evolutionary process, by educating men to desire it; a
very main obstacle to social advance will then have been
removed.

> " The world's Great Age begins anew,
>   The Golden Years return ;
>   The Earth doth, like a snake, renew
>   Her winter-weeds outworn :
>   Heaven smiles ; and faiths and empires gleam
>   Like wrecks of a dissolving dream."
>
> .   .   .   .   .   .
>
> " The world is weary of the past ;
>   Oh might it die—or rest—at last."

APPENDIX I.

WE have already remarked upon the identity that we have since discovered between many of the suggestions made in this essay, and the propositions set forth by Mr. W. Morris in his *Hopes and Fears for Art:* we may, therefor, without further preface, take this opportunity of quoting two or three passages which are very relevant to the discussions in this last chapter and in Chapters IX., X., and XI. Says Mr. Morris—" Nothing can be a work of Art which is not useful; that is to say, which does not minister to the body when well under command of the mind, or which does not amuse, soothe, or elevate, the mind in a healthy state.

" *What tons upon tons of unutterable rubbish*, pretending to be works of Art in some degree, would this maxim clear out of our London houses, if it were understood and acted upon!" (p. 31.)

" *Simplicity of life*, begetting simplicity of taste, that is, a love for sweet and lofty things, is of all matters most necessary for the birth of the new and better Art we crave for: *simplicity everywhere*, in the palace as well as in the cottage." (p. 32.)

" As to the bricklayer, the mason, and the like—these would be *artists*, and doing not only necessary, but beautiful, and therefor happy, work, if Art were anything like what it should be! No; it is not such labor as this which we need to do away with, *but the toil which makes the thousand and one things which nobody wants.*" (p. 63.)

" —— troublesome superfluities that are for ever in our way: conventional comforts that are no real comforts, and do but make work for servants and doctors; if you want a golden rule that will fit everybody, this is it: *Have nothing in your houses that you do not know to be useful, or believe to be beautiful.*" (p. 108.)

One might easily multiply quotations from this delightful book, but the foregoing are sufficient to show how strikingly Mr. Morris's conclusions—from the side of trained Art—bear out our own: and we will only instance—without quotation—his directions for house-decoration and furnishing as bearing out our own pleas for *simplicity of Life:* in fact, much of Mr. Morris's book may be taken as an illustration of what we have said in Chapter IX. as regards *choosing the least evil.*

To one apparent point of marked divergence we have already alluded (p. 216 footnote *supra.*): and in conclusion we can only say to everyone whose heart is set upon social betterment—*Read him: read, mark, learn, and inwardly digest, with a modicum of critical sauce, certainly,* that *Golden Book* (15th February, 1893).

Still more recently we have had an opportunity of reading Mr. Lewis Day's *Art in Every-day Life*, and must take the opportunity of cordially recommending a perusal of this book in company with Mr. Morris'. It was uncommonly satisfactory to us to find Mr. Day insisting on what has for some time been a pet notion with us—the utter absurdity, we mean, of giving up a room in every house, however small, as a " drawing-room " for use on state occasions! This is a silly piece of ill-bred snobbishness that, with Mr. Day, we wish, rather than expect, to see disappear.

APPENDIX II.

QUITE recently we have come across, in Wallace's *Malay Archi-*

pelago, a passage bearing so strongly on the subject-matter of this work, that we must give ourself the pleasure of transcribing it. We need scarcely add that with nearly every word of the following admirable remarks we are in the very heartiest accord.

" What is this ideally perfect social state towards which man ever has been and still is tending? . . . . In such a state every man would have a sufficiently well-balanced intellectual organisation to understand the moral law in all its details, and would require no other motives but the free impulses of his own nature to obey the law.

" Now it is very remarkable that among people in a very low stage of civilisation we find some approach to such a perfect social state. I have lived with communities of savages, in South America and in the East, who have no laws or law-courts but the public opinion of the village freely expressed. Each man scrupulously respects the rights of his fellow, and any infraction of these rights rarely or never takes place. In such a community all are nearly equal. There are none of those wide distinctions of education and ignorance, wealth and poverty, master and servant, which are the product of our civilisation ; there is none of that widespread division of labor which, while it increases wealth, produces also conflicting interests : there is not that severe competition and struggle for existence or for wealth which the dense population of civilised countries inevitably creates ; all incitements to great crimes are thus wanting, and petty ones are repressed, partly by the influence of public opinion, but chiefly by that natural sense of justice and of his neighbor's rights, which seem to be, to some degree, inherent in any race of man.

" Now altho we have progressed vastly beyond the savage state in intellectual achievements, *we have not advanced equally in morals.* . . . . It is not too much to say that the mass of our population have not at all advanced beyond the savage code of morals, and have in many cases sunk below it. *A deficient morality is the great blot of modern civilisation, and the greatest hindrance to true progress*" (*Malay Archipelago,* p. 595-6 : 7th edition, 1880).

Again "we should now clearly recognise the fact that the wealth and knowledge and culture of *the few* do not constitute civilisation, and do not of themselves advance us towards the ' perfect social state.' Our vast manufacturing system, our gigantic commerce, our crowded towns and cities, support and continually renew a mass of human misery and crime *absolutely* greater than has ever existed before. They create and maintain in lifelong labor an ever increasing army, whose lot is the more hard to bear by contrast with the pleasures, the comforts, and the luxury, which they see everywhere around them, but which they can never hope to enjoy ; and who in this respect are worse off than the savage in the midst of his tribe.

"This is not a result to boast of or to be satisfied with ; and, until there is a more general recognition of this failure of our civilisation—*resulting mainly from our neglect to train and develop more thoroly the sympathetic feelings and moral faculties of our nature, and to allow them a larger share of influence in our legislation,* our commerce, and our whole social organisation—we shall never, as regards the whole community, attain to any real or important superiority over the better class of savages. . . . . We are the richest country in the world, and yet one-twentieth of our population are parish-paupers, and one-thirtieth *known* criminals. . . . . We allow over a hundred thousand persons known to have no means of subsistence, but by crime, to remain at large and to prey upon the community, and many thousand children to grow up before our eyes in ignorance and vice to supply trained criminals for the next generation. This, in a country which boasts of its rapid increase in wealth, of its enormous commerce and gigantic manufactures, of its mechanical skill and scientific knowledge, of its high civilisation and its pure Christianity—I can but term a state of social barbarism. We also boast of our love of justice, and that the law protects rich and poor alike; yet we retain money-fines as a punishment, and make the very first steps to obtain justice a matter of expense—in both cases a barbarous injustice or denial of justice to the poor. Again our laws render it possible that, by mere neglect of a legal form, and contrary to his own wish and intention, a man's property may all go to a stranger—and his children be left destitute. . . . We permit absolute possession of the soil of our country—with no legal rights of existence on the soil to the vast majority who do not possess it. A great land-holder may legally convert his whole property into a forest or a hunting ground, and expel every human being who has hitherto lived upon it. In a thickly-populated country like England, where every acre has its owner or its occupier, this is a power of legally destroying his fellow-creatures; and that such a power should exist, and be exercised by individuals, in however small a degree, indicates that, as regards true social science, we are still in a state of barbarism" (*Malay Archipelago:* 7th edition; p. 596-8).

APPENDIX III.

WE have recently had an opportunity of reading Mr. Ruskin's *Munera Pulveris*, and gladly take the opportunity to quote the following passage, which shows that, in some respects at any rate, Mr. Ruskin by his own road has arrived at precisely the same goal as political economists and various scientific sociologists have guided us to.

Says Mr. Ruskin: "The only final check upon it [1] must be *radical purification of the national character.* . . . But in this more than in anything, Plato's words . . . are true, that neither drugs, nor charms, nor burnings, will touch a deep-lying political sore any more than a deep bodily one; but only *right and utter change of constitution;* and that they do but lose their labor who think that by any tricks of law they can get the better of those mischiefs of commerce, and see not that they hew at an hydra" [2] [5/7/93].

[1] We are not to be understood as endorsing the context of this passage.
[2] P. 101; edition 1880. Italics our own. We would like to express our vehement agreement with Mr. Ruskin (*Crown of Wild Olive*, p. 41-42) as to the wickedness of lending money to fighting powers (such as Russia) who are raising war-loans.

MISCELLANEOUS WORKS OF HERBERT SPENCER.

SOCIAL STATICS. New and revised edition, including "The Man *versus* The State," a series of essays on political tendencies heretofore published separately. 12mo. 420 pages. Cloth, $2.00.

CONTENTS.—Happiness as an Immediate Aim.—Unguided Expediency.—The Moral Sense Doctrine.—What is Morality?—The Evanescence [? Diminution] of Evil.—Greatest Happiness must be sought indirectly. Derivation of a First Principle.—Secondary Derivation of a First Principle.—First Principle.—Application of the First Principle.—The Right of Property.—Socialism.—The Right of Property in Ideas.—The Rights of Women.—The Rights of Children.—Political Rights.—The Constitution of the State.—The Duty of the State.—The Limit of State-Duty.—The Regulation of Commerce.—Religious Establishments.—Poor-Laws.—National Education.—Government Colonization.—Sanitary Supervision.—Currency, Postal Arrangements, etc.—General Considerations.—The New Toryism.—The Coming Slavery.—The Sins of Legislators.—The Great Political Superstition.

"Mr. Spencer has thoroughly studied the issues which are behind the social and political life of our own time, not exactly those issues which are discussed in Parliament or in Congress, but the principles of all modern government, which are slowly changing in response to the broader industrial and general development of human experience. One will obtain no suggestions out of this book for guiding a political party or carrying a point in economics, but he will find the principles of sociology, as they pertain to the whole of life, better stated in these pages than he can find them expressed anywhere else. It is in this sense that this work is important and fresh and vitalizing. It goes constantly to the foundation of things."—*Boston Herald.*

EDUCATION: Intellectual, Moral, and Physical. 12mo. Paper, 50 cents; cloth, $1.25.

CONTENTS: What Knowledge is of most Worth?—Intellectual Education.—Moral Education.—Physical Education.

THE STUDY OF SOCIOLOGY. The fifth volume in the International Scientific Series. 12mo. Cloth, $1.50.

CONTENTS: Our Need of it.—Is there a Social Science? Nature of the Social Science.—Difficulties of the Social Science.—Objective Difficulties.—Subjective Difficulties, Intellectual.—Subjective Difficulties, Emotional.—The Educational Bias.—The Bias of Patriotism.—The Class Bias.—The Political Bias.—The Theological Bias.—Discipline.—Preparation in Biology.—Preparation in Psychology.—Conclusion.

THE INADEQUACY OF "NATURAL SELECTION." 12mo. Paper, 30 cents.

This essay, in which Prof. Weismann's theories are criticised, is reprinted from the *Contemporary Review,* and comprises a forcible presentation of Mr. Spencer's views upon the general subject indicated in the title.

New York: D. APPLETON & CO., 72 Fifth Avenue.

SOCIALISM NEW AND OLD. By Professor WILLIAM GRAHAM. 12mo. Cloth, $1.75.

"Prof. Graham's book may be confidently recommended to all who are interested in the study of socialism, and not so intoxicated with its promises of a new heaven and a new earth as to be impatient of temperate and reasoned criticism."—*London Times.*

"Altogether Mr. Graham has given us a useful discussion, and one that deserves to be read by all who are interested in the subject."—*Science.*

"Prof. Graham presents an outline of the successive schemes of three writers who have chiefly influenced the development of socialism, and dwells at length upon the system of Rousseau, that of St. Simon, and on that of Karl Marx, the founder of t e new socialism, 'which has gained favor with the working classes in all civilized countries,' which agrees with Rousseau's plan in being democratic, and with St Simon's in aiming at collective ownership. . . . The professor is an independent thinker, whose endeavor to be clear has resulted in the statement of definite conclusions. The book is a remarkably fair digest of the subject under consideration."—*Philadelphia Ledger.*

DYNAMIC SOCIOLOGY; or, *Applied* Social Science, *as based upon Statical Sociology and the less Complex Sciences.* By LESTER F. WARD, A. M. In 2 vols. 12mo. Cloth, $5.00.

"A book that will amply repay perusal. . . . Recognizing the danger in which sociology is, of falling into the class of dead sciences or polite amusements, Mr. Ward has undertaken to 'point out a method by which the breath of life can be breathed into its nostrils.'"—*Rochester Post Express.*

"Mr. Ward has evidently put great labor and thought into his two volumes, and has produced a work of interest and importance. He does not limit his effort to a contribution to the science of sociology. . . . He believes that sociology has already reached the point at which it can be and ought to be applied, treated as an art, and he urges that 'the State' or Government now has a new, legitimate, and peculiar field for the exercise of intelligence to promote the welfare of men."—*New York Times.*

"A fundamental discussion of many of the most important questions of science and philosophy in their bearings upon social economy and human affairs in general. It does not treat directly these current questions in any department, and yet it furnishes the basis in science and in logic for the correct solution of nearly all of them. It is therefore exceedingly opportune, as there has never been a period in which greater activity existed in the direction of thoroughly working out and scientifically settling the problems of social, national, and individual life."—*Washington Star.*

FREELAND: A Social Anticipation. By Dr. THEODOR HERTZKA. 12mo. Cloth, $1.00.

"A treatise on social economics somewhat on the plan of Bellamy's 'Looking Backward.' Dr. Hertzka has actually founded a socialist colony in Africa, upon the lines laid down in this book, and 'Freeland' is the imaginary history of the future of the colony. It will doubtless be the cause of much comment and discussion."—*San Francisco Evening Post.*

"A politico-economic romance in which is elaborated a comprehensive and philosophic scheme of social reorganization. Its author is a Viennese economist of eminence. . . . Dr. Hertzka's conception of an ideal social state, his 'Anticipation' is well worth careful and sympathetic reading."—*Detroit Tribune.*

"In the end Freeland reaches a state of universal prosperity and contentment now unheard of. Dr. Hertzka assures the reader that he has drawn no Utopia, but a practicable community, such as a sufficient number of vigorous men can establish in other eligible parts of the world as well as in the highlands of Africa."—*Cincinnati Times Star.*

New York: D. APPLETON & CO., 72 Fifth Avenue.

EVOLUTION OF MAN AND CHRISTIAN-ITY. New edition. By the Rev. HOWARD MACQUEARY. With a new Preface, in which the Author answers his Critics, and with some important Additions. 12mo. Cloth, $1.75.

"This is a revised and enlarged edition of a book published last year. The author reviews criticisms upon the first edition, denies that he rejects the doctrine of the incarnation, admits his doubts of the physical resurrection of Christ, and his belief in evolution. The volume is to be marked as one of the most profound expressions of the modern movement toward broader theological positions."—*Brooklyn Times.*

"He does not write with the animus of the destructive school; he intends to be, and honestly believes he is, doing a work of construction, or at least of reconstruction. . . . He writes with manifest earnestness and conviction, and in a style which is always clear and energetic."—*Churchman.*

HISTORY OF THE CONFLICT BETWEEN RELIGION AND SCIENCE. By Dr. JOHN WILLIAM DRAPER. 12mo. Cloth, $1.75.

"The key-note to this volume is found in the antagonism between the progressive tendencies of the human mind and the pretensions of ecclesiastical authority, as developed in the history of modern science. No previous writer has treated the subject from this point of view, and the present monograph will be found to possess no less originality of conception than vigor of reasoning and wealth of erudition."—*New York Tribune.*

A CRITICAL HISTORY OF FREE THOUGHT IN REFERENCE TO THE CHRISTIAN RELIGION. By Rev. Canon ADAM STOREY FARRAR, D. D., F. R. S., etc. 12mo. Cloth, $2.00.

"A conflict might naturally be anticipated between the reasoning faculties of man and a religion which claims the right, on superhuman authority, to impose limits on the field or manner of their exercise. It is the chief of the movements of free thought which it is my purpose to describe, in their historic succession, and their connection with intellectual causes. We must ascertain the facts, discover the causes, and read the moral."—*The Author.*

CREATION OR EVOLUTION? A Philosophical Inquiry. By GEORGE TICKNOR CURTIS. 12mo. Cloth, $2.00.

"A treatise on the great question of Creation or Evolution by one who is neither a naturalist nor theologian, and who does not profess to bring to the discussion a special equipment in either of the sciences which the controversy arrays against each other, may seem strange at first sight; but Mr. Curtis will satisfy the reader, before many pages have been turned, that he has a substantial contribution to make to the debate, and that his book is one to be treated with respect. His part is to apply to the reasonings of the men of science the rigid scrutiny with which the lawyer is accustomed to test the value and pertinency of testimony, and the legitimacy of inferences from established facts."—*New York Tribune.*

"Mr. Curtis's book is honorably distinguished from a sadly too great proportion of treatises which profess to discuss the relation of scientific theories to religion, by its author's thorough acquaintance with his subject, his scrupulous fairness, and remarkable freedom from passion."—*London Literary World.*

D. APPLETON & CO., 72 Fifth Avenue, New York

MEMOIRS OF PROF. E. L. YOUMANS.

*E*DWARD LIVINGSTON YOUMANS, Interpreter of Science for the People. A Sketch of his Life, with Selections from his Published Writings, and Extracts from his Correspondence with Spencer, Huxley, Tyndall, and others. By JOHN FISKE. With Two Portraits. 12mo. Cloth, $2.00.

"Whether as a memorial of a noteworthy man, or as a record of a most important phase of intellectual life in our own time, the volume is entirely admirable, and must be given a high place in the honorable list of recent biography."—*Philadelphia Times.*

"His life was at once inspiring and interesting. His career gave to manhood in America an ornament as well as a potent example. While he lived, he helped to enrich thousands of lives. Now that he is gone, Prof. Fiske's beautiful biography not only shows us how noble the man himself was, but how great was the public loss, and how precious must remain the possession of such a memory."—*New York Times.*

"It was eminently proper that the biography of Mr. Youmans should be written, and certainly there could not have been chosen a fitter man than Mr. Fiske to write it. An acquaintance dating back thirty years is itself a qualification, and when to this are added Mr. Fiske's ability and the lucid method which characterizes his work, the elements for a satisfactory memoir are all present."—*Philadelphia Bulletin.*

"To enumerate Youmans's achievements in the dissemination and interpretation of scientific truth is to sum up the record of an epoch from the view-point of the gradual enlightenment of the American people. When Mr. Fiske reminds us that the discovery and propagation of truth are functions seldom united in one person, and that science, like religion, must have its apostles, he speaks as one having experience and authority ; and no one will dispute his competence to define and applaud the services which his friend rendered in the capacity of a breaker of the bread of science to the multitude."—*New York Sun.*

"The selection of Prof. John Fiske as the biographer of the late Prof. Youmans was the best thing that could be made. Prof. Youmans has done more for the dissemination of scientific information, and the cultivation of a taste for such knowledge, than any other American of his day."—*Cleveland Plain Dealer.*

"We shall not be misunderstood as agreeing with all the views recorded here by Prof. Youmans, from whom we were often compelled to differ while he lived, when we say that we have read the book with great interest, and are thankful that one who truly and unselfishly labored in the cause of popular science has so worthy a memorial."—*New York Observer.*

"He had the broad democratic spirit, and the absolute unselfishness which it reveals at every moment and in every act of his life; and Mr. Fiske has written a biography which is tender and true, and rich and strong. To it are appended some of his writings which have a fitting place here, and fully illustrate his mental gifts and convictions."—*Boston Herald.*

"Edward Livingston Youmans was a remarkable character, and the world could ill afford to lack a history of his life. Fortunately, the best biographer possible has undertaken to write that history, and all thoughtful readers may rejoice thereat ; for John Fiske came to this task well fitted in every way by his intimate personal acquaintance with Mr. Youmans, extending through many years."—*Chicago Inter-Ocean.*

"Prof. John Fiske has performed a labor of love for the friend whose name is its title, and one of whose closest intimates he was. The volume is a good example of friendly but not unwholesomely laudatory biography."—*Boston Congregationalist.*

New York: D. APPLETON & CO., 72 Fifth Avenue.

NEW EDITION OF PROF. HUXLEY'S ESSAYS.

COLLECTED ESSAYS. By Thomas H. Huxley. New complete edition, with revisions, the Essays being grouped according to general subject. In nine volumes, a new Introduction accompanying each volume. 12mo. Cloth, $1.25 per volume.

"Mr. Huxley has covered a vast variety of topics during the last quarter of a century. It gives one an agreeable surprise to look over the tables of contents and note the immense territory which he has explored. To read these books carefully and studiously is to become thoroughly acquainted with the most advanced thought on a large number of topics."—*New York Herald.*

"The series will be a welcome one. There are few writings on the more abstruse problems of science better adapted to reading by the general public, and in this form the books will be well in the reach of the investigator. . . . The revisions are the last expected to be made by the author, and his introductions are none of earlier date than a few months ago [1893], so they may be considered his final and most authoritative utterances."—*Chicago Times.*

"It was inevitable that his essays should be called for in a completed form, and they will be a source of delight and profit to all who read them. He has always commanded a hearing, and as a master of the literary style in writing scientific essays he is worthy of a place among the great English essayists of the day. This edition of his essays will be widely read, and gives his scientific work a permanent form."—*Boston Herald.*

"A man whose brilliancy is so constant as that of Prof. Huxley will always command readers; and the utterances which are here collected are not the least in weight and luminous beauty of those with which the author has long delighted the reading world."—*Philadelphia Press.*

"The connected arrangement of the essays which their reissue permits brings into fuller relief Mr. Huxley's masterly powers of exposition. Sweeping the subject-matter clear of all logomachies, he lets the light of common day fall upon it. He shows that the place of hypothesis in science, as the starting point of verification of the phenomena to be explained, is but an extension of the assumptions which underlie actions in every-day affairs; and that the method of scientific investigation is only the method which rules the ordinary business of life."—*London Chronicle.*

New York: D. APPLETON & CO., 72 Fifth Avenue.

EVOLUTION SERIES, NOS. 1 TO 17.

Popular Lectures and Discussions before the Brooklyn Ethical Association.

EVOLUTION IN SCIENCE, PHILOSOPHY, AND ART. With 3 Portraits. Large 12mo. Cloth, $2.00.

CONTENTS.

Alfred Russel Wallace. By EDWARD D. COPE, Ph. D.

Ernst Haeckel. By THADDEUS B. WAKEMAN.

The Scientific Method. By FRANCIS E. ABBOTT, Ph. D.

Herbert Spencer's Synthetic Philosophy. By BENJAMIN F. UNDERWOOD.

Evolution of Chemistry. By ROBERT G. ECCLES, M. D.

Evolution of Electric and Magnetic Physics. By ARTHUR E. KENNELLY.

Evolution of Botany. By FRED J. WULLING, Ph. G.

Zoölogy as related to Evolution. By Rev. JOHN C. KIMBALL.

Form and Color in Nature. By WILLIAM POTTS.

Optics as related to Evolution. By L. A. W. ALLEMAN, M. D.

Evolution of Art. By JOHN A. TAYLOR.

Evolution of Architecture. By Rev. JOHN W. CHADWICK.

Evolution of Sculpture. By Prof. THOMAS DAVIDSON.

Evolution of Painting. By FORREST P. RUNDELL.

Evolution of Music. By Z. SIDNEY SAMPSON.

Life as a Fine Art. By LEWIS G. JANES, M. D.

The Doctrine of Evolution: its Scope and Influence. By Prof. JOHN FISKE.

"The addresses include some of the most important presentations and epitomes published in America. They are all upon important subjects, are prepared with great care, and are delivered for the most part by highly eminent authorities."—*Public Opinion.*

EVOLUTION SERIES, NOS. 18 TO 34.

MAN AND THE STATE. Studies in Applied Sociology. With Index. Large 12mo. Cloth, $2 00.

CONTENTS.

The Duty of a Public Spirit. By F. BENJAMIN ANDREWS, D. D., LL. D.

The Study of Applied Sociology. By ROBERT G. ECCLES, M. D.

Representative Government. By EDWIN D. MEAD.

Suffrage and the Ballot. By DANIEL S. REMSEN.

The Land Problem. By Prof. OTIS T. MASON.

The Problem of City Government. By Dr. LEWIS G. JANES.

Taxation and Revenue: The Free-Trade View. By THOMAS G. SHEARMAN.

Taxation and Revenue: The Protectionist View. By Prof. GEORGE GUNTON.

The Monetary Problem. By WILLIAM POTTS.

The Immigration Problem. By Z. SIDNEY SAMPSON.

Evolution of the Afric-American. By Rev. SAMUEL J. BARROWS.

The Race Problem in the South. By Prof. JOSEPH LE CONTE.

Education and Citizenship. By Rev. JOHN W. CHADWICK

The Democratic Party. By EDWARD M. SHEPARD.

The Republican Party. By Hon. ROSWELL G. HORR.

The Independent in Politics. By JOHN A. TAYLOR.

Moral Questions in Politics. By Rev. JOHN C. KIMBALL.

"These studies in applied sociology are exceptionally interesting in their field."—*Cincinnati Times-Star.*

"Will command the attention of the progressive student of politics."—*Pittsburg Chronicle-Telegraph.*

Separate Lectures from either volume, 10 cents each.

EVOLUTION SERIES, NOS. 35 TO 48.

FACTORS IN AMERICAN CIVILIZATION:

STUDIES IN APPLIED SOCIOLOGY. Popular Lectures and Discussions before the BROOKLYN ETHICAL ASSOCIATION. 12mo. Cloth, $2.00. Separate Lectures, in Pamphlet Form, 10 cents each.

This volume is uniform with the two previous volumes of the series, entitled respectively "Evolution in Science and Art" and "Man and the State."

CONTENTS.

"One can hardly speak too highly of the work which is being done by the BROOKLYN ETHICAL ASSOCIATION. Its plan is to bring within definite compass and knowledge some of the largest subjects which can occupy the minds of thoughtful men. It has found students and thinkers who are equal to this task, and here we have some of the best work on subjects of the highest meaning that has been done by Americans."—*Boston Herald.*

New York: D. APPLETON & CO., 72 Fifth Avenue.